American Quartet

Also by Warren Adler

Options
Banquet Before Dawn
The Henderson Equation
Trans-Siberian Express
The Casanova Embrace
Blood Ties
Natural Enemies
The War of the Roses
The Sunset Gang (short stories)

American Quartet

A Novel by
Warren Adler

ARBOR HOUSE / *New York*

For A.L., J.A.G., W.B.M., and J.F.K.

The author would like to express his warm thanks for the patience, insight and help of Detective Judy Roberts of the Metropolitan Police Department of the District of Columbia. Also indispensable to the research was the able assistance of George R. Wilson, Chief of the MPD Firearms Identification Section, and Firearms Examiner Sgt. John M. O'Neil.

But O heart! heart! heart!
O the bleeding drops of red,
Where on the deck my Captain lies
Fallen cold and dead.

—Walt Whitman

American Quartet

I

THE AIR conditioner sucked in the steamy Washington air, wheezed, faltered, then regurgitated a dank iciness into the interior of the coffee shop. The establishment, as Fiona had observed countless times, had the air of a comfortable old street lady, shabby but serviceable, a touch world-weary but still aiming to please the customer.

"How the hell would you know?" Teddy said, in his cop's rasping croak.

"Osmosis."

It was a game they played; one of many, a professional duet, after nearly six months as homicide partners.

She watched the widening spear of sunlight illuminate the coffee slicks on the formica table. Through the smeared window, the leaves were still, and the trendy rehabilitated townhouses appeared appropriately eighteenth century in the morning light. Capitol Hill itself had the look of a sleepy village.

Sherry's, with its plastic and chrome booths, its Scotch-taped Naugahyde lounge covers, was a good spot for on-duty hiding and always, at this early morning hour, filled with coffee-gurgling police and loners fleeing from their crumbling rooming houses.

"The kids excited?" Fiona asked.

"Yeah," Teddy shrugged. He was always tight-lipped in the morning, which gave his wife Gladys fits, and his children's possessiveness was absolute and draining. They were going to Ocean City for the Fourth. He looked warily at the portable radio on the table, their umbilical cord to headquarters.

"I promised Bruce the whole weekend," Fiona said. "With his kids at camp and the House out . . ." Crazy, she thought, how their lovers' time was dictated by outside forces. She was proud of him, a member of Congress, although she detested politics. For his part he admired her cop career as an exercise in female pluck, although she suspected that deep down he considered it an aberration.

They had planned to live together experimentally for the summer while his kids were away. She hoped it would be a vacation fantasy, July Fourth to Labor Day, like in a lazy resort holiday. Her bags were packed.

"If we make it through August, we might get married," she said. She and Teddy were intimate the way strangers on a train are intimate. She looked across the table at him, a brooding, hulking man, the genuine Teddy. His bigness gave her security. She wondered if he resented her; her youth, her education, her femaleness.

Being partners wasn't random selection. They were together only because they were Caucasians. The eggplant, the division chief, had "married" them, to keep down the salt-and-pepper tensions in the department. He always took the line of least resistance, hence the vegetable nickname.

"Quiet?" Sherry asked, coming from behind the counter to refill their cups. The spotted apron accentuated her girth.

"We hope," Fiona said, looking at the black box, which gave out static. "We both have weekend plans. But you never know in this business."

Teddy grunted indifferently. His private thoughts seemed always to be on home problems, making ends meet, raising a family of four on twenty-two five.

12

The radio crackled suddenly. They leaned forward, the adrenalin charging.

"The National Gallery of Art?"

"Shit." Teddy put a buck down and slid out of the booth. He was still cursing as he gunned the motor. The police car moved deftly through the traffic on First Street, past the Library of Congress.

"Goddamn tourists," he mumbled as the car slowed behind a busload of them headed toward the Capitol parking lot. The interior of the police car had heated up in the morning sun and the air conditioning was still blowing hot air. Fiona felt a moustache of sweat form on her upper lip. Three police cruisers were lined up along the plaza between the National Gallery and the Hirshhorn Museum. A knot of gawking tourists had gathered near the fountain. She was dripping with perspiration as they arrived at the side entrance of the National Gallery.

"It's your scene," Teddy grumped at her. It was police homicide procedure to rotate scene and witness interrogation between partners. Today was her turn.

A glistening black face under an MPD uniform cap waylaid them. Behind him, a purring ambulance, a red light revolving on its roof, partially blocked the entrance.

"He got out this way," the black cop began excitedly, pointing to a narrow path between the bushes. Across Constitution Avenue an audience of hardhats were perched on a steel superstructure, watching the action.

"Faded into thin air," the black cop said. Fiona nodded to the uniformed policemen at the entrance, then raced through the glass doors, relieved by the sudden blast of cold air. At the top of the stairs was a small round balcony where an elevator was stalled, its door open.

"Here." Another uniformed policeman pointed as she turned into one of the gallery rooms. An apple-faced intern in crisp whites kneeled beside the body. Above him stood two paramedics, flanking a stretcher on wheels, poised to move the body.

"Is he dead?" The intern looked up and frowned. He was pale and beads of sweat covered his forehead. Not a moment too soon, she thought. The medics were always damaging physical evidence.

"Is he dead?" she repeated.

"Not yet."

The victim was a bulky man in his late forties, with a trimmed full beard. Kneeling, she quickly chalked an outline around the body, then stood up and watched as the medics lifted the victim's unconscious body and gently laid it on the stretcher. By then Teddy had arrived.

"I better go with them," he whispered. "Maybe he'll say something on the joyride."

She knew the dilemma. It was too important to trust to an untrained uniformed cop and the homicide backup hadn't arrived yet. The wounded man, if he regained consciousness, would be their best witness.

"Everything sealed off?" she asked, then suddenly shouted at one of the paramedics, "Dammit, don't step on that blood." By the book, she was in charge.

"I'll be back as soon as I can," Teddy growled, following the wheeled stretcher.

"I don't want anyone in this room." A startled MPD policeman reluctantly shooed away the growing crowd.

"Bullshit," a voice boomed.

Turning, she confronted a red, glowering face.

"This is my beat, baby. You can't keep me out of here." He flashed a badge and an ID. "I'm Barrows. Chief of Smithsonian police."

She let herself cool, standing her ground. In the distance the ambulance siren was already screaming.

"Just securing the scene," she said calmly. "I'm FitzGerald, MPD Homicide."

He watched her, unsure, still angry. She knew what his tongue wanted to say: "You little uppity twat." Conditioned to the reaction, she waited for him to regain control.

"The lab team will be here shortly." It's a publicity case, she realized suddenly. They'll all be here, including the eggplant. Inside she groaned.

Barrows watched her helplessly. She opened her shoulder

pocketbook and slid out her notebook. Legally, she preempted him.

"What is this place?" she asked firmly. Barrows's tongue probed nervously under his lip. His eyes roamed the room, betraying his unfamiliarity with it. Others, claiming authority, were sure to follow. The eggplant would be thirsting for notoriety, making pronouncements, playing take-charge. She'd have to finesse that as well.

When the lab team came in with their equipment, she excused herself and filled in the known details.

"From the way he fell, he was shot in the back."

"It's a big room, pretty pictures," Flannagan said. He was the head of the lab team. Between them was the ethnic bond so dear to her father's heart. But that was New York PD, another place, another era, her father's time.

Barrows partially recovered his sense of authority. He brandished a map in his chubby hands, his fingers shaking slightly.

"It's gallery sixty-seven, American Art."

Fiona was sketching the scene in her notepad. Pausing, she stared at John Singer Sargent's "Portrait of Mrs. Chamberlin." It was a powerful painting, reaching out to her, deflecting her concentration. The centerpiece on the side of the room in which the victim had been killed was called "The Bersenglien." A painter she had never heard of—Lukas. It was a colorful street scene bedecked with flags. The man had fallen at the foot of the picture beside it—"Allies Day, 1917," by the impressionist Childe Hassam. The scene was familiar, Fifth Avenue, New York. She recognized St. Patrick's Cathedral. American flags waved in the breeze.

Next to it, near the entrance to the gallery, an enigmatic observer, "Edith Reynolds," painted by Robert Henri, seemed to mock Fiona's gruesome task. At the other end of the wall, a second Henri, "Young Woman in White," stared out with haughty indifference.

Why here? she wondered. She braced herself for the uproar to come, complicated by the onslaught of the press and TV. The Washington tourist scene was sacrosanct. With twenty million tourists a year, it was the capital's major industry. A murder in one of the choice landmarks could send the media wild.

She proceeded with her hasty sketch, carefully recording the paintings. She noted two additional Sargents, making a klotch of mute ladies confined forever in their gorgeous immortality. She also noted "Mother and Mary" by Edward Torbell and one entitled "A Friendly Call" by William Merit Chase.

Then she paced off the measurements of the large room, penciled in the bench in the center of her sketch and estimated the length of walls from floor to ceiling. By the time she had finished, Barrows had fully recovered his sense of command. She had expected it. As a woman, the best she could ever hope for was a stalemate. How else to survive in the steamy pool of police machismo?

"There were two shots," Barrows said gruffly. She took notes as if to validate the importance of his information. He made a sour face at her shorthand but went on with his account. "My boys heard both. He ducked out through gallery seventy-one. A passel of high school kids were coming up the stairs. He threaded through them and out the door."

"Past the guards," she interrupted. They were merely bodies and this was not one of their textbook possibilities.

"They didn't want to endanger the kids," he said, biting his lip.

Low-paid, inefficient flunkies, she wanted to tell him but checked herself. She hoped the man would live. Then it wouldn't be her case. Only if death occurred . . .

She dreaded interviewing the teenagers, looking for reliable witnesses. Older kids were notoriously unreliable. As for the guards, boredom had dulled their powers of observation. But Barrows was not to be deterred.

"Nevertheless," Barrows said, as if he was about to impart a bombshell, "the guard at the east door thinks he saw a white man with a moustache and long hair. Youngish. Medium height, wearing dark jeans and dark shirt . . ."

She half-listened, searching the crowded gallery entrance for Teddy, who suddenly lumbered toward them.

"It's ours, Fiona. He was DOA." He read from his notebook. "Joseph Damato. Age forty-eight. He was a high school teacher from Hagerstown, Maryland. Taught art. No record."

Crime of passion perhaps, she thought, already concocting theories. A search for theory began early in an investigation.

"We're knee-deep in eyewitnesses," Teddy said.

"We got a pretty good description from our door guard." Teddy nodded at Barrows without interest and left her to finish the sketch. The mobile lab team had laid out their equipment and camera flashes popped in the room like tiny match fires.

Nearly an hour later, the eggplant himself, Homicide Captain Luther Greene, arrived, resplendent in a tan summer suit and Yves St. Laurent tie, a perfect accompaniment to his dark chocolate complexion. Tiny splashes of gray on the tie went well with his distinguished temples. He was decked out for the press.

"What have we got, Fitz?" he asked in a pleasant, purring voice.

She told him in accurate homicide language. She could almost sense him composing the press statement. In the role of spokesman, he was perfect casting.

"No theories?" It was the eggplant's usual opener.

"Too early." Fiona looked down at the rough chalk line she had drawn. A flash popped, blinding her for a second, giving her just enough time to throw him raw meat. She was not above a special kind of pandering. Besides, he needed a good script for the media.

"The way he fell, he might have been looking at the Hassam."

"The what?"

"Childe Hassam. The American impressionist." She remembered the name from an art appreciation course at Brooklyn College. He squinted at the brass plate that identified the picture.

"Some kind of a celebration somewhere," he mumbled.

"New York City. During World War One."

"Does it connect?" he asked.

She shrugged.

Teddy joined them. Despite his size, he had a knack of making himself appear neutral. He was also good at anticipating questions.

17

"He was tall and short. White and black. Blond and dark. There were two shots. Three shots. One guy heard four. The only consistency was facial hair. He had a moustache." He paused. "And male." He grinned at her. It was another banter bit in their duet. Murder was a man's game. A woman killed only in passion.

"Next of kin?" The eggplant always asked the right questions for a performance. What he meant was, should he reveal the man's name to the media? It always added a little suspense to keep it hidden. The line went: "We can't reveal it until the next of kin is notified," in response to: "Was the victim important?"

The eggplant seemed pleased. Not that she and Teddy were experts who performed under his care and feeding. He defied experts. All his brains were in his ego and all his energies were directed at making himself look good to his superiors. The next step for him was inspector. Beyond that, chief. They all knew where he was heading. He swaggered across the gallery to the nearest exit, already posturing to face the press.

"A lineup might light a spark," Teddy said. "We're making arrangements. I've also asked the guard to come downtown. Maybe with an artist, we might get lucky."

"An Italian high school teacher from Hagerstown is shot in the back while viewing a work of art. Why here?" She knew it was a rhetorical question. Teddy watched her, his eyes gloomy with disappointment. The son of a bitch had ruined his July Fourth weekend.

II

PUZZLES ALWAYS made her appear distant. Her unconscious became heavily involved. She had developed this characteristic early and it had a profound effect on her relationships with other people, especially men.

"Fiona's daydreaming again."

It was her mother's favorite rebuke. Her father, as always, was kinder.

"She's a deep one, that one," he would say. There was a broguish lilt to the way he said it, although he was born in Brooklyn. Grampa FitzGerald had brought the brogue all the way from Limerick and died crying it on his lips, gunned down in Bedford Stuyvesant, three weeks from NYPD retirement.

She was five years old at the wake, but the memory still prompted total recall more than a quarter of a century later. Beery, sodden cabbage smells. Big red veiny faces. Swollen bloodshot eyes. Moving shadows in the dimly lit living room where old Fitz was laid out, rouged and smiling, as if he had confronted his killer, daring him to ship him off to Gaelic heaven. To them, it was the only respectable way to die.

To Grampa Fitz, and to her father, the police department was always the "farce," and all FitzGerald males were expected, indeed decreed, to "jine the farces." Retribution to her father came in the form of three daughters. Coupled with the sexual revolution and the radicals in the church, especially the language change in the liturgy, the poor man was rendered punchy, always on the edge of rage, by the time she, the youngest daughter, began to menstruate.

She grew up with threats of "mortal sin" and "you'll roast in hell" burning in her ears—it was the only preventive medicine her parents knew, to make her preserve her virginity for some nice Irish boy. It was a losing battle. She saw them, beginning in her teens, as quaint relics of Irish myth. They abominated the freedom of contemporary life; it was all murky darkness, redeemed only by a sliver of light that was their love for her, and she forgave them everything.

Events in her life seemed to happen in mysterious apposition. She moved to Washington to escape the family. Then, after a stint as an FBI office worker, she joined the Washington police "farces" as if to redeem herself in their eyes.

It was not, of course, a woman's place, and her father ranted and raved over such effrontery to the male imperative—until the day he saw her in uniform, and then he collapsed in tears of pride. Her two older sisters had, in their way, followed the family's wishes. They had both married cops and were busily producing future members of the "farces," as if the new techniques of birth control had never existed.

Once she had gained family approval, she took a further step, a master's in criminology at American University. This turned out to be a brutal attack on the maleness of her brothers-in-law, who had only their high school diplomas, creating family tensions.

"Goddamned niggers, spics and broads are invading the forces," one of her brothers-in-law, deep in his cups, had railed at her one day. Surprisingly her father had stood up for her.

"She can't help it if she was born a girl," he shouted. "Besides, there's more niggers in Washington. At least, she's Irish. In my day we kept the kikes and niggers out. Before the politicians mucked things up."

She hadn't the guts to introduce Bruce Rosen to her parents. He was the embodiment of all their pet hates. Jewish, a politician, a liberal, divorced and, frosting the cake, about to live with her in sin. They would find this out soon enough. Why hassle them? As she carried her two suitcases up the walk to his Georgetown townhouse, she felt the tug of guilt, the old trepidations. Bruce's presence steadied her.

"I left the light burning in the window," he said, opening the door before she could insert the key.

"You shouldn't have." She let him embrace her, annoyed by her own gaminess after a long sweaty day's work. "I smell awful."

"Au naturel," he said. He smelled beautiful, like a bar of lime soap. He was wearing a velour robe, which he drew slightly open to show his eagerness.

"I've got a headache," she giggled, making no move. She felt his surety, his comfort. He kissed her hair. He could wait.

He released her to bring her suitcases in and carry them up the stairs of the three-story house. His ex-wife had decorated the house with charcoal gray carpets and red throwaways. She had arranged it around their collection of Chinese "Bloods," antique sixteenth-century vases. His wife had thoughtfully left him three or four, although she had taken most of the antiques, which had tripled in value since their divorce settlement three years earlier.

He hadn't done much with the house since, and the divorce had left a big dent in his bank account. It was, he told Fiona, a ransom just to have the kids half-time. Also, it foreclosed on a nasty divorce proceeding that could have affected his political career. From the moment she met him she understood that as a "given."

Soaking in the hot tub, Fiona felt her body soften. It was her ritual to have a long soak after the day's grimy work. It was as if she were washing away the film of human filth that daily clung to her.

In her work she floated in a sewer of human degradation, a scum of horrors, aberrations, cruelties. She was always fighting a battle with herself to maintain professional indifference, the same standard of a surgeon operating on a cancer, leaving the emotions to others. But sometimes the tide of human horror flowed through all too vulnerable chinks of her being. A sexual mutilation, a child ripped apart solely for gratification—you never were too hard-boiled for that. Sometimes the utter madness of crime crashed through the ramparts of her defenses. When she faltered, she would pray it was not because she was a woman. Compassion was the enemy of homicide cops.

Yet there was something bizarre, something oddly clean about murder by gunshot, like killings in a cowboy flick. Pain without tears. As she lay in the tub, she felt the distance growing between her and that day's murder. Her eyes were closed and she did not notice Bruce until he stood above her, holding a drink.

"Pour that in your snout," he said, clinking the ice in the glass. She took the glass and held it against her face, feeling the cold. She sipped, watching him, the aesthetic aquiline nose, the full lips and strong cleft chin. Above his high forehead the bed of steel-gray curls began in endless ripples, tight but soft.

In his flecked hazel eyes she saw the intensity of his own drama, predatory when it came to political ambition, a trifle too shrewd at times, frightening when he was on the attack. She preferred watching them on the threshold of pleasure.

He was so well made and he made her feel so good. Yet, in many ways, they were opposites. She was light, thin-skinned, with veiny networks under her patina of freckles. Her hair burned auburn in the right light and her pubic bush was carroty and, she thought, unfetching. She loved the lush black jungle mysteries of him.

In any light her eyes were Kelly green, matching the Irish flag. They carried their own inner lamps, he once told her. She had a good straight Gaelic nose, unfleshy, with nostrils that quivered when she restrained anger. Her Irish was a beast on a leash, she knew, and she could let it out when her turf was invaded. She could also slip into deep brooding dark moods, like the most morose black Irishman.

"The boys downtown should see you now," he said, soaping her breasts. She reached out for him.

"And you your constituents." She kissed him there. "Good old Johnson."

"What?"

"Police nomenclature." She laughed. "You'd get every lady's vote."

"I'm going to need them in November." She caught a tremor of anxiety.

He helped her out of the tub and toweled her off like a baby, adding light oil and sliding his palms over her skin.

"God, it's good to feel like a woman again," she whispered. He hitched her to him and carried her to bed. She was surprised at the fury of her pleasure after such an exhausting day. When it had subsided and his soft breathing found its sleeping rhythm, she lay beside him, energized, unable to sleep. In that state the puzzles always surfaced, like a submarine emerging from the deep.

She had carried away from the scene a half-made image, a negative aborted in mid-development. Later, she had watched Dr. Berton do the autopsy and had seen the killer bullet extracted. They had a corpus delicti with a history. He was a painter, frustrated by failure, a common ailment, who taught art history to teenagers and haunted museums, presumably searching for the missing link to his own talent.

"Who would kill Joseph?" the victim's wife had gasped. Surely not her. She was bogged down by three young children, overwork, and her husband's perpetually lit fuse of unrequited artistic ambition.

Fiona would have to go up to Hagerstown and ferret out more details. Poor Teddy. He'd have to go as well, courting Gladys's wrath and jealousy. Fiona always went out of her way to make Gladys feel secure, but nothing helped. It was simply a hazard of the industry.

"She thinks that women get into police work so they can get laid a lot," Teddy had confessed. "Even though she likes you."

Can't be helped, she had decided. It hadn't been her motivation. Police males hardly made a dent in her libido. For that reason she tried to neuter herself, not an easy task in a sea of men who played with guns and their precious Johnsons. The uniforms, the camaraderie, the occasional brutality were all a man's game. That, she knew, made homicide all the more challenging.

Whatever the motive, it was an unlikely setting for a killing. The National Gallery of Art! Nobody ever murdered anybody in an art gallery. And why in that specific spot under Childe Hassam's painting? She made a mental note to check out Hassam. And the crime lab reports would tell them a great deal. When she grew drowsy, she fitted herself against Bruce's body, two embryos, and let her mind idle. Soon she was asleep.

His hands wakened her, their movements sensual and probing, lifting her out of the mud of unconsciousness. At first her sense of place was confused, but soon a warm wave of pleasure overtook her, and she yielded to its power.

"I love this woman," he whispered as his lips smoothly glided over her body. No one should be allowed such joy, she told herself, with a nod at the old Catholic guilt. It had long lost the power to inhibit her. She threw herself into the sexual duet with fierce joy, hearing the echo of her cries of pleasure in the cool room.

"A regular screamer," he laughed, biting her earlobe. She felt her heart pounding against the hand on her breast. "And very much alive."

"Maybe it's compensation for all that death around me," she said, and instantly regretted saying it. "Sorry. I'm getting too analytical."

A buzzing began, and Bruce reached over and pressed the clock button, which threw a time reading on the ceiling. It was after nine.

"I forgot to shut it off," he murmured. He embraced her again. "A whole weekend," he sighed.

"Not all of it, I'm afraid." She realized that she had blurted it out too soon. It struck right at the heart of their major point of contention . . . time together.

"You're getting to be an Indian giver," he said, releasing her.

"You can't schedule a killing," she said. "I had scene."

"After the weekend, I'm going to be hounded until November. I've got a race on my hands. A Hispanic lady with a Harvard law degree, who talks street talk. Her name is Rodriguez. Her brother is married to a Rosenbaum. And she has a voice like Lauren Bacall."

"And her looks?"

"Disgustingly attractive."

"You're just running scared."

"Scared?" He got up and opened the blinds, squinting into the sun. "I'm petrified. I need this win. Otherwise, I don't have a shot at the Senate seat."

"Doesn't a dozen years count?" she asked.

"They count for change. The district's gone to seed."

She could see the fine glaze of his long slender body, the hairs swathed in the glow of bright light. His manhood was still engorged. She patted it.

"You'll make it. Eight the hard way."

"In craps, it's not an easy roll to make, Fi. I just got the poll yesterday. Only twenty percent even know who I am. I've been their congressman for seven terms and only twenty percent know who I am. Can you believe it? That's not merely a disaster. It's a catastrophe."

"When the going gets tough, the tough get going," she mumbled foolishly.

"You're trivializing it."

He went into the bathroom and she heard the steady gush of the shower. She started to brood, then picked up the phone and called a man at headquarters.

"Odd as hell," Jim Hadley said in his Baltimore twang. He was one of the examiners in the Firearms Examination section. "A forty-four. From the lands and grooves it could be either an English Bulldog or a Wembley. It's the ammo that bugs me. Ancient. Like maybe a hundred years."

"What does that mean?"

"Nothing probably. Anyway, that's your job to find out."

She hung up, then dialed Flannagan, whose cheery "Yo" defied his gruesome task.

"Prints?"

"An army."

As she listened to other details, Bruce came out and without looking at her left the bedroom. When she finished with Flannagan, she called Teddy at home. Gladys answered, her voice distant and angry.

"I'm sorry," Fiona said.

"Speak to my kids," Gladys snapped. Teddy was on the extension and shouted for his wife to get off the line.

"It's on page one," he growled. "And there's a picture of the eggplant. The mayor is very defensive. And the Board of Trade is raising hell. We're all on the griddle. Got to find the bastard."

"They want things safe in their Disneyland," she murmured. Even if she wanted to, she couldn't cancel the weekend. "He'll want something every day now."

"He just got off the phone with me. I got a pep talk and he's authorized overtime."

"The eggplant? What makes him so generous?"

Bruce came in wearing a short striped robe, his curly hair glistening. He put a cup of coffee on the bedside table and threw the *Post* on the bed. She picked up the paper and read the headline: "MURDER AT THE NATIONAL GALLERY."

"It'll sell papers," she told Teddy. "Pick me up in an hour. I'm at Bruce's." She hung up and jumped out of bed.

"Sorry I blew up," Bruce said. "I got greedy."

"I like you greedy," she said, cuddling him.

"Previous experience gets me edgy. My ex-wife's career became her everything."

"No comparisons, please." She felt the brief panic. It was bad enough being secretly, sometimes vociferously, jealous. It's a dead ember, he had protested.

"It's my morning for apologies. I wanted us to start out on a perfect note."

"It did," she said, caressing him.

"At least arrange it so you can be with me to see the fireworks at Remington's. From his place you get a clear view."

"I like the fireworks from here," she said, insinuating her hand under his robe.

"It's an annual thing. Everybody is coming."

26

"Everybody?" She knew he loved surprises like this. "I'll settle for just us coming." It was the kind of double entendre they both loved.

But suppose he does lose his seat in Congress, a voice inside her speculated. It didn't wait for an answer.

III

"THERE," MRS. Damato whispered. "A life."

They peered into the cramped room, heavy with the acrid smell of paint. Pigments permeated the warped wooden floor that creaked as they stepped forward. Painted canvases lay helter-skelter along the walls, mostly city scenes. She flipped through them hurriedly, recognizing the Hagerstown main street.

"I thought they were good. Nobody else did."

"Did he?" Fiona asked. Teddy and Inspector Al O'Leary from Hagerstown PD still thumbed through the paintings. O'Leary pulled one out and slanted it to catch the gray light of a fading rainy summer day.

"Harper Street. I grew up there," he said in his flat Maryland accent.

Mrs. Damato's eyes were watery in their deep padded sockets. Her grief seemed to have resharpened her features, which had run to flesh. Her olive skin was pinched and when she spoke, she showed yellowed teeth with large gaps. Whatever money was left over obviously had gone to feed her husband's artistic obsession.

"Maybe I was too supportive," she shrugged.

"They weren't bad," O'Leary said, still looking at the pictures.

"Too photographic," Mrs. Damato complained. "That's what they told him. In twenty years he never sold a single one for more than fifty bucks." Her reddened nostrils quivered, and a sour odor emanated from her body, familiar to Fiona. She had often observed a particular smell about the grief-stricken, which undermined her professional indifference. She was better, cooler, with the dead.

Teddy had begun to take Polaroids of the paintings.

"His work was the most important thing in his life," Mrs. Damato said regretfully.

The paintings were failed attempts at expressionism. The memory of Hassam's "Allies Day" popped into Fiona's mind, a complete image, powerfully stated. How Damato must have envied the painter's talent.

"And in there?" Fiona asked gently, nodding toward a door. She turned the knob. The door was locked.

"A closet. He had the key. This was his place," the widow said harshly, revealing the battle lines of their marriage.

Fiona fiddled in her pocketbook, checking the make of the lock with the keys on her ring. They were Damato's. She found the correct key and opened the door.

"I never touched his things," Mrs. Damato whined.

There was no light in the closet, which was filled with canvases placed face-in. Fiona drew one out and brought it out to the light. Behind her, Mrs. Damato coughed nervously. Teddy stopped taking pictures.

"Jesus," O'Leary gasped.

Fiona felt the exhilaration of surprise. The girl in the picture was nude, her flesh and blond hair luminous in its natural grassy setting. She was just this side of puberty, a bud opening, glorious and unmistakably erotic. There were nearly half a dozen paintings in the closet, all depicting the same girl. As Fiona laid all the paintings against the wall the effect was startling. It was the dead man's artistic apogee.

Mrs. Damato stared at the pictures, making gurgling sounds.

"You know her?" Fiona asked gently. Mrs. Damato did not respond. So this was Damato's dirty little secret, Fiona thought. He had certainly put his heart into it. From the way Mrs. Damato glanced away, Fiona sensed the recognition. The point had to be pressed slowly. The trail had now begun.

Mrs. Damato moved back and sat heavily on a wooden chair, as though her own weight had become too much of a burden.

"They're beautiful," Fiona said. "Your husband was a talented man." It was designed to be a con, but she really meant it. By comparison, the other paintings seemed pale wasted images.

"She doesn't look more than fourteen," O'Leary said angrily. "The whore. I got girls in that school."

Mrs. Damato was playing with her fingers, watching them blankly. The dead, Fiona had learned early in the game, always took their revenge on the living.

"Maybe he did it from imagination," Fiona said, stalking now.

"The hell he did," O'Leary shouted.

"Will you please . . ." Fiona snapped. She touched the woman's shoulder. Mrs. Damato lifted helpless lugubrious eyes. "You do, don't you?"

The girl in the picture seemed to reach out of the canvases, revealing her arrogant disdain, shattering the myth of innocence. The nipples on her rising young breasts seemed rouged in the exquisite sunlight, and between her legs was the hint of a pout.

"We're looking for your husband's killer, Mrs. Damato," Fiona said. It was time to confront reality. The man's guilt had died with him.

"It looks like Celia Baines," Mrs. Damato said hoarsely. "One of his students. I think two years ago he gave her private lessons." The effort exhausted her; her voice was a whisper.

"Yeah," O'Leary croaked. "Dirty-minded somebitch."

"Will you please shut the hell up?" Fiona snapped again. Teddy told him to take it easy.

"Hotshot big city cops . . ." O'Leary sneered.

"It's bewildering," Mrs. Damato said, finding her voice again.

"He was not like that at all." It was a confession of a lifetime of sexual indifference. The smell of the woman seemed to fill the room, stifling the odors of the paint.

"I thought I knew him."

They found her behind the counter of the McDonald's on the edge of town. She was older, fuller, and although attractive in a teenage way, hardly the powerful pubescent image in the paintings. There was, however, no mistaking her identity. When she opened her mouth, she completed the destruction of the dead man's fantasy.

"Let me," Fiona had urged. "You two gumshoes will frighten her."

The place was nearly empty and Fiona and the girl, Celia, sat in a corner booth away from the two men, who munched on Big Macs. Occasionally, O'Leary would glower at them from across the restaurant.

Her police badge had frightened the girl at first, but Fiona recognized she was a sieve to vanity.

"I wish I had hair like that," Fiona said. It was the color of a wheat field in the morning sun, a perfect articulation of the painter's image. Fiona wasn't sure she meant the painting or the reality before her. Up close, the girl was duller, her blue eyes clear but reflecting a dim intelligence.

"You got nice red hair," the girl said. Fiona nodded her appreciation.

"A terrible tragedy about Mr. Damato," Fiona began slowly.

"Yeah. Jeez."

"Mrs. Damato said you took lessons."

"Yeah. I like to drore."

"Was he a nice man?"

"He was okay. A little creepy."

"How so?"

"You know, funny."

"Funny-looking?"

"You know. Woppy."

She felt sorry for the girl. Her looks had obviously spoiled her. A pampered darling of the working class. She was the kind of girl whom hard hats whistled at and greasers pawed in drive-in movies. In towns like this, no one was a virgin past thirteen. She could imagine the scenario of seduction. "You ain't getting into my pants," a protest that would be moot ten minutes later. Fiona laid the Polaroids on the table like a called poker hand.

"Dirty wop bastard." Her eyes didn't leave the pictures and she flushed down to her neck, leaving a scarlet blotch on the soft skin under a cheap gold chain.

"You want to tell me about it?"

"Why should I?"

"The man was murdered." Fiona let it sink in. The girl's lips snarled. "Maybe your old man found out about it."

"Sheet," the girl said, showing a lipstick-stained smile. It was obviously the wrong tack.

"Where were you last Tuesday?"

She was an unlikely suspect, yet the question jarred her. Like everyone else, she, too, had secrets.

"You think it was me?" The girl seemed genuinely startled.

Fiona shook her head. She needed to calm the girl. Her frail defenses were no match for a professional attack. Besides, Teddy had already talked to the manager, who reported she had worked the breakfast shift that morning. But guilt came out of specifics. Everybody felt guilty about something and Celia was no exception.

"You won't tell?" the girl asked in a sly voice. It was the modus operandi of her young life: not telling. It had only made whatever guilt was inside her more painful.

She spoke calmly, her eyes shifting, glancing occasionally at Teddy and O'Leary. The girl didn't tell everything, Fiona was certain; but enough to provide the remote possibility of a motive.

Damato had persuaded her to pose. She had done so reluctantly, but it felt good. They would go up to this secluded place in the Cumberland mountains. Not far. He played with himself, she admitted. It was as far as she would go. "I wouldn't let him put his greasy hands on me."

"Did he try?"

"They all try," the girl said bitterly.

"Did he try with any of the other girls?" Celia's concentration had already wandered.

"Do I look pretty?" she asked, fingering the pictures. "He said I was a masterpiece. He said I was very special."

"You look magnificent," Fiona agreed.

"Really?" The girl's eyes brightened, emerging momentarily out of their dullness. She sighed. "Why would anyone want to kill him? He wasn't that bad."

"Did you feel sorry for him?" Fiona asked.

"Yeah. Yeah, I did." The girl had grabbed at that and Fiona knew instantly that Damato had indeed put his hands on her. "He was like a big baby. When I got tired, we played."

"Played?"

"You know," she shrugged.

Fiona knew. She also knew that the poor girl would soon be hounded, humiliated. There was no protecting her. Hagerstown was a small town with a single newspaper. The best she could do to postpone the inevitable was to impound the paintings as evidence.

"I'd appreciate it if you'd keep it out of the papers." She tried to charm O'Leary, knowing it was a futile gesture.

"It'll hurt the investigation," Teddy pressed. But she had already seen the small town cop in O'Leary chomping at the publicity bit. It was impossible to control the situation. She had made a bad mistake in offending O'Leary.

"I'll work with you," the cop lied transparently. He hadn't forgotten her put-down.

"My fuse is getting too short," she told Teddy as they drove back through the Maryland countryside. A fog had risen in the high spots as Teddy moved the car cautiously through the almost impenetrable haze.

They had moved fast, interviewing as many people as they could. Damato's students. His fellow teachers.

"When it hits the papers, they'll all clam up," Teddy said. "And they'll make a pervert out of the poor bastard. Juicy stuff."

33

They had packed the six paintings into the back of their car. Mrs. Damato showed no reluctance to part with them. Her life was already in flames.

"I feel sorry for her kids," Fiona sighed. "The garbage slops over."

"It's never clean," Teddy agreed.

They had combed through the house, the yard, everywhere, looking for other pictures of young girls. And they had talked to Celia's mother, carefully avoiding the truth of her daughter's relationship with Damato. They'd find out soon enough. The girl's father was an alcoholic drifter, with neither the will nor the energy to seek revenge. Besides, his alibi was airtight. He was home sleeping off a drunk. Mrs. Damato, too, was well accounted for.

"It's a motive," she said. "Especially if we find an outraged parent with an old revolver hidden in a drawer. The eggplant will love it." Fiona closed her eyes, beat.

"O'Leary will be pissed off when he finds we took the pictures," Teddy mumbled.

In her mind, she was speculating, following the trail. Damato had tried it again. He was caught at it. He was followed to the museum and shot. Open and shut. Simple logic. Too simple. It simply didn't mesh with her instincts. The car's rhythm nudged her to sleep.

IV

BRUCE ROSEN was not in a good mood. He was sitting in the gloomy half-light of a television set, slumped in a leather chair. Beside him was a half-filled highball glass. The scene did not augur well for the future of their experiment.

She pulled the chain of the table lamp, throwing a yellow splash of light against the paneled walls and rows of leather-bound books. It was a "Wasp" room, down to the nineteenth-century landscape that hung over the fireplace, a touch that bespoke deeper American roots than had been sunk in a couple of generations. She hated spotting details like that. Cynicism was an occupational hazard, like spotted lung to miners.

"It was the loneliness that bugged me the first time around," he said, lifting heavy-lidded eyes. In the ten months she had known him, he had never seemed so vulnerable.

"What the hell is it, Bruce?" She poured herself two fingers of Scotch and sat on the arm of the chair, putting her hand on his head. The curly touch of it warmed her.

"There's a kinky rhythm to our work," she said softly. "Murderers work odd hours, too." They had been through that before. In their time as lovers, politics had made her a grass widow as well.

"And I don't control it, baby," she said, kissing his neck.

Bruce picked up his glass, emptied it and squeezed her buttock with his free hand. It reassured her that her absence alone was not the reason for his depression. A talk show was in progress and she got up to shut off the inane chatter.

"I think I'm going to get knocked off in the primary," he said. "I saw the polls today. The bitch has got me by the balls."

She let it pass. The New Woman had scorched the earth, leaving behind her a race of injured men. They simply could not adjust to a nonmaternal woman. Was Bruce going to be one more victim? She wished his opponent was not a woman.

"So you'll fight it. You're a pro. It's not the first trip to the well."

"Too late. The fucking districts are changing. More black faces. Spanish is a second language. I've always been lousy at languages. The bitch . . ." She hated the word. She wondered if he was baiting her.

"But it's not over yet."

"She poses as a tough spic street broad. They love it. Maybe Jewish is out of fashion."

"Not to me. I'm just getting into it," she said lightly.

"Dumb mick." He gathered a palmful of flesh and squeezed affectionately. "Always at the tail end of a trend."

She kept silent, afraid to go too lightly. It was his life. Sixteen years. It was the only occupation he wanted. Once, just once, she had asked him why.

"I like the glory," he had said. "It fulfills my thirst for recognition and power, for manipulating others. I like to see my name and picture in the papers. I like to make decisions. I like to touch the levers of power. It makes me feel alive." It had come out like a confessional laundry list and she had actually felt like a priest peering out at him through the veiled opening. Say three Our Fathers, three Hail Marys and a sincere act of contrition, she had wanted to say, but it was too close to all those exposed nerves.

"You could do with a little more Irish." She poured more whiskey into his glass. "Here's a temporary cure. Irish medicine."

"I just don't want to be beached here," he said. "I can't go home anymore. Home has disappeared. I'll have to stay. Be a 'usta.' I'll get a couple of invitations with honorable on the envelope. Probably lobby for big oil or the potash industry."

"You are down," Fiona said, biting his earlobe. There was something to this Jewish mommy bit, she had learned years before, during her first sorties out of the Irish ghetto. Jewish boys were puffed up with confidence by their mamas. Sooner or later, it came out in the wash. They expected their wives, or mistresses, to perform the same service.

"You'll make it," she said earnestly. "You always have. So you'll run scared."

"Petrified," he said. "I'll run petrified."

Her own mother would have put it all in the hands of providence. Her father would have called it a conspiracy of the Protestants and, of course, the kikes.

"I needed a shoulder to cry on tonight," he said, resting his head on her bosom.

"That's not my shoulder." He seemed to be making an effort to come out of it.

"Every compulsive achiever is paranoid." He was quiet for a long time and she felt him listening to her heartbeat.

"I was thinking of Remington earlier," he said. "He was assistant secretary of the navy under Kennedy. Practically a kid then. Ran for the Senate from California. Lost. Now he throws parties. Goes everywhere. But he doesn't count."

She had seen his name in the social pages of the *Post* and the *Washington Dossier* countless times. Thaddeus Remington III. Good old Tad. He lived in one of the great houses of Washington on Linnean Drive. Not important?

"Remington depressed you?"

"He's loaded, but he can't really buy his way in. It's power that counts. Oh, they kiss his ass. He gets his brownie points. Ambassadors suck up to him because he's a kind of social catalyst. He brings the mighty together, but he's never mighty himself. You know what I mean. He's a celebrity, true, but without power or achievement. Beached."

It was the second time he had used that word. Thwarted, she supposed he meant.

"An empty life," he continued. "Every four years, he becomes the new version of a fat cat. A fundraiser for others. But never a kingmaker and never a king. Even his dough can't insulate from the corrosion of his failure."

"I can't see him as an object of pity."

"If I go down in November, I kiss the Senate seat good-bye. It would be rough."

"But not the end of the world."

"The end of my world. In politics, to win is everything. All else is sudden death. All campaigns make me crazy, Fiona. I'm not fit to live with. None of us are. We'd shoot our mothers to get reelected."

"Would you really?"

"My mother's already gone." He caressed her arm. "Bear with me. Pay no attention. This is not the real me."

"Who is it then?"

"Some gluttonous monster without a shred of integrity. I have this man Clark. A hired gun. He's figuring it out. I'll do what he tells me."

"Anything?"

"Almost."

He was obviously having an anxiety attack. A hurt child, she thought. Either that or male menopause.

"I'm forty-five," he murmured, as though reading her thoughts.

"Eisenhower was an obscure colonel at fifty-two, before Marshall picked him and lightning struck. Nixon was a has-been in 1960, in disgrace a little more than a decade later. And still bouncing back. Where is your instinct for survival?" She felt like a cheerleader. "I thought you were Jewish. Besides, you haven't even begun to fight back."

"I'm waiting for Clark to tell me how."

She let him wallow in silence, caressing him.

38

"And how was your day?" he asked suddenly, turning to her. He began to unbutton her blouse. She let him. This was, after all, what a relationship meant. At least she was only tired, not down. His strength was one of his great attractions. He's not really weak, she assured herself, just manic.

"My day? I found myself a motive." She edited herself. "A possible motive." She explained succinctly. He was a good listener.

"How do you stand it?" he said. "Death morning, noon and night. At least old Papa Hemingway liked it only in the afternoon."

"A matinee man."

He laughed. She was drawing him out. It pleased her to see the dynamics of their relationship, she filling his need. When it was her turn, she hoped he wouldn't let her down.

Finally he had freed her breasts and buried his face between them. She felt the tickling roughness of his chin.

"My bubby," she said, pressing his head against her flesh.

Death had brought them together. The suicide of Carol Harper, one of his receptionists.

"We have to investigate every death in D.C., natural or otherwise," she had told him in his office. Like all politicians, he was wary. She knew he was wondering how it would affect his image. He was divorced, handsome, visible. A good story. She was wearing a Wedgwood blue suit and a high-collared blouse. Very neuter. Very professional.

Only three months in homicide, the only woman, Fiona was still shaky in her role, especially without the protection of her uniform and those clumpy sexless men's shoes she'd had to wear. She had another white partner then, Al Short, who let her do the talking. The man was a congressman and Al was heading for early retirement in a month or two and not inclined to rock any political boats. At that time, she was still naive, learning the homicide trade.

"You saw the medical report," Bruce told her. "An overdose. No question about that."

"Did you see her socially?" The question infuriated him.

"What are you trying to make of it? Your implication is a little presumptuous."

She had been tempted to apologize, but he wouldn't let her break in.

"She was a damned receptionist. I barely knew her. I was strictly her employer. I feel rotten that she did this thing, but I had nothing to do with it. Nothing."

She could see the color rising under his deep tan. She let him work it out.

"It's just routine, sir." She was rocked back by his tongue-lashing.

"Is she a confirmed suicide?" he asked, suddenly gentle.

"No question about that. She took an overdose of sleeping pills and left a note in her own hand to her parents, asking for forgiveness. Just a couple of scrawled lines."

"All right, then. Why bother me about it? There's no question of foul play?"

"No."

He seemed fully relieved now. What she did not tell him was that the girl was the closet mistress of an important senator, although she was certain he knew that. In the capital, young vulnerable girls were passed around by powerful men like pieces of meat. Few made it to the altar. Most remained in the closet, sometimes all their lives. Police files were filled with information about similar suicides. It was, as she had told him, routine. The juicy details were kept hidden forever, largely to protect appropriations or to be used for subtle blackmail. Even the press, with occasional lapses, joined in the conspiracy, unless they had targeted an enemy or needed the hapless lecher as a source.

"She was stupid, throwing away her life," Bruce Rosen said with disgust. "Don't you think?" His yellow-flecked hazel eyes probed at her. She felt his minute inspection, and involuntarily she pressed her thighs closer together. Inexplicably, the man moved her.

"I try to stay away from emotional judgments," she said. "It confuses the facts."

Al Short, sensing the tension, said: "I think we got all we need from the congressman." He stood up and put out his hand. The congressman shook it with obvious political sincerity.

"Glad to oblige," Bruce said, winking at her. She had learned to ignore these little macho bits. But she couldn't dispel the pull, the magnetic attraction. It annoyed her. It interfered with business. Perhaps she hadn't been trying hard enough to be neuter that day. She found out why a week later.

He called and asked her for dinner at Tiberio's. She said yes, perhaps too quickly. Was she transparent? she wondered. She was irritated by her vulnerability. They met at the restaurant, where he was waiting for her in the little alcove bar.

"I was nasty," he said, offering his little boy's abashed look. She had gone off to Loehman's and bought a new dress for the occasion. "You look smashing for a cop."

"Just routine." She giggled, feeling clumsy and unsophisticated.

Julio put them side by side at a table under a bright floral painting that matched the colors of the flowers on the table. It was late October and Washington was enjoying one of its golden fall seasons. The air was clear and crisp and the moon was full. She would always remember that.

After two Scotches, she felt braced enough to face the routine litany. Men simply could not rest without knowing why she had become a cop. Knowing what? At least it was something that made her interesting.

"I'm not good at explaining it," she confessed. She had avoided the nuances of street talk, taking care with her language; she was trying to impress him. People came over to shake his hand and he reacted in practiced political style. But there was no mistaking his interest in her, and she was loving it.

"Maybe nostalgia. Maybe some instinctive filial urge because of my family being cops. Maybe it was also a deliberate attack on the concept of a woman's place. Maybe I've got an urge to be a heroine."

"Maybe it was opportunism," he said shrewdly. "You're a double minority."

"You noticed."

"There must be a lot of pressure."

41

Because he was a congressman, she resisted telling him about the poor morale, the promotions based solely on race, her gripes against the eggplant. The D.C. government still depended on Congress for its money. The department, despite its flaws, carried a special brand of loyalty. The eggplant would have loved her tact.

"I'm all for women going as far as they can," he said, a trifle unctuously. He appeared to her then as a beautiful, elegant man, secure in his manhood, filled with an obvious sense of male superiority. It might be intellectually repelling, but his explosive sexuality could not be denied. Soon he was telling her about his first wife. She listened, trying not to betray her impatience. God, get the preliminaries over with, she thought.

"It was my wife who wanted out," he said over the linguini. "There's a certain type of New Yorker who could never be transplanted. She could never hack it here. Went back to the Big Apple. Anyway, we had had it. No problems with the kids. It's not a good divorce. Not a bad divorce. We're strangers with memories."

"I never found the right guy," she told him. The Chablis had loosened her tongue. Maybe it was the sense of power in him that goaded her. His aura. It acted on her like an aphrodisiac. Suddenly she felt a disturbing kinship with poor dead Carol Harper.

"Maybe it's the distribution system," she sighed. "I'm not exactly in the perfect mating environment. I don't think I could go home every night to a cop. They're depressing. There's a kind of stink about them. Comes from human misery."

"Does it get to you?"

"You learn to insulate yourself. Maybe I can hack it better because I am a woman. Most of the bad guys are men."

"I never thought of it that way."

He seemed to have lost his smooth edge and she worried that she had turned him off. He became introspective, less talky.

In the car, driving to his place for a nightcap, he admitted some confusion.

"I was watching you. I saw a beautiful woman. I looked into your eyes and suddenly realized what horrors you see every day. Autopsies. Bruised bodies. Every conceivable aberration. Death everywhere. It scared me." Reaching out, he took her hand and lifted it to his lips.

"You saw that?"

"I want to love away the pain of it."

"I told you. I keep the pain at bay."

They were silent until he opened the door of his townhouse and they stood facing each other in the vestibule. He took her in his arms. Deep inside she felt the great tidal wave surge.

"Just don't love away the joy," she said. She felt the wave crest, carrying her forward on its inexplicable power.

The memory of that first conflagration always thrilled her. Now she stretched out beside him, her body pressed against his, her fingers tapping along the length of his long lank body. He stirred. A hand reached behind him, caressing.

"Don't work late tomorrow. Let's see the fireworks at Remington's." She understood. He didn't want to be alone, without her, another night.

V

A FULL-LENGTH painting of Thaddeus Remington III hung over the fireplace, reaching upward almost to the beamed ceiling of his Linnean Drive mansion. The portrayal was heroic, a handsome young lieutenant, junior grade, in dress whites, his naval cap cocked with nonregulation jauntiness, a blond lock of hair spilling over his forehead. The eyes, bluer than the sea in the background, looked confidently out to the horizon, as though in search of an impossible dream.

The strong square jaw offered a target to all takers, and the high glistening cheekbones set off the straight proud nose and delicate nostrils. The elegant body showed the strength and power of youth at its finest, most glorious, moment. Inscribed on a solid gold plaque were his name and the words, "At Inchon, Korea, 1950."

Until his mother's death six years before, it had hung over the fireplace in her Nob Hill townhouse.

"My golden boy," Mrs. Remington would tell visitors, her eyes lingering over the portrait with wistful pride. "A gift of God," she would sigh. It was the first thing guests were shown in the elaborate house, a shrine to young Tad.

Later, he would explain why he had placed the portrait so prominently in his Georgetown home.

"I put it there more as a monument to her than to satisfy my well-known egocentricity." Indeed, the *Post* had dubbed him "the Golden Host," despite the fact that the shock of shimmering finespun blond-gold hair had turned mustardy with age. His real life pose almost surpassed the heroic posturing of the young war hero, complete with Navy Cross with clusters on his chest.

"I'll say one thing for him. He's got style." Everybody who compared the portrait with the original agreed on that. But they couldn't pin him down. They asked themselves and one another, what does he do with his days? When the question was put to him, he would respond with a wink: "Drink a lot and read financial statements," thereby implying a private knowledge of deep financial entanglements, of spider-webbed interlocking directorships.

Because he was single and squired some of the capital's spectacularly beautiful women, as well as imports from New York or Beverly Hills, he was always an object of rumor, and ladies no longer on his escort list were not above exchanging little confidences. He was too charming and, by their standards, too important, for real malice. He was also generous. Trips to Paris or Newport or even safaris to Africa were not gifts to be ignored by women over thirty swimming in the treacherous eddies of the Washington social stream. A date with Tad Remington was a brownie point in an arena where a brownie point counted for more than the gold star of achievement.

Remington's home, reflecting his style, added another note, pure Americana. The neo-classic house's architecture, with its solid fluted columns, reflected a time when American architects put a distinctive Grecian stamp on the capital's architecture. Inside, the antiques, autographs, paintings, photographs and framed letters bespoke vast collectible wealth.

The house was filled with exhibits of scrimshaw and marine decorations—stern pieces, taffrails, trailboards, paddle-wheel covers and pilot house carved American eagles. One fierce version was perched ominously on the heavy oak headboard of his oversized bed; other carved wood colonial pieces filled the master bedroom, and a curious collection of small antique mirrors filled an entire wall. The bedroom contrasted sharply with the American Empire style furnishings of his parlor, including an array of bowfront cabinetry, relics of the time America went mad for Hepplewhite.

There was also a profusion of mirrors elsewhere in the house, some of them topped with carved eagles or other early American motifs, and guests always seemed surprised to come upon them in odd nooks and crannies.

Along the corridors Tad Remington had hung his most prized possessions of Lincolniana, including several interpretations of the assassination as drawn by contemporary artists. A Currier and Ives print in a gold frame hung on the wall of an ornate powder room, with the legend: BOOTH KILLS LINCOLN, GOOD FRIDAY, APRIL 19TH, 1865. Scattered around the house were framed letters signed by "A. Lincoln," some of them dealing with unbelievably trivial matters. Apparently the Great Emancipator loved writing letters, as though he sensed their special value to future generations. Behind the bar in his large paneled den were photographs of Tad with John Kennedy, two handsome golden boys, sometimes formal, sometimes mugging for the camera, but always signed "With Thanks, Jack."

He owned other letters and framed memorabilia signed by Andrew Jackson, Garfield, both Roosevelts, Truman and McKinley, as well as a collection of gilt-framed portraits of these Presidents. His library, floor to ceiling, offered even more presidential lore with complete leather-bound sets of books by and about the chief executives from Washington to Nixon.

There was also what he called the "Rustic Room," dedicated to his prowess as a hunter, with stuffed antlered heads and a huge prized head of a grizzly, with bared, ominous long teeth. Two glassed-in gun cabinets graced a far wall, one for long guns, the other showing a collection of hand guns. Tiger rugs covered the stepped plank floor, kept glossed and shiny by his housekeeper, a dark Spanish lady.

Because he treated his possessions with a self-deprecating

humor, he was able to soften the awesome effect of its spectacular profusion.

"Here," he would tell guests. "Take the catalogue and look around. I'm bored being the museum director."

He was fond of stitching together his history, as if following some intricate needlepoint pattern, although the morgues of various California newspapers contained fairly documented accounts of his official, personal and family background. There were nonofficial accounts, too, mostly dredged up during his ill-fated Senate race in 1964, a year too late for the other golden boy, mowed down by Oswald's bullet, to be of much help to him.

He had done rather badly in that contest. Postmortems attributed it to his boyish, patrician manner. The voters didn't take him seriously enough and his opponent had somehow got the message across that there was something Scott Fitzgeraldish about him. He had tried to point out that he was not Gatsby, that he came from three generations of authentic old money, cattle, oil and real estate, but the voters went cold. Perhaps he was too handsome, too rich. His mother blamed his defeat on jealousy, the press, the ignorant voters, the communists. Because he had divorced when he was twenty-three and never remarried, the rumor mill portrayed him as kinky, or homosexual. It was, his mother assured everybody, a deliberate attempt at character assassination.

"One thing about him," some of his ex-girl friends had later confided, always with a sigh of regret, "he knows how to make a woman feel good." But even that kind of comment carried with it something mysterious and provocative. It certainly didn't keep the girls away.

"He takes them to the best places. He gives them a glimpse of an elegant life-style, and when he travels he lets them have their own room. That's class." Perceptive Washingtonians agreed.

To the senators, congressmen, ambassadors, cabinet ministers and others in the high ether of Washington society, he carried a glow of undefined importance, earned by fifteen years of glossy entertaining. His invitations were heeded less for himself than because a guest was sure to make an important connection, the real currency of the capital. He was a catalyst, his lavish home a crucible, even though everyone knew that real power was denied him.

Aside from charm, most of his guests agreed he was interesting and slightly eccentric, an image he assiduously cultivated, and a going joke was that if reincarnation existed the men would be happy to return as Thaddeus Remington III. When he heard the joke, he took it as a compliment and retorted that he would foreclose on that possibility by living forever.

Bruce had described him to Fiona long before the July Fourth fireworks party; because he had been single for more than five years, Bruce was an ideal extra man when Remington invited unattached females to his elaborate dinners. When he became attached to Fiona, the invitations ceased temporarily, but now that the Washington grapevine had officially recognized the liaison, the invitations came again, appropriately stated: *The Honorable Bruce Rosen and guest.*

"Well, we made it," he told her.

To Fiona, Remington was an apparition, foreign to her social world which, up to then, had revolved around cops and their milieu. She had learned early that Bruce, despite all his high-minded liberalism, loved the closed circle of the Wasp world and enjoyed the privileged social access to important people.

"I admit it," he had agreed. "I'm bathing in bat dung and loving it."

He was also a gossip. She had found that hard to accept; it was too rarified, too inside, as hers had been when she talked about the eggplant, the chief, the black mafia in the department and some juicy morsels gleaned from the sex squad.

"Sometimes I dated the girls he did," Bruce once confessed during a long postcoital discussion. "They usually skipped any references to Tad's virility as if it were a conspiracy of silence. But they had a lot to say about that damned eagle watching over them on his big bed. Perform or else. One of them had a fantasy that if she faltered, the damned thing would swoop down and bite off her nipples."

48

"Gross."

"One of them said it was the eagle that really turned her on. She wouldn't dare not come."

"Who was that?"

"None of your business."

"Your business is my business. Especially this business."

She patted him fondly there, a signal for the beginning of a new cycle.

"You're just about the most wonderful thing that ever happened to me," he said, and their sexual stirrings altered every nerve end.

"Must be love," she whispered.

"Must be." Only this could stop him talking.

"Just don't introduce me as 'My Homicide Honey,' " she whispered as they passed through Remington's heavy paneled door. He was receiving in the vestibule in front of a large oil of Frederic Remington, a cowboy with a droopy moustache on a horse. The host claimed distant cousinship to the artist, although no one had checked its veracity.

"Wearing your gun?" Bruce asked. He could never accept the fact that she always brought her gun with her to parties. It was regulation for an off-duty cop to have his piece handy when in the District of Columbia. Because it was summer, she had put it in a shoulderstrap purse, the daintiest and dressiest she could find.

"In here," she patted the purse. "Less chic than serviceable. But it does the job."

"If they only knew what was in there."

"Well, if you can carry a hidden weapon, I can."

He had wanted to respond in kind but Remington was upon him, offering his handsome face with a broad smile.

"I see you brought your daughter," Remington joshed. He knew how to pay a compliment.

"I didn't want to compete in your range," Bruce countered, introducing Fiona.

"Ah," he said admiringly. "A daughter of the old sod. I'm really glad you could come."

"He's got the best view in town," Bruce said. "Had the house moved to accommodate the spectacle."

"Well, it's patriotic at least," Fiona murmured. The house had begun to weave its awesome spell, adding to her discomfort. Her trained detective's eye swept the room, revealing no one she knew, although faces were vaguely recognizable. Bruce introduced her around and picked two Scotches off a silver tray being passed by a waiter. In the dining room, she saw portraits of somber ex-Presidents overlooking waiters in black tie who were preparing a buffet.

"There's Senator Moynihan," Bruce said suddenly. "Got to do my thing. I need the guy in my campaign. Mind?"

"I'm not a child," she said. She actually felt like a child suddenly caught in the rain in an open field. There seemed no place to hide.

It was Remington himself who came to the rescue. His wary host's eye had apparently sensed her discomfort.

"We can see the fireworks from the rear lawn," he said. "Considering the distance, the display is surprisingly clear, although we don't hear the boom boom."

"I love your house," she said. It was the most appropriate remark she could think of.

"A bit of a barn," he said modestly.

He smiled, but his blue eyes, despite his charm, seemed layered with ice, confusing her. Perhaps the voters had also seen the chill beneath the facade. His portrait above the fireplace revealed a gorgeous youth and he was aging perfectly, like a well-turned roast, wrinkling in just the right places. His chin was still firm. Beneath his fitted pin-striped suit, he appeared lithe and muscular.

"This is Fiona FitzGerald, Sean," he called suddenly to a youngish man with a ceremonial air.

"Sean Ambrose, the Irish ambassador. This is Miss Fitz-Gerald."

"Cork," he said.

"On the money," she replied. "My father is a professional Irishman."

"So am I. That's what I get paid for."

Even his laugh had a touch of brogue, reminding her of her grandfather, underlining once again the ethnic brotherhood. No one ever leaves Ireland, he had told her once when she was a young girl. How he would have envied her now, facing, almost touching Himself, the representative of the Old Sod?

"To my grandfather, the Irish ambassador was more important than the pope," she said. "Or at the least, the apostolic delegate."

"He's over there," the Irish ambassador said, indicating a man with a priest's collar in the crowd on the lawn. "Tad collects diplomats, whatever the relationship between countries." He pointed out the Russian and Saudi Arabian ambassadors.

"I did my gig," Bruce said, coming up to her. He chatted for a moment with the Irish ambassador, who soon disengaged. She noted how practiced they all seemed, making contacts, moving on, like summer insects around a candlelight, never quite close enough to the flame to get really burned.

Several guests sauntered over to discuss the central topic of all political discussions, reelection.

"Safe?" someone asked him.

"Duck soup . . . if the President can hold our cranky Democrats in line." He looked at her, showing a tiny tremor of anxiety. He is really scared to death, she thought.

"If he don't, we can all run for the hills," the man replied, walking away.

"What is he?"

"An appointee," Bruce replied. "One of nearly three thousand paranoids running around loose, hoping the President will win."

"The perils of democracy," she snickered. He frowned, obviously in no mood to be further reminded of his plight. Meeting peers obviously increased his tension.

"It's the Washington zoo," he whispered, trying unsuccessfully to remove himself from the pack. He ran with these bulls, somewhere in the middle, nondescript. What he wanted was to speed up and get into the lead.

He spent the next half hour pasting titles on the guests. Senators, congressmen, ambassadors, socialites. It wasn't quite the full "A" group, he told her with mock derision. Although Congress was in a short July Fourth recess, many of his colleagues had fled the oppressive Washington humidity. Each title was accompanied by a bit of gossip.

"And there's Tweedledee," he whispered, pointing to an attractive woman in her forties. There was a nervous air of discomfort about her, as if she didn't quite belong there and knew it.

"Used to be one of Jack's girls."

"Jack?"

"Kennedy."

It was one of his affectations to call famous people by their first names. The Johnson landslide in '64 had brought him his first term. But the photograph in his den of Bruce when he was an eager beaver Kennedy advance man gave him, she supposed, special rights.

"He had two White House concubines. Tweedledee and Tweedledum. Just two kids in the typing pool. They serviced him when the wife was away, which was frequently."

There it was again. Closet lechery. A favorite Washington syndrome. The closet image brought back memories of poor Damato, festering in his Lolita fantasy. Had it really killed him in the end? She dismissed the speculation. Mysteries, she had learned, could spawn obsession.

"Louise Padgett Sharp is her name," he said. "Haven't seen her in years." He lowered his voice. "Can't imagine what she's doing here."

Suddenly he spotted someone behind her.

"Good to see you, Mr. Ambassador." He stuck out his hand to a large jolly man. It was the Soviet ambassador. He quickly introduced Fiona. The big man smiled graciously and moved on.

"It's a United Nations," she whispered.

"Just Remington doing his thing."

It was darkening and the guests had begun to crowd the buffet table, taking heaped plates of lobster, roast beef, salad and brie to tables on the lawn, decorated in red, white and blue. Waiters in black tie poured vintage wines. Remington chatted with Mrs. Sharp, giving her more attention than was due a single guest, but it seemed forced. The woman was agitated, she looked furtive and confused.

"He seems interested." Fiona tugged at Bruce's sleeve, but he did not respond. Remington's reaction to the woman was out of kilter. His mask of charm had disappeared, revealing a flash of temper. She felt like a voyeur and quickly turned away.

A collective sigh went up on the lawn. The fireworks had begun, big bursts of colored sparks sprinkling in the humid air. The spectacle seemed to go with Remington's private vision, a tintype with an earlier American flavor.

She also felt patriotic, admiring a spectacular burst that had replicated white stars against a blue field, like the flag.

"Miss FitzGerald," a Hispanic female voice intruded, Remington's maid. "Telephone."

"Dammit," Bruce said irritably.

"Woman's work is never done, Bruce." She had expected this call all evening.

It was the eggplant, and his anger sputtered over the wire.

"You had no right to take those paintings," he shouted as soon as she had identified herself. "A reporter from the Hagerstown Daily Bugle or whatever just creamed all over me. Not to mention their bush league PD and that prick, O-something."

"O'Leary."

"Yeah, him," he mumbled. She let it pass.

"I did it to keep them out of the press. They're going to make the man a pervert."

"Maybe he was."

"He was the victim, remember? Why poison his wife and kids? It could be important evidence." She did not tell him that she also wanted to protect the semi-innocent nymphet.

"I don't like these interdepartmental hassles," he growled. "I also don't like my poker games interrupted."

"Better that we release it properly to our press," she said, sure of her ploy. "We'll look better. Besides, they are Mrs. Damato's property. She let me have them." It was stretching the truth slightly. The poor woman wanted no part of them and would have burned them.

"I want a break in this case, FitzGerald, and I want to come out on top."

"Of course."

Was he uncertain whether to let her continue on the case? But she knew that she was less of a threat than some of the more ambitious black detectives. "I want you to brief me first thing in the morning," he said, surprisingly calm.

There was a pause, then a throaty chuckle at his end.

"What you doin' there with all them fancy dudes, mama?" The jive talk showed his jealousy, also his special form of ridicule.

"Watchin' fire in the sky, man," she shot back, wanting to add "mufucker." The loud click as he hung up tickled her eardrum.

What she did not tell him was that her instincts were rebelling at the idea that Damato was shot by an outraged parent. But the eggplant hated intuition, the despised female taint. Perhaps black men in general hated women, all women. She loathed the generalization, but working in the MPD was teaching her aberrant lessons. She choked off the unworthy thought and a burst of brilliant fireworks helped dismiss it from her mind.

VI

IN THE brief flare of her cigarette, Remington had seen the predatory beak of the wooden bird above them, its carved wingspread hovering over the bed, its beady wooden eyes almost alive, bearing witness. Reaching out, he caressed the smooth ridged claws.

That first time with Louise had set the match to the dry tinder in his soul. The beginning! It had barely been a week, the memorable date, June 29. Eons ago.

He had come across her by accident. She had materialized, a face out of the dim past, at one of those summer obligatory "in honor of" parties on a sprawling Potomac lawn. She had been in his peripheral vision before, but always at a distance. She had never really been part of the scene, always someone to be hidden in a closet, one of Jack's girls.

Perhaps it was the wide-brimmed hat, which cast her face in the shadows, making it look younger, sharpening the image of what she once was. Cute. Time hadn't brightened her intellectually either. Not that he had ever really talked with her in those days. She was just a girl in the typing pool.

"It's destiny," he had told her. She had flushed with pleasure.

"And a very sensuous lady." He had reserved her then, right under a huge tulip oak. She was leaning against it, drink in hand, straightening to make her bosom rounder, a gesture which told him she was available. She had just separated from her second husband, she volunteered. "A real loser." But she had the golden President's mark on her and who could come up to that? Tad had taken her home, calling ahead to Mrs. Ramirez to unfreeze a batch of chili and toss up a salad, which they ate with iced champagne in the Rustic Room. The champagne had made her giggly and the flattery, talkative, as if he were really interested in her pedestrian life. Remington let it all pass through him, waiting for the moment when she would trust him enough to tell him what he had to know.

Everything had been building to this, waiting for just the right moment, the sign. Louise Padgett Sharp was that sign. She wanted more champagne, but he did not open a second bottle. He needed her clear memory. To stimulate her, he showed her pictures of him with the golden President.

"He was lovely," she said, tears brimming over her lids and onto her cheeks. He licked them away, tasting their salt. Then he found her lips, parting them, his eyes open to the photographs.

Upstairs, in his bed, with the wooden eagle as witness, under the approving gaze of its eyes, he did it, as if it were a holy ritual. His tongue explored, probed, searched those places where the golden President had been. Her pleasure was excruciating and he let it occur to her again and again, his own hardness unfaltering.

"My God," she gasped finally.

She had placed her cigarettes on a night table beside the bed. Sliding one out, she groped for a match. Finding none, she opened a drawer and found a little silver gun. "No," he said quickly, "it's not a lighter." She studied it and then tossed it back in the drawer. "I hate them," she said. "They always remind me."

Her matches had dropped to the floor. Finding them, he lit her cigarette and watched as she sent the smoke in spears through her nostrils. Like a miracle, the gun had appeared to bridge the gap. A sign!

"What was he like?" he had asked, no longer tentative. He had won the right to command her.

"Fun," she said, after a long pause.

"I mean, how did he do it?"

"How?" She seemed startled, puffing deeply.

"It turns me on," he said, hating the vulgarism.

"You like to talk it," she laughed. He knew then that he had broached the intimacy. She must like that as well. Perhaps, too, she felt the power of the experience. It was not, he was sure, the first time that she had told it.

"Did he do it straight? Missionary-style?" he coaxed.

"Every way, mostly sitting on his lap. Once he got me in the Oval Office like that. Also, I'd do him under the big desk." She put out her cigarette and rolled over on her side, tracing her nail along his chest.

"Was he big?"

"About like you," she said, looking down. "My God, you're curious." She giggled. "You're making me feel guilty."

"What was his best way?"

"Doggy-style in that room right next to the office," she said without hesitation. "I really loved that."

"What was his face like when . . . you know?"

"He smiled. I made him happy."

He had wanted to ask her more, but her tongue was busy elsewhere. Gently, he eased her away.

"How did he smell?"

"Smell?"

She seemed confused. He repeated the question, sharp, like a scolding teacher.

"Like a man," she said.

"Like me?"

"No. He was an Aqua-velva man." It was meant to be a joke. It irritated him.

"Like a man, Tad," she said in a whining, placating tone. "Like you. I don't have a good memory for smells. He smelled good." She sniffed his body. "Like you." But she did not begin again, squatting at the foot of the bed, watching him, losing the spirit of the game. But he couldn't stop. There were things he had to know, and the trail was endless.

"And how did he feel? I mean, the texture of his skin."

In the darkness across the bed, she moved her legs Indian-style, perplexed but patient. His big toe played with her, reassuring her that it was still play.

"His skin was thick. He had longish hairs on his arms and legs. He was slender, beautiful really." She paused and moved her body forward. "Like you."

A new wave of feeling began, tiny shivers at the base of his spine, radiating through him. She crawled forward and began her tongue's work again.

"And taste," he cried, knowing, certain that some angel was touching him, that he was transcending self, merging with the other golden man, that he was him. Him! The explosion pounded in his brain, surged. His essence flowed upward, forced by the power of the earth, spending in great squirting plumes. Above him, the great eagle flapped his wings, the beak snapped closed and carried him upward. It was, he had no doubt, the final sign.

"Like you," he heard her say. A lifetime had passed. "Like you."

At that moment his plan, resurrected from its suspended state of abstract longing, was irrevocably set in motion, his will inexorably set on its tracks. He knew the time had come.

He devoted most of July 1 to assembling props, going over the minute authentic details. It would be as near perfect as possible, a replication of pristine inspiration. He rechecked his notebook, which he stored in the locked closet of the library along with other items needed to perform these acts.

The bulky man was shot at exactly 9:25 A.M., July 2, ninety-nine years before. Again a sign. Nine and nine. The number eighteen. Arriving at the Baltimore and Ohio Railroad Station five minutes before, the man looked happy, relaxed, anticipating his July Fourth holiday. The other man, Guiteau, wearing black, his droopy moustache and scraggly beard moist in the summer heat, had pumped two bullets into him, the fatal one into his back. Remington checked his *Gray's Anatomy*, also among his props. The .44 slug from the pearl-handled English Bulldog pierced the pancreas, but the big man had miraculously survived when a clotted sack formed around the wound and continued the blood's circulation. That would be impossible to replicate. The other bullet had pierced the man's sleeve, harmlessly.

Guiteau had practiced firing at saplings near the Potomac and Remington had secretly done the same. The authenticity was absolutely necessary, preordained. Otherwise, the signs would disappear. But the context was ninety-nine years after the killing and whoever was ordaining it would also have to make allowances.

That evening he put on the clerical garb, his own symbolic invention, the turned collar tightly grasping the folds of his neck. He studied himself in the myriad mirrors of his bedroom as he put on the black wig, the moustache, the scraggly beard; he packed the gun, the tumbler oiled, with the bullets inserted, a few pages of writing paper, a copy of *The Berean*, that Biblical revision of Guiteau's former cult.

"I am Charles Guiteau," he told his splintered images in the mirror. "And what I do, I do for the good of the country." He let out a childish giggle. It was thrilling. He discovered he had an erection.

He had telephoned to reserve room 222 at the Hotel Washington at Fifteenth and G. It was close enough to the site of the old Riggs House to be acceptable. The fact that the hotel had a room 222 was still another sign. He took his white Volkswagen bug (the other was a Bentley) out of the garage and drove downtown. He had bought it solely for this one task, a chariot of death, waiting for the moment.

The clerk hardly looked up as he checked in and took his cash; he had no credit cards and would stay for only one night. Even the request for room 222 hadn't phased the clerk. Room clerks, Remington had learned, were totally disconnected and indifferent. He signed the card: The Rev. C. J. Guiteau. It was a title his precursor had once assumed.

In the room the air conditioning coughed and sputtered and he could sniff the vague scent of disinfectant. At the writing desk he took a ballpoint pen from his pocket and began to recompose the letter that had pulsed in his memory.

"The President's tragic death was a sad necessity, but it will unite the Republican party and save the Republic. Life is a fleeting dream and it matters little when one goes. A human life is of small value . . ." He paused, studying the words, proud of the flourish of his handwriting; he felt waves of delicious excitement beginning at the base of his spine, radiating out. The exquisite power of it transcended everything, the room with its pedestrian furnishings, the immediacy of time, the other reality of himself. Addressing the envelope to himself as Remington, he sealed and stamped the letter.

He slept like a baby, a leaden, dreamless sleep, and wakened ravenously hungry. He showered, shaved and carefully applied his wig, moustache and straggly beard. He put on khaki pants, a khaki shirt and workman's shoes. He moved close to the smiling image in the mirror.

"I am a stalwart of the stalwarts," he whispered, watching his breath patterns on the glass.

Once more he checked the revolver, making sure that the cartridges were in their proper places. He buffed the pearl handle against his pants, then pointed the gun toward his image in the dresser mirror.

"The President's nomination was an act of God. His election was an act of God. His removal is an act of God."

He felt a tingle of pleasure in his crotch, then put the gun in his left hip pocket. He must, he knew, follow the pattern exactly, as Guiteau had done on that fateful morning.

The air was still crisp, but the sun was already a brilliant glow behind the Capitol in the distance as he walked leisurely through the deserted streets, past the East Gate of the White House in which the President and his family slumbered peacefully. An occasional car passed by on Pennsylvania Avenue. Posting the letter in a mailbox, he crossed to Lafayette Park and sat down on one of the benches facing the White House. The sun, rising quickly now, threw long columnar shadows along the front portico. A spark of light caught the hanging brass lamp, transforming it into a burst of glitter. The panes shimmered like still waters as the sun's rays washed over them.

Stretching, he put his legs in front of him, felt the reassuring weight of the gun and looked about, gratified that he was, except for the squirrels and pigeons, the only living figure in the park. When a bum who might have just risen out of the shrubbery sat on a nearby bench, he left and walked back to the hotel. He had a leisurely breakfast of eggs, bacon, toast and coffee and read the *Washington Post*.

What did Guiteau read ninety-nine years ago to this day? What was Guiteau's state of mind? Had he found the hole of delicious calm, the eye of a hurricane? Had the newspapers told him that the vigorous, bearded ex-soldier would take off for the July Fourth weekend to escape the oppressive heat of the capital?

"More coffee?" a waitress asked politely.

He nodded, studying her as she walked away, annoyed by the patched imperfections of her net stockings. It was the first sour note of the morning. Abruptly he paid the check and left, determined to recapture the symmetry of the illusion.

By nine o'clock, he had parked the Volkswagen in a tight corner of a construction site where the workers parked their cars. He checked the hard hat stored on the back seat, patted the gun in his left hip pocket and set off for the mall entrance of the gallery. The full edge of his excitement had returned and he felt his blood surging, his heart pounding.

"I am alive," he murmured. "Alive. Alive. Alive."

Having rehearsed the moment so many times before, he knew that he would arrive inside the gallery at 9:10, perhaps at the exact moment that Guiteau had arrived, filled with the same potent degree of excitement and fear. He knew it was the missing link in himself. Guiteau, fearing reprisal, the malice of the crowd, had even gone to inspect the accommodations of the District jail. Remington acknowledged a different kind of fear. But events were now in motion, and nothing must prevent him from going full circle.

The gallery had opened at nine. The tourists had begun to

crowd inside; groups of high school students, the retired old people in long Bermuda shorts hanging low over scaly bare legs, cameras swinging from their hands. The rotunda was cool, its fluted columns rising like great stone stalks from the black marble floor. He saw in his own mind the old Baltimore and Ohio Railroad Station that had once stood on this site.

Remington's eyes roamed the vast rotunda, certain that all vectors would intersect. The signs had all proven it. Everything was irrevocable now. As he moved toward the American galleries, he searched for the ultimate sign, a heavy black-bearded man, nearly six feet tall, in his late forties, a physical copy of the original.

As he neared the entrance to the American galleries, a nest of rooms at the outer edge of the west gallery from which he planned his exit, he was suddenly confronted by two men, both bearded, both physically perfect for his purposes. A double sign. Two! He hadn't counted on such a windfall. They were both moving purposefully toward the American section. Which one? He had not counted on choices. According to the plan, he had to act at precisely 9:25, ninety-nine years later to the minute, even at the very second, when the big man had entered the B & O's waiting room. He reached into his pocket, positioned the revolver in his hand, his fingers curling around the cool trigger.

When one of the bearded men trailed off to other galleries, he knew that providence had decided. Miraculously, now, the American galleries were almost empty, the guards lost in a haze of boredom. He had calculated the time it would take to fire and fade away; he had counted on a crowd pushing forward as he scurried down the marble steps to the mall that led to the east wing. He had done all he could do. Now it was up to the unknown force to provide.

The bearded man moved slowly to gallery twenty-six, lingered over the famous George Bellows painting of the battling boxers, then moved to the north wall. At that moment Remington saw the flags, unfurling and flapping in the breeze. Allies Day! Still another sign.

The bearded man paused, studying the painting. Remington

let the seconds pass, then lifted the gun slowly from his hip pocket. The guard had just completed his circle of the room and was wandering off to an adjoining gallery. The room was deserted. The second hand on his watch intersected the six. Crotch tingling, blood surging in his veins, he lifted the gun and stretched out his arm. He sighted along the gun barrel to the spot on the man's body that he had previously plotted, then squeezed the trigger. The report exploded the silence. He pulled the trigger again. The man faltered, staggered and sank to the floor.

He was out of the gallery with the sound of the echo. The gun heated his upper thigh as it rested again in his side pocket. He threaded through a group of high school students, rushing eagerly upstairs. Using them for protection, he moved swiftly to the entrance, turning right through the path between the bushes. Joining a crowd crossing the street, he insinuated himself into a line of pedestrians, using them as a second shield. He made it quickly to the Volkswagen, removed his shirt and put on his hard hat.

Moving close to the construction site, he paused, waited, listened. In the distance he heard the faint sound of an ambulance siren. It grew closer, the sound more raucous. The cacophony of construction sounds splintered the siren's wail. He got out of the car and hiding behind a steel girder, he saw the ambulance pull up to the entrance. A group of Smithsonian guards were rushing about. Several crossed the street, skirting the construction site, going through the confused motions of a search. He snickered. The bureaucratic mind was appallingly unimaginative. Risk nothing was the bureaucratic watchword. He waited until they had dispersed, then calmly got back into the Volkswagen, put the gun in the glove compartment, and drove slowly through the traffic, accelerating only as he turned into Massachusetts Avenue, then into Twelfth Street heading north.

The BMW stood in the glaring late morning sun. Behind the picture window, the rustle of curtains told him that Louise was watching. By now, the flowers, a dozen American Beauty roses had arrived, and the note, along with the car keys in the envelope.

"With gratitude," the note had read. Gratitude? That idea would haunt her forever. He had promised to see her that morning, as if he could not bear to be away from her. Actually, it was a half-truth. The desire for her was overwhelming, necessary and immediate. He needed her to cap the volcano.

Louise opened the door before he could ring and drew him inside, kissing him deeply. The material gift had readied her and he could sense her wetness. Behind him in a cracked vase he saw the long-stemmed roses.

He was ready. The pleasure had been there all morning, waiting, fermenting. He pushed her against the wall of the foyer and almost in one fervent step parted her panties, inserted himself and lifted her by the buttocks. Her legs closed around his waist and she shivered, contracting.

"Yes," she cried as he pumped. He remembered Guiteau's deadly pointed barrel. He felt her paroxysms, heard her screams in gathering crescendoes. His own pleasure lingered, gaining strength like breaking waves.

"More," she gasped as he slid down against the wall. He turned her over roughly, rolled down her panties to her ankles, pressed against the tight small opening. She went down on her knees, helping him as she spread herself and he pounded into her. He held her viselike as she tried to squirm away from the pain.

"Am I him?" he shouted. She screamed out, incoherent words.

"Him?" feeling the eruption begin.

"Him?" he shouted again.

"Yes! Yes!"

He collapsed over her, spent, and she whimpered below him, kissing his palm. She had served her purpose. She was part of the grand design and did not question it. The forces that moved him had their own momentum, their own logic. He would never question, only obey.

VII

THE EGGPLANT was furious. Always, when the chief had berated him, his eyes were bloodshot with anger and his thick black hands shook. He had assembled the entire shift, their faces glum against the sickly green paint of the long office with its rows of mismatched desks and chairs.

He had his back to the blackboard, erased to some parody of cleanliness by one of the frightened officers, Garber, the only white lieutenant, desperately trying to serve out the last seven months of his twenty. Suddenly the eggplant whirled around to the blackboard and squeaked out a word with a nub of chalk.

Assholes.

Fiona had never seen him so angry. They must have really shoved him around upstairs. That meant special trouble for her. She had braced herself, had seen it coming, but had vastly underestimated the fury.

"Assholes," he shouted, looking directly at her.

"You can cut the heart out of a smacked-up nigger on the strip. You can rape some honkie teenage floozie in some back alley. You can waste some hood in front of the White House. That's okay for open cases. But if we can't close a killing in a

65

public building, a fucking public building filled with tourists, then we all belong in the shithouse."

He sucked in a deep breath and tried to calm himself. His hands were still trembling.

"Tourists are the business-blood of this city. Next to government, the second biggest industry," he said almost in a normal voice. He was no longer looking at Fiona. It was obviously the way the chief had put it to him.

Because of the pressure from upstairs, the case had resulted in confusion and paranoia within their department. There were other open cases, but the glare of publicity was on them, and the eggplant, angry and frustrated, had passed it on down, especially to Teddy and her.

It was his special way of coping with upstairs pressure. When things got too hot, he had to perform in front of his available underlings, focusing his anger on specific cops. It was obvious that this brief meeting was called for their benefit alone, a kind of public trial.

"I hate mysteries," the eggplant shouted to the assembled group, forcing her to tune him in again. What he also meant was that it was bad for the percentages. Last year they had closed more cases. Soon they, the ubiquitous white enemy, would blame it on the fact that too many blacks were running the show, even though they had deliberately kept Fiona as the point lady. Now the eggplant was actually ducking press conferences and had changed his home number.

"In an election year we have to be especially responsive to the community," he continued, his eyes wandering, deliberately avoiding Fiona's and Teddy's. "And we live in a society where everyone craps on cops. It's a national pastime. That's why we need to maintain a good public relations attitude and set up priorities." Finally, his gaze rested on Fiona. "And my priority is to pour our maximum effort on those cases directly relating to large bodies of people. Do I make myself clear?"

Fiona nodded eagerly. It was the expected response. Apparently Teddy had been less demonstrative, and the eggplant turned to him with visible fury.

"There is a tendency around here for long-termers to take

things for granted, waiting around to draw retirement. I won't stand for that. Everybody puts out to the end, down to the last second of the last minute of the last day. You all get that." The *all* was superfluous. Everyone knew whom he meant.

Poor Teddy. He didn't have the protection of her sex. He became inert, fear-ridden, and it showed.

"You can't leave me hanging by my thumbs," the eggplant had shouted at him after the meeting. The door of his office was open. He wanted everyone to hear.

She had read and reread her notes, badgering Flannagan at the lab and Hadley in ballistics. Had they missed something? They interviewed eyewitnesses again and again. There simply were no clues. She couldn't come up with a single theory. Their trips to Hagerstown had led nowhere.

As she had predicted, the hapless Damato was savaged in the press as a pervert and the nymphet, Celia Baines, had attained a dubious notoriety. But there was nothing concrete, except the blank walls that ended every investigative path.

The eggplant had tried brutally to force the issue. It was already late July and he had begun to feel the first sharp needles of pressure. The press had turned ghoulish, and had exaggerated the episode. The *Post* had run a series on crimes in public buildings, and a television station did a three-part series about Washington tourists who had died under mysterious circumstances, going back over more than 150 years of history.

The District government, meaning the mayor and his staff, already paranoid in a presidential year, saw a conspiracy to hound them out of getting their just budget rewards. As always, the police hierarchy saw the media campaign as an attempt to prove their incompetence on solely racial grounds. The chief and his major deputies were all black.

His superiors accused the eggplant of creating the limelight so that he could dance in the circle of glory. It was one of the hazards of the publicity seeker. Being caught in the white heat of that spotlight also made one a target. Fiona got little satisfaction from such wisdom. The politics of the bureaucracy had its own wisdom.

A few days later she was summoned to the eggplant's office

alone, an ominous sign. It was raining, a driving summer rain that tapped out a drumbeat on the dusty windows of his office.

He sat behind his desk, on which piles of cigarettes filled his numerous ashtrays. For some reason he did not empty them, as if they were there to illustrate his displeasure.

"That Baines girl," he grumped. "You let her off the hook. You didn't even sweat her. Or her old man." He was matter-of-fact, although she felt the capped pressure. Bloodshot eyes scowled at her.

"The manager vouched for her that morning. Teddy covered that base. She was working the breakfast shift. The old man was sleeping off a drunk and the mother . . ."

"Sheet," he interrupted, punching out yet another cigarette, the nicotine yellow deep against his black gnarled fingers. He picked up a sheaf of papers, read the first page, then threw it back on his desk. She braced herself.

"Hagerstown PD got another story. The assistant manager was on duty, not the manager. According to him, she didn't show till noon. That, smartass lady, is bad police work."

As senior detective, Teddy had given her latitude and it had blown up in his face. She knew the eggplant had her. She was sorry for that, guilty. But she had indeed overlooked a confirmation. Why? Had she dismissed the girl as innocent too quickly?

"You and your goddamned Master's degree."

"Maybe I goofed," she said, opting for quick surrender. "Maybe I was too intuitive. It was my own damned fault."

"Women's intuition," he smirked. "Magic bullshit. As if it were something holy. You all should stay out of police business."

"I don't appreciate the generalizations," she snapped. The door to his office was closed. No witnesses. His word against hers. She braced for more abuse.

She watched him struggle to cap the temper. His disdain hung in the room like the after-stench of a fire.

"I want that bitch sweated. And the manager. And the mother. And her old man. And I want you to sweat her . . . And another thing. I'm divorcing you and Teddy. I think you got his balls in your hand."

"What the hell does that mean?"

He watched her, then showed his large teeth in what passed for a smile.

"I'll put it another way, mama," he said softly. "You've pussy whipped him. He's lost his . . . ," he groped for a professional touch, ". . . his initiative."

"You'll be humiliating him," she said. Her stomach tightened. "That's not fair."

"Fair? Fair is for games. Not murder."

She braced herself for more.

"I'm putting Jefferson on your case."

"*Jefferson.*" It came out as an oath.

Jefferson was a swaggering egomaniacal black stud with a mouthful of ghetto sewer talk. The Ape, they called him in the department. Worse, he was proud of it. He had been a Ranger in Vietnam in the early days, cultivating the image of the cruel avenger. They called him the Ape, someone had told her, because of that old joke.

"Where does that big Ape sit?"

"Anywhere he wants."

He had a reputation for uncompromising cruelty to criminals, especially black ones, and he was an outspoken honky-hater. She knew that he considered women a subspecies, and white women unclassifiable, although it was rumored that he would use them, if opportunity knocked, for their only obvious function.

Jefferson had been brought up on so many disciplinary charges that they were considered pro forma. They were always dismissed with a slap on the wrist. Apparently his misdeeds were merely the fantasies of other black cops saddled with the job of patrolling a jungle where their brothers were the principal enemy.

She had barely talked to him, although he always gave her a lascivious look, accompanied by a grab at his Johnson. The gesture, she knew, was so endemic among black men that she began to feel that she was the only one it offended. Despite his faults, Jefferson was marked as a good cop. But the idea of working with him did not appeal to her.

"Not him," she muttered. "Not Jefferson."

The eggplant observed her squirm, enjoying her discomfort. Finally he stood up and leaned over her, pointing a big finger, almost touching her nose. She confronted it, unblinking. She knew he was itching for her to show some insubordination. Controlling her anger, she let the confrontation become a checkmate. It was futile for both of them. They had no witnesses and, if he had the room bugged, she wasn't going to give him any evidence. Besides, it was a case that no one wanted. It was doomed to be a standoff, like a bad Irish Catholic marriage.

The eggplant suddenly turned to his telephone and dialed a number. His rudeness was an obvious dismissal.

She was surprised to find Jefferson standing outside the door, waiting. His lugubrious heavy-lidded eyes matched her mood. His lips were tight with contempt.

"It ain't my idea, mama," he said, observing her like a meat inspector.

"Ours is not to reason why."

"Ours is but to do or da," he took up the beat, showing off. So he was not as dumb as he looked. She also was struck by his ghetto accent, slightly awry, as though it were forced.

He drew air through the spaces of his teeth and offered her a mocking smile.

"All I ask from you is professionalism," she said.

"Say what?" he said, scratching his crotch.

"And I'd appreciate it if you stopped that disgusting habit."

"Got to be sure it stays put, mama." Jefferson swaggered to the door, his large tight bulging rump moving like chunks of granite under his jacket.

The other detectives were eyeing them. The blacks seemed to snicker, the whites wore an air of futility. They turned away, avoiding comment. She saw Teddy in a corner, typing with fierce concentration, obviously too ashamed to look up. Shrugging off a biting guilt, she followed Jefferson's big rump down the hall.

"But you said you were working," Fiona said gently, although she had been at it for nearly half an hour. Celia's fingers shook as she lit a cigarette from the butt end of another. Jefferson leaned against the wall at Hagerstown Police Headquarters, watching them. The girl was obviously lying. Jefferson was growing restless, scornful of her method of interrogation.

"I was," the girl repeated for the twentieth time.

"Your mother says you weren't."

"She was sleeping."

"And your father agrees."

"He was drunk."

They had the manager cooling his heels in another room. So far they had prevented the Hagerstown police from getting into the act, particularly O'Leary. Even Fiona had to admit that it was Jefferson's awesome presence that had done the trick. He knew how to use his power and could produce an intimidating scowl on demand. On the way to Hagerstown she had made some effort to connect with him, but his grunts told her he was in no mood to meet her even halfway.

The wife of the McDonald's manager had told them her husband had gone fishing that morning. It was his day off and he had caught some trout from a mountain lake which they had had for dinner. They in turn did not tell her that the manager had taken unscheduled leave.

To Fiona, the connection between the two seemed obvious, and she sensed that the girl was frightened of Jefferson.

"Maybe if you left us alone . . . ," she suggested as they conferred in the corridor.

"No way," he sneered. "It's bad enough ahm lettin' you do it to her."

"I suppose you can do better."

"Sheet." She did not want him to have a go at the girl. Left to him, the poor kid would confess to anything.

"She's just not guilty. The chief is wrong. Dead wrong."

"If you don't do it . . . ," he said menacingly.

"You think she's guilty. Or the other one." She motioned to where the manager sat glumly on a nearby bench.

"Sheet, no. Ah jes want to hear it so we can get the fuck outa here, mama."

"So you know it's an exercise in futility?"

"It's bullsheet."

When they came back in, Fiona went up to the girl, who looked pale and forlorn in the harsh light.

"You're not helping yourself," she said. The girl shrugged stubbornly.

"You want me to sic him on you?" She pointed to the scowling Jefferson.

"I ain't gonna let no nigger cop mess with me," she cried. Jefferson grabbed his bulge in his big hand and clicked his tongue.

"It's disgusting," Fiona said. Jefferson accentuated his gesture. Irritated, Fiona looked at the girl, who glared at Jefferson and sneered.

"You were shacking up with the manager. He told us," Fiona snapped. She had wanted to be gentle, but the girl's arrogance and Jefferson's obscenities now irritated her.

Celia's eyes opened wide; her jaw dropped.

"He didn't tell you nothin'," she said angrily. At that point Jefferson exploded, moving his big bulk to within a hairsbreadth of her, crotch high, confronting her with his raw maleness. He opened his jacket, revealing a Magnum .44, snug in its holster, hanging down his right side. On his left side, under his armpit, she could see his regulation .38. The exhibit, Fiona knew, was also for her benefit.

"You little honky cunt. Dumb ass. Ah gonna give you a clue . . ."

"She'll talk," Fiona objected. "You said you'd stay out of it."

"Sheet. You want us to take you to DeeCee and put you in a room with a bunch of nigger cops like me? They'll pound your ass dry. Now you stop this bullsheet, mama, cause I'm gonna do that." He waved a big black fist in front of her nose.

"I'll scream," the girl gasped.

"You do that," Jefferson said, caressing the length of the Magnum. "And ah know jes where to put this."

What little blood was left by then drained from the poor girl's face. Before Fiona could react, the girl spoke in a rush.

"So I was shackin' up. So what? I never killed no one."

It went quickly after that, the manager capitulating easily. It would be all over town soon.

"I'll lose my job. Maybe my wife," the frightened manager said when they confronted him. Fiona felt unclean.

"You are one mean bastard," she said to Jefferson in the car. The two statements in manila envelopes lay between them on the front seat. "I could turn you in for that piece. Also for the way you leaned on her."

"Ain't nothin' but a woid," he said, turning toward her, revealing the shrewdness under the macho pose. "You do that to me?" He put his big hand on her thigh and squeezed it.

She quickly reached for her gun and pointed it at his crotch.

"I could invent a good cover story."

He ignored her and accelerated the car.

"Did you wanna waste your time with all that bullsheet? Jes because that asshole at headquarters got a bug up there? We got killers to catch, mama."

"I'm not your mama," she said sharply. "Unless you're not sure yourself." The gun felt useless in her hand and she slipped it back in its holster.

He laughed, for the first time, indicating a softness behind the glowering ebony facade.

"Jes wanna see how tough you are." He winked.

"I don't like tests."

"In a pinch, you'll be glad I'm around, woman," he said.

"There's another test I don't want to take," Fiona said. But all the same she found it an oddly reassuring remark.

She had tried. She had put her heart into it. Her last conversation with Mrs. Damato the night before she left Hagerstown for good eliminated any possibility of a hard theory. Jefferson had left them alone, swaggering out to get a few beers.

"Maybe whoever did it put him out of his misery," Mrs. Damato said, her face bloodless, her eyes dry.

"We'll find out who did it," Fiona said, catching the rhythm of the woman's pain.

"He had this dream that he was going to be great, a foremost

American impressionist. Ever since I married him. The worst thing is that I believed it." She sighed sadly. "A case of more ambition than talent, I guess. I gave up everything for that idea. I bought it whole. I guess I can start living for myself again." She shook her head and played with her fingers. "And the kids." She looked up at Fiona. "I envy you. Out there living life."

"The grass is always greener," Fiona said.

"Don't ever get mixed up with a man with an impossible dream," Mrs. Damato said, her eyes misting. The warning found its mark.

"I never graduated college," the woman said. "I gave it up to make him a family."

"Maybe you can go back now." Fiona wondered what her own regrets would be ten years from now.

"I envy you," the woman repeated.

"You'll be fine," Fiona said, letting Mrs. Damato hug her. Fiona smelt her acrid odor. At least, she had had her husband's dream. Better than nothing. A sob welled up in Fiona's chest. She was happy Jefferson wasn't around to see her unprofessional compassion.

What was worse, the woman had forced her to look at Bruce in a new light. Was he, too, chasing a futile dream?

By then it was apparent that Bruce's opposition was formidable and he had to spend more and more time in his Queens constituency. Fence-mending, he called it, but on the days she went up to New York with him, she saw what he was really facing. The demographics of his district, which hugged the borders of Brooklyn, were changing rapidly.

"There aren't any fences to mend," he confessed. Although he kept an apartment in his district, the air conditioning was broken and they stayed at the New York Sheraton. He was restless, hyped up by his frenetic activity and the frustrations of his campaign. Even the party system had broken down and his opponent had opted not to try to beat him in the primaries, but to run on an Independent-Liberal ticket, tempting a Republican to further split the vote.

"I'm being squeezed from both ends," he would tell her, usually in the middle of the night, sitting up in bed.

"You'll be stronger if you win. Then no one can ace you out of the Senate race."

"If I win."

"You can't lose your confidence."

"It's around here somewhere," he said with sarcasm. The fear of losing had made him a different person.

"I really need you, baby. More than ever."

She was flattered. But the summer's tension was taking its toll.

"My mind is elsewhere," he confided. She also retreated from sharing her professional frustrations. The campaign absorbed him completely.

"Hasn't that fellow found the answer?"

"Clark? He's working on it."

An air of desperation seemed to cling to him.

"Maybe I can put a contract out on the lady." He had first raised the point as a joke, but when he repeated it she caught an undercurrent of wishful thinking.

"Like your friend at the gallery. Bing bang. Not a clue."

"I told you that in confidence," she rebuked him.

"A random shot by a hired killer. Sounds to me what happened to your gallery man."

"The finger would point right up your nose," she said. "You'd be suspect number one."

"I've thought of that."

He spent much of his time in New York, trying to save his political life. Her work kept her in Washington. Mostly she rattled around in the Georgetown house by herself, waiting for his calls.

"I need you here. Not there," he would plead.

"I have my work."

"But this is really a crisis. Really important."

She dismissed such selfishness as being caused by panic.

"This campaign is life or death for me, Fi. I need the woman I love beside me."

"I wish I could."

"But you can." He was really saying that his career was the more important of the two. She promised that she would take her vacation in late October and be with him at the height of the campaign. It didn't placate him.

"I need you now."

"I can't, darling. I really can't."

What she did not tell him was that she had been on the verge of asking the eggplant for leave. Unfortunately the timing was out of the question. She had to stay on the Damato case, if only to resist hearing him rave about the unsuitability of women cops.

"Always something," she imagined he would say. "If it's not your damned periods, it's your love life or your damned pregnancies or abortions . . . or whatever. Always something going on down there."

"If you really loved me, you would," Bruce whined.

"But I do," she protested.

"You'd also benefit," he said. "Especially if we got married."

"Is that a proposal?"

He hesitated. "After I win."

"Suppose you lose?"

He didn't respond. She sensed the manipulation and it offended her. What did one thing have to do with another?

VIII

STANDING IN the foyer of his home, Remington greeted each man in turn, flashing the patrician smile. He had accepted the fundraising assignment for the presidential challenger with joy and relief. Through the month of July, he had waited for another sign. None came.

The candidate himself had called him right after the Republican convention. Remington had sent him a polite telegram and an offer of support.

"I need you, Tad." The candidate had responded with a phone call, his trained television voice warm, charming. Here was a personal involvement. The man himself had called. Was it the sign?

"I'm ready," he had promised the candidate, assuring him that he could muster at least a hundred thousand dollars if he would appear at his home to press the flesh. The candidate had agreed instantly.

"Is he coming?" someone asked. The man was a banker, he needed instant reassurance.

"Yes," he said emphatically, although the man in charge of appearances had been suspiciously tentative, undermining the clear-cut sign. If he doesn't show, Remington vowed, the sign would be a false omen. He had set himself a deadline of September 5. Today! To provide the essential replication, the deed would have to be achieved by the afternoon of September 6. Tomorrow!

As the hour of the candidate's arrival approached, he became increasingly nervous. The voices in the room grew louder and eyes gazed anxiously toward the door.

"He'll be here," Remington assured those who asked, glancing at the large grandfather clock poised to sound its ten chimes. The candidate was already half an hour late. Many of his guests would not ever have been granted access to his house without having paid the political price of admission, one thousand dollars. They were the cream of merchant Washington, the bankers, brokers, drug and retail tycoons, real estate developers, the backbone of the city's commerce and, with the exception of a few, not social equals, certainly not among the capital's permanent elite.

"Money has its limits," he mused, looking over the crowd.

They were his father's words. He looked up at the portrait of the golden hero, searching for reassurance. His father's persistent mocking reverberated in his mind.

"Joe Kennedy gave his kids the political drive," his mother had protested to the old man. "All you do is inhibit Tad's."

"Politicians are whores," his father had replied. There was a thirty-year difference between them, and by the time Tad was certain of his calling, the man was doddering. To the end, his father fought his mother's ambition for him.

"He has everything," his mother had contended, an assessment that he secretly believed himself. His mother's judgment had, by then, become infallible.

"Who is going to run this business?" his father had protested. He was a great believer in blood. To him, Tad's future was preordained.

"I married you for heirs."

"I'm not a brood mare," she had told both of them more than once. It took him years to understand what she really meant, and by that time his father had died and he had won his first race for the state senate of California. He was twenty-three years old, fresh from Korea.

"I wish the old bastard could see you now," she had said on that election night, at a party for two hundred in her big Nob Hill house.

"This boy will be President," she had told the crowd while standing on a chair in her stockinged feet. "And I'm being perfectly objective." The crowd had laughed, but he was sure that she was absolutely correct. She had always believed that.

The power and enormity of her drive had always been Tad's guiding force. It was she who had stepped in to run the business —cattle, oil, real estate—amassing a considerable fortune that had been enhanced by three generations of Remingtons.

After his father's funeral, she had taken him along to the old man's massive office near the vaunted Pacific Club, detouring from the cemetery. She had summoned his top men.

She looked wonderful, he remembered, dressed in black, her sculpted cheekbones subtly rouged and her pouting sensual lips painted lightly with pink lipstick. Her eyes were his. When he looked into hers he saw his own, long lashed, deep, as blue as a spring sky.

Lifting her veil, she settled into the soft brown leather swivel chair. The young Tad stood beside her, his hand in hers, feeling the power of its grasp, their shared secret, safe and warm, between them.

His father's six top executives, uncomfortable in their mourning pinstripes, faced her. She did not ask them to sit down, and they shifted and harrumphed in discomfort as her blue eyes searched their frightened faces.

"This is my company now," she said quietly, her free hand stroking the polished mahogany of the ancestral desk.

The men facing her were granite faced and solemn, and nervously glanced at each other.

"All decisions will be mine to make. All."

He remembered the silence in the room. His admiration was absolute. A thrill had charged through his body.

"We'll help you all we can," one of the men said, a big red-haired fellow who towered over the others. His height seemed to give him added authority. "Rem had his finger on everything." His implication was clear.

"So will I."

"There's a lot to it, Mrs. Remington," another man said. "There's a great deal at stake."

"What's at stake," she said sharply, "is mine." She had squeezed Tad's hand and looked at him lovingly. "And my son's." He was, after all, the only progeny, the golden boy.

"I can't believe that Rem meant for you to take an active role in day-to-day management," the red-haired man said. His tone was patronizing.

"Why not?" she asked in a silky voice.

"He would have wanted you protected. This is a complex business, full of intricate details requiring sophisticated decisions." The big man shifted from one leg to another, his confidence rising with his words. He was obviously expressing a consensus of all the executives. Certainly, while his father lay dying, they had discussed it, planned for it. His mother's shock tactic had temporarily discomfited them, but they were quickly recovering.

"You give me options. I'll decide," she said, her lips smiling sweetly. How delicious, he remembered. She had their balls in her hand.

The red-haired man surveyed the faces around him.

"It's not as simple as that," he persisted, his courage fully returned as he looked down at her.

"I know," she said. "And I appreciate your candor." She was calm, revealing not a ripple of tension. "And you're presenting me with my first options. That's why I'm firing you."

The big man was stunned, his pale skin flushing almost to the color of his hair. He swallowed hard.

"I helped build this business," he whispered hoarsely.

"You have our gratitude," she had replied. He had seen big tears well in the man's eyes as he turned and staggered out of the room. By the time she was finished, three others had also gone.

"Do we understand each other?" she asked the remaining

three men. They nodded grimly and left the room, backing out as if she were a figure of royalty.

"That's power, my darling," she said, embracing him. He could still smell her delicious freshness, still feel the glorious special aura of her. Her eyes had always been his mirror.

"Mama will show you, my sweet wonderful boy."

He had tried. He had given it his best and when Kennedy had appointed him an assistant secretary of the navy, both he and his mother were sure he had a foothold on the political ladder.

It was a perfect time to marry Ann Fairchild, and the golden boy and his fragile wife were given a wedding send-off that made headlines in every social page in America.

"A reasonably good choice," his mother had admitted.

Mostly it was her decision; an appropriate wife was essential to a rising politician with his eye on the White House. With her credentials as an heiress to one of the great old American families, Ann seemed perfectly crafted for the role.

"She'll be of great help," his mother had assured him.

"She's not much in other departments," he had confessed. She had not stimulated him either physically or intellectually.

"She'll be good for you in Washington. You just can't get anywhere being single. You'll want to entertain. Be seen."

Unfortunately, Ann had barely made a dent in his life, although she obediently plodded through his first years in Washington. After three years of mutual boredom, they decided to divorce, but then the Senate chance had come up.

"You should wait until after the election," his mother had said. "You owe it to yourself."

A fleeting memory, his mind could barely find Ann's outline. The divorce after his defeat was a relief to them both.

"Good riddance," his mother had told him then. "Her indifference lost you that election. Don't worry, the chance will come again." Her dreams would not admit defeat.

Remington was growing more irritable by the moment. The candidate was very late. Had he not been forceful enough in demanding the candidate's appearance? He tried to rein in his anxieties, to keep that Pandora's box closed.

"I can't stay much later," the banker collared him again. "You said he'd be here."

"He promised, and I promise you he'll be here."

"What's a politician's promise?" the banker sneered.

Remington could no longer cope with the anxiety of waiting. He went up to his bedroom and searched his faces in the many mirrors, moving close to one of them, as close as he could get without losing focus.

"I need this sign, mama," he whispered, probing into his mother's blue eyes. He had made such careful, elaborate plans. He resisted going to his closet, to touch the gun hidden there. What had gone wrong? A wave of tremors wracked his body. His mouth went dry. What had he done to incur such a defeat?

"Mama," he pleaded, searching her eyes again.

The door chimes clanged like the clarion of church bells. Racing down the stairs, he appeared in time to be the first to greet the candidate, to touch the cool flesh of his hand. A lightning shock passed through him, eliminating anxiety.

"Tad," the candidate said, pressing his hand, palms touching, fingers intertwined. He did not want to let go. The man's energy flowed into him.

"I'm sorry I'm late," the candidate said, looking around at the faces of the waiting men, awed and silent now. "Sorry, guys," he waved, pressing into the crowd. Remington's hand was locked around one arm. He introduced the candidate to every man in the room. The candidate, picking up the cues, smiled boyishly, nodding as he caught and repeated each man's first name.

Remington felt the muscle of the man's upper arm, strong, hard, like his own. When they had made their rounds, the candidate was given a drink and sat down on the couch. Remington made his introductory remarks.

"This man is our next President." He lingered over the words, feeling every man's eyes on him. He felt the candidate's presence beside him, their mingling energy. *We are one,* he wanted to say.

Instead he said: "We are of one mind. One mind—in philosophy, outlook, vision and hope. The future of our country is at stake. We've come forth with our money to support this man in whom we believe." He had wanted to say love. "But our dollars are only one small part of what support he must have. Money has its limits." He was surprised that the familiar words had come out, as if by divine fiat. Surely, it was yet another sign.

As the candidate rose, Remington's heartbeat leaped, his armpits flooded, and a pleasurable tingle began at the base of his spine. He felt the sheer power of himself.

"This is one helluva fella," the candidate said, putting an arm around Remington. He felt as if he would swell up and burst with pleasure. He was glowing, with a perfect blue flame.

The sign had come, validating his motives, the rightness of his projected act. Tomorrow, he thought happily. September 6.

IX

WITH ALL suspects checked out and eliminated, the Damato case became a gnawing embarrassment. Thankfully, the press turned its attention to other matters. The hostage crisis. The declining economy. The presidential campaign.

The eggplant assigned them to the boring routine of checking out natural deaths, which did not improve Jefferson's disposition. He didn't like being part of the punishment to Fiona. What she learned later through the grapevine was that Jefferson, too, was being disciplined for a brutal beating he had given a drug dealer involved in an earlier murder.

But the Damato case continued to bug her and, when she found the time, she would mentally retrace the investigation. Was there something she had overlooked? It was not a subject she cared to discuss with Jefferson.

She pressed Hadley, the firearms examiner, on the question of the gun and the bullets. He was a tall ascetic man, not given to speculation.

"As my report says, from the lands and grooves, it could only be an English Bulldog or a Wembley. Hard to tell the age. They stopped making them in '39."

"When did they start?"

"The design was first manufactured in 1880, a historic piece. Qualifies as an antique."

"And the bullets?"

"Old. Made, I'd say, about that time."

"Why a bullet that old?"

"I just identify them," he shrugged.

"You don't think it's odd?"

"In this business, everything's odd. Old ammo is not that rare. It hangs around. Sometimes it's not reliable."

"This was."

"Shows how good they made 'em back then."

"But why would someone go out of his way to use old bullets if he could get new ones?"

"You're the detective," Hadley said.

At the autopsy, she had watched Dr. Benton's strong dark fingers deftly slice into the cold alabaster flesh. In the glare of the overhead light the corpse looked like a bloated fish. Dr. Benton's rich voice, with its Louisiana back parish accents, fell soft and melodious in the quiet room as he dictated his findings. Deftly he extracted the bullet where it had lodged in the pancreas. It had severed a main artery, and the man's life had quickly hemorrhaged away.

"Destructive devil," Dr. Benton said as the bullet pinged into a metal pan. His hair was white and cottony, his carriage stooped and scholarly, an authentic wise man's mien. Of all the men that she had met in police work, he seemed to have the widest understanding of human nature.

"It's as if he aimed straight for that artery," he said, pointing to the shredded lifeline. Autopsies had never made her queasy, although she gagged when she had to put the garbage in her apartment's compactor chute.

"Purely accidental," Dr. Benton said. Gently, he opened the man's lids as if he were still alive. The eyes were glazed, as dead as his living dreams. "It was a fluke shot. A smaller projectile might have missed it."

"What kind of a person shoots another in the back?" she had

asked him over coffee at Sherry's a few weeks later.

"A guilty man, perhaps."

"Of course he's guilty."

"I mean guilty of something else other than the crime. Why then not face his victim? Normally, your garden variety killer would shoot from the front, finding the heart. A contract killer, on the other hand, would go for the head on a rear shot. No. This man is guilt-wracked. Driven."

"You learned that from the autopsy?"

"From living. From seeing so much violent death. This was no random shot."

"Sounds more like instinct than science."

He sipped his hot coffee, smacking his lips.

"Science is nothing without intuition," he muttered, staring off into space.

He was a widower and lived in an attached house in Northeast Washington, a few blocks from Capitol Hill. It was stuffed, floor to ceiling, with books and magazines. Occasionally he had invited her in for Sunday afternoon tea. He had been deeply attached to his late wife, a lawyer, and memories of her were framed throughout the house: her degrees, photographs, awards.

"You don't think it was a crime of passion or revenge?" Fiona pressed.

"No. It wouldn't explain the rear shot."

"Maybe it got out of hand. Maybe he only wanted to maim?"

"It was not the gunman's to control," Dr. Benton said.

"Do you think the victim knew the killer?"

He was always open with her, treating her as an equal. She attributed that to a general respect for women, a by-product of his happy marriage. He was the closest thing to a "rabbi" that she had in the department. Unfortunately, as a medical examiner, he was far outside the chain of command and of little practical help.

"I don't think so," he said, mulling over the question. "If it was an act of passion or revenge, the killer would not forego the psychic pleasure of direct confrontation. The dramatist knows this, and he is right. This man killed for other reasons."

"And therein lies an enigma." The frustration was eating badly at her.

The enigma lingered in her mind, waiting to be supplanted by other more pressing concerns. And, they came, they always did.

She had promised Bruce she would go with him to New York for the Labor Day weekend, the deadline for their experiment in communal living. Outside pressures had intervened, making any definitive decisions impossible. He hadn't expected to be confronted with a formidable challenger and she had not expected things to go badly in her work. The gallery case remained unsolved. Nothing was going right.

When the duty roster came down, marking her for the entire Labor Day weekend duty, she stormed into the eggplant's office.

"I need this weekend," she said abruptly.

"I can't spare you." He did not look up from the pile of papers on his desk.

"It's okay with Jefferson," he growled. She stood over him a long time, fighting to control her anger. He looked up and smiled a big toothy grin, goading her.

"I won't beg you."

"I know," he said calmly. She could have called in sick. It was too late now.

"You're being unfair," she said.

"I'm being a boss."

A bastard, she thought.

"It's a big weekend. We need all hands." Although he was being official, his eyes told her otherwise. It was rumored that the chief had given him the deadline of Labor Day on the gallery case, but things had quieted down. He was beginning to believe that the crisis was passing and he was celebrating the event by showing her who was boss. He picked up the telephone, dismissing her.

"You could have helped me out," she told Jefferson as they cruised the city on routine patrol. Their verbal back-and-forth had been so scanty that she realized she had never even broached the subject.

"You never asked, mama."

"I won't ask you for squat."

"You sure are an uppity woman," he grinned.

"I'm a cop, not a woman."

They had maintained a kind of professional truce during their weeks together and she had steadfastly avoided confrontations, hoping that nature would take its course and this unnatural alliance would fall apart on its own volition. Sooner or later they would have to be separated. But both knew the timing for such a divorce was still a long way off. It had become, for both of them, a test of patience.

"I can't wait for the day," she muttered.

"I'm jes gettin' to like it. Nothin' like a challenge."

"It's a dead end for both of us."

"Ain't nothin' but a woid."

"Those stupid ghetto expressions. They make me sick."

"Jes don't throw up on the seats, mama."

When she told Bruce about their lost weekend, he fell into one of his hurt child moods.

"What are you trying to prove?" he asked, after an evening of icy indifference. They were sitting on the patio of his townhouse, having their after-dinner coffee. She had cooked him a meal before breaking the news. "Call in sick. Ask for a transfer. Quit. Anything. Why should you let those bastards control your life?"

"I'm a professional," she mumbled.

"It's not worth the candle."

"You're asking me to understand your war. Understand mine."

"Dammit, Fi, you could be a senator's wife," he fumed.

"I don't like titles, especially 'wife' of . . ."

"Better than having to take shit from a bunch of shmoogies. Besides, you're lost in a man's world, the lower depths at that, strictly blue collar. Cops got no class."

"Bad for your image, you mean," she snorted. "The great liberal. At least we're not hypocrites."

"What is it you women want?" he shouted.

"That's what Freud asked," she said calmly.

The saucer shook, clattering the cup. He seemed to be making an effort to soften his anger.

"How about what I want?" he said more gently.

"I know what you want, Bruce."

"So then, why all this . . . stubbornness?"

"I'm not going to let the bastards do me in."

"At my expense?"

"I'm sorry. I have battles, too."

He took her hand.

"I can lean on them, you know. There's a way to horse-trade." He looked into his cup. "If I lose, I also lose the clout. That's the name of the game. Clout."

"You miss the point. What the good Dr. Freud couldn't know was the answer. I want . . ." She paused, clicked her tongue. "My own."

"Your own what?" He paused, observing her. "Penis?"

"Jesus."

"He had one."

"My God."

"Him, too."

The wisecracks loosened him and he framed her face in his hands.

"I love you and admire you." He kissed her lips. "You're a beautiful sexy lady. How did you get mixed up in such a macho business? Your sex is an intrusion. Don't you understand that? I mean there is a difference. A cop is a father figure. It's a no-win career. And most of them are not even your intellectual equals."

"Who's the bigger bigot?"

To argue further would get them nowhere. Besides, she came from a long line of thick-headed micks who felt something sacred about their calling.

"Maybe I'm just a dumb Irish cop," she said.

"Well, if we don't have the weekend . . ." He moved closer and his warm breath tingled her ear. "We'll just have to compress the timeframe," he said, biting into her neck.

She moved out on Saturday morning. There were no tears or recriminations. No sad words; no bad words.

"We've got too much on our plates just now," she told him. "Maybe later."

"You're still my girl," he said, turning to embrace her as they lay in bed. She traced his profile with her fingers. Before she moved in, they had rarely spent full nights together. He had wanted to be home when the children wakened and the delicious luxury of the morning was lost to them. Now they both clung to it.

"Still your girl," she said.

"Maybe when we both stop trying to make it . . ." he began, his voice trailing off as he kissed her deeply. Make what? she wanted to ask, but held back, disinclined to start down that path again, questioning the priorities of their lives.

"Every once in a while, we'll run away," she breathed into his ear.

"To where?"

They made love, but the sense of loss weakened the pleasure; it was less sensual, more cerebral. It was a sharing neither of them could articulate. And in the end it boiled down to an airport farewell.

"I'll call you when I get back on Tuesday," he said. He kissed her lightly and picked up his bags.

"I'll be waiting."

When he left, she packed quickly. She did not want to stay in his house alone anymore.

X

I N THE downpour, the old gingerbread State Department Building still retained a gloomy dignity; despite its name, EOB, Executive Office Building, old Washington hands still referred to it as Old State. To the east, the White House seemed like a varnished wedding cake preserved intact long after the nuptial party had left the ceremony.

The image amused him as he walked, head down against the rain gusting into his face. Government, with all its paraphernalia, its restrictions, its inhibitions, was not natural to the human condition. As Tad he might have thought otherwise. But as Czolgosz, he had to flog himself to accept that perception. Czolgosz believed that. It strengthened his motivation and goaded him to make his own historical contribution.

Remington's hand slid into the right pocket of his raincoat. His fingers touched the cold barrel of the 32-caliber Ivor Johnson revolver, then moved deftly over the hard-rubber grip and the outline of the owl's head stamped on either side. Another instrument of the grand design.

He had found it, miraculously, among his father's effects, one of the many revolvers he always kept fully loaded at home.

Once he had thought it a weird eccentricity. In those days he did not fully comprehend his father's paranoia. But his father was acquisitive and greedy, his substance and energy fully devoted to the pursuit of more and more wealth. Once, too, Tad had resented being the beneficiary of such largesse, finally to appreciate it only when his mother put it at the service of her grand cause. Himself.

He lingered near the guard house that stood sentry at the parking lane between the White House and the Old State building. He wanted to take a short cut through the alley, which came out on the ellipse, cutting the distance to the Pan American Union Building where he was headed. The guard studied him for a moment then turned away, waving a car through the corridor.

I am Leon Czolgosz, he whispered; he pronounced it "Cholgosh," in correct Polish, for the guard's benefit. It was like a child's dare, but the man was too far away to hear it. Moving past the spiked iron fence, he turned on Seventeenth Street and headed south. The west side of the Old State shielded him and he walked erectly, ignoring the rain, still fingering the gun. With his other hand he groped for the handkerchief in the left side pocket of his raincoat, rehearsing again what he had to do.

He had done it at home four times that morning, standing stark naked before his mirrors, observing himself while doing it: wrapping the handkerchief around the gun in his hand and then pulling the trigger of the empty gun. It had excited him and, as before, he had had an erection.

Last night had erased all doubts. The candidate had come, had touched him, indented his flesh with the mark of himself. On one of the mirrors, Tad had written in soap, JOHN DOE, the name Czolgosz had used when he checked into that Buffalo hotel nearly eighty years ago. He had decided not to go to Buffalo— surely the fates would allow him some leeway. He had learned enough authentic details to win approval from the great cosmic judge who was testing him for his obedience to courage and truth.

The ellipse was empty and silent. Few people were in the streets and the weather had foreshortened the perpetual line

.

around the Washington Monument. The rain laid a glistening sheen on the grass and the manicured trees. He walked on the landscaped side of the street, which afforded him a clearer view of the Pan American Union Building, with its green rotunda and Spanish architectural style.

He glanced at his watch, then quickened his pace. It was nearly four. Ten minutes to go. The fact that it was a Saturday had caused him a fretful anxiety. Suppose the building were locked? It was another test that had to be passed. But as the day wore on, his anxiety had faded. Nothing could stop what he had to do. Not now.

As he moved closer to the Pan American Union Building, the tall ornate metal entrance doors opened and shut. A man came out, walking slowly. The building was obviously open for business. Why had he ever doubted that?

When he reached a point on the street directly across from the building, he looked at his watch again. Another six minutes. At ten after four, they had, all those years ago, put down the ropes and let in the crowd. Withdrawing his handkerchief, he wrapped it around the right hand that held the revolver, then replaced it in the pocket of his raincoat. With his free hand, he smoothed down the moustache he had pasted on his face and pulled the rainhat brim over his eyes.

He had rehearsed it so many times. The raincoat was reversible. Afterward, he would remove his hat, walk calmly out the front door, turn the corner, and slip into Constitution Hall a block away. There, he would wait in the men's room until the rally was over. It was the site this afternoon, he remembered, of a religious convention. Another gift from providence. Odd, how little planning was needed, how perfectly things were programmed to fall into line. All he had to do was imagine them.

How laughable it was, all that newspaper and television attention given the shooting at the National Gallery of Art. A bonus for him—did they really think he could be stopped? And how laughable was that obtuse police captain proclaiming his department's expertise. "We'll find the perpetrator," he had said, cocky and arrogant, his dark face threatening. How could they possibly understand that Damato was merely a surrogate, irrelevant to the grand pattern?

Again he looked at his watch, feeling the adrenalin surge, the tingle at the base of his spine, the suffusion of blood in the center of his body.

He tightened his finger on the trigger and walked across the street. There would be no hesitation, but this time he had to look into the man's eyes; he had to see him. The connection had to be complete. At the exact moment, he was sure, a man would appear, a big man. The choice would be made for him.

He mounted the steps. The rain had quickened. Rivulets cascaded down the brim of his hat, and with his free hand he wiped away the moisture from his eyes.

Opening the door, he saw the guard eye him perfunctorily, then turn away. It didn't matter. He knew he was immune. In front of him was a large atrium with a fountain in the center. On either side were huge symmetrical winding marble staircases. The interior was surprisingly light and he could hear, faintly, the staccato of the rain on the rotunda.

The place was deserted and the guard turned back to his newspaper. He sat at a wooden table near the staircase to the right.

Then there was a clicking sound, a man with leather soles moving swiftly as he descended the stairs on the left. Remington felt his heart pound in a thrill of discovery. The man was big, dark haired, middle-aged. He moved swiftly down the stairs, his hand on the brass banister. Remington walked forward and waited at the landing. He probed the eyes of the oncoming man. There was the faintest tremor of recognition. Perhaps, he wondered fleetingly, he knew this man, but he could not remember.

The man offered a tentative greeting, a neutral smile, and Remington pressed forward, lifting his handkerchiefed hand as though to return the greeting. He felt an intense joy as the man came toward him, still smiling. A mysterious power radiated from his core through the muscles of his right hand, then down to his fingers.

"*Buenos dias,*" the man said.

His response was the pressure of a finger. He felt the jerk as the bullet left the chamber, aimed directly at the man's chest. Calmly, he pointed the barrel leftward to the man's abdomen and fired again, and suddenly felt the handkerchief catch on fire.

It was still burning as he opened the doors and ran down the outside stairs, not looking back. Turning the corner, he ran into an alley, smothered the flames with his coat, reversed it, removed his hat, then moved calmly through the street until he reached Constitution Hall.

People milled in the lobby. He found the men's room, ducked into an empty booth and sat fully dressed on the toilet seat. His hand was badly singed, the skin blackened and painful.

"Something burning," someone said. He looked through the crack in the booth. Two men searched the towel bin for signs of fire, then, discovering none, left the men's room. He left the booth, washed his hands, and felt the pain as the water hit the burned flesh. Lifting his eyes, he saw himself in the mirror. The moustache was awry. He tore it off and flushed it down the toilet along with the remnants of the singed handkerchief.

In the distance, he heard the wail of sirens. A man came in and stood in front of a urinal. The sirens grew louder.

"Trouble," the man mumbled. "Satan's work."

"God's," Remington said hoarsely. The man stared at him with raised eyebrows, then returned to his business.

Men crowded into the lavatory after the religious rally ended. They were somber, colorless, like figures carved from the same bar of soap. He left unobtrusively. People jammed the lobby, escaping from the driving rain. He could see policemen in slickers searching the crowd. Had they a clear description of him? It hardly mattered. The signs were clear; he was divinely protected, the only bona fide messenger of God in the crowd.

For all his sense of invulnerability, the police observation urged caution. He looked around at the faces in the crowd. Next to him, an older woman stared glumly into the rain.

"Summer rain," she said. "It was nice when we came in."

"God's will," he said.

The lady wore a straw hat with faded flowers and a black

print dress. She looked at him through sad pinched gray eyes set in chicken skin sacks.

"My car is two blocks away."

He saw his escape clearly now. The policemen in their slickers studied the departing crowd. Occasionally they would stop someone, males about his height and build, and ask questions.

There was a moment when the rain eased and the crowd in the lobby surged outward. He took off his raincoat and put it over his head.

"Duck under," he said to the woman. She stooped under him and they edged forward into the rain. With the lady in tow, he walked through the police gauntlet. They crossed the street without incident. Yet another sign, he thought.

"That was very kind of you," the woman said. He continued to hold the raincoat over her as she opened the door of her car.

"Can I give you a lift?"

He nodded his thanks and slid in beside her. Surely an invisible hand emerged at every turn to guide him.

"I live in Arlington," the woman said, jockeying the '75 Chevy out of the parking space. The car moved past the new State Department Building, made a left on Twenty-Third and headed for the Memorial Bridge.

"This is fine," he said as the car reached the Lincoln Memorial circle. He had not intended to leave the car at that moment. The memorial was not in the most convenient spot. He thanked the lady and got out.

The rain had become relentless again and the great Grecian shrine to the martyred President glistened in the milky light. A few tourists carrying umbrellas trudged up the long staircases to the majestic sculpted figure deep in reflection.

Rain cascaded over his bare head, down his neck, wetting his back. As if drawn by a magnet, he ascended toward the giant seated figure.

Towering above him was the Great Emancipator, the Captain, the Commander-in-Chief, the man who saved the Union. He looked up at the somber bearded white figure, high in his lofty chair, eyes brooding under the massive brow. He searched the man's face and felt that Lincoln was watching him as well.

Again the cosmic connection surged through him, touching every nerve, every sensor in his being. The hand of the martyred President seemed to reach out, touching him.

He did not know how long he stood there. When he recovered his sense of place, it had turned dark, the rain had stopped. The memorial was deserted. Lincoln, too, had cast his eye elsewhere.

He moved toward the bridge, past the massive brass horses shining in the reflected lamplight. Cars drove swiftly past him as he walked at a steady pace over the footpath. Occasionally, he glanced over the stone railing at the murky Potomac beneath him. He darted through the traffic on the Virginia side and cut across the grass island to the Arlington Cemetery station of the Metro.

In the deserted station he waited patiently for a train. He felt thrill after thrill of pleasure, signs of validation. He alone had been chosen to execute the grand plan. As he stepped into the train he felt radiant, gloriously alive.

XI

THE BODY of the dead man, Jorge Perfidio, flesh peeled away like a banana skin, innards exposed, lay in the glare of the bright fluorescent lights on the medical examiner's autopsy table. With so many spectators crowded around the action, it looked like a demonstration for a cooking class, a lesson in butchery. Out of a corner of her eye, Fiona observed the eggplant, his face glistening with perspiration, scowling at the corpse as Dr. Benton's fingers maneuvered an instrument into the carcass of the dead man, his apron stained with bile and blood.

Directly in front of her were two men from the FBI, an official from the Executive Protection Agency and another neatly dressed intense man, whose officious look marked him unmistakably as Central Intelligence Agency. There were others—Roy Howard, the chief himself, God Almighty in their special police universe, an unsmiling middle-aged black man. Beside him stood two nervous men from the Argentine embassy. In the background she caught a glimpse of Teddy's gray, gloomy face. Jorge Perfidio was the Argentine representative to the Organization of American States.

Fiona was deliberately hanging back, not wishing to appear conspicuous. Teddy had called her, wakening her from a sound sleep. She had come off duty at midnight and found it impossible to sleep until ten, keeping busy by cleaning her apartment, dusty from her summer's absence. Their paths had not crossed since their separation.

"It reminded me of the Damato case, Fi. I got scene." He sounded agitated, talking police shorthand. He explained that a man had been shot in the lobby of the Pan American Union Building, and sketched in the details. To both of them, the Damato case had been traumatic, changing the course of their police careers. It was a natural impulse on Teddy's part to seek vindication in some way. There was no doubt why he had called.

"He was DOA," Teddy said. "There was a guard witness. This one had fantasies. Said that the killer's right hand spit fire."

"Like an avenging angel." The comment reminded her of her father and his vivid religious imagery.

"We got a height and sex fix. A man in a raincoat. Medium height. He was bundled up. Wore a hat." Teddy paused as if reading from a notebook. "Apparently the Argentinian was walking down the stairs. Then bang bang."

"And the gun?"

"If it's the same one, the shit will hit the fan. The eggplant will have a hemorrhage. Why the hell did it happen to me?"

"Hell, you could close it. Be a hero."

"No way. There's not one fucking real clue. But I know they're connected. I know it."

"Take it easy."

"I just thought you'd like to know. Maybe you can help."

"Maybe." But she doubted it.

"Look at it from my point of view. I tell you, Fi, it's going to be like last time."

Had they missed something? It had nagged at her, a lingering itch that would not go away.

She knew what he meant. Destiny had struck the poor bastard a rotten blow. It was okay to abuse a woman, to ridicule her ability, but fate had set him up to be a scapegoat. A white male!

"The body is over at the medical examiner's now. I'm going. Everybody's going."

"So am I," she said, jumping out of bed.

But when she started to dress, she realized her tactical stupidity. It wasn't her case, it wasn't her business. She was about to give them something else to resent about her.

Dictating into a small microphone headset, Dr. Benton described the wounds, traced the path of the bullets, one of which had punctured the heart. The other had struck the left side of the abdomen and passed through both the outer and inner walls of the stomach.

As he paused in his dictation, Fiona noted that his eyes had squinted, had become reflective, as if his mind had paused to contemplate something he couldn't pin down. She didn't have time to wonder about it. The ping of an extracted bullet on a metal tray alerted everyone in the room.

"A thirty-two," one of the FBI men said.

"Sure?" the eggplant asked. The FBI man nodded. The eggplant's sense relief was tangible and he lit a cigarette. He looked over to Fiona and smiled, obviously relieved by the lack of connection to the previous killing. Her own feelings were ambivalent. Had she actually wished for the connection?

"This one looks political," the eggplant said, clearing his throat.

"Well, it's finally come," the chief agreed.

The Argentinians looked at each other as if they possessed some secret knowledge.

"Everything is political," one of them said.

"So far, we've pretty well managed to avoid this terrorist shit. Hate to see it happen here," the eggplant said.

He was going to great pains to sell the idea. Lucky bastard. She could understand the ploy. No need to stir up dying embers. Suddenly Dr. Benton popped another bullet into the metal tray.

"Same," the eggplant said.

"You can go home now." The eggplant had edged over to her. "I thought . . ."

"I know what you thought," he interrupted. His nicotine breath washed over her. "The other is a goddamned open case."

"At least the heat will be off of us," she said. It was an effort to be ingratiating. She detested the reflex.

"Me," he retorted, patting his chest. "Off me."

Teddy had been watching them from a bench in the far corner of the room. Autopsies always made him queasy.

"I hope that guy's right. I was praying for anything but a forty-four." His eyes were sunk in deep dark circles. He reminded her of Bruce, confronting his own abyss. His weakness irritated her and she turned back to Dr. Benton. He untied the back strings of his apron, then lit a cigarette, pinching it between thumb and forefinger.

She hung back until the other men had finished their inquiries and left the room. The corpse lay on the metal table, covered with a rubber pad. For some reason, Benson struck her as being more thoughtful than fatigued. A nest of wrinkles etched his brow.

"What is it?" she asked softly. He did not reply at once, and glanced around the room, as if to assure himself that they were alone.

"The two shots," he whispered. There was a touch of the bureaucrat about him. His reports were always concise and accurate, never speculative, and he rarely volunteered extraneous theories to his superiors. Because she admired him, she liked to think this reticence was wisdom but she knew better. He was a brilliant man but no hero.

"Why would a murderer fire a second bullet at close range in the man's belly, after blowing apart his heart?"

"You know that?"

"Know?" He looked at her. "Suspect. It is different. It's something one doesn't put in a report. Not precise enough."

"Maybe he didn't know about anatomy."

"But why actually lower the gun? The belly shot wasn't the fatal one in the first place. Why not just shoot the bullets into the chest and head, the places of sure death?"

"Accident," she countered. "Or he simply couldn't stop himself. Who knows what was in the man's mind?" A killer's logic, she had learned, never traveled in a straight line.

"A terrorist would be thinking only of elimination. Why waste a shot? He was already at close range."

"Just because the eggplant . . ." She corrected herself, not wanting to draw him into her private war. ". . . Captain Greene said it was. Doesn't mean it's so." Out of respect for his caution she did not elaborate.

"And if a terrorist was looking for an insurance shot, why move the barrel out of range of the vital organ?" He was repeating himself as if to emphasize the point.

"Are you on this case?" he asked suddenly, his cool eyes alert and cautious.

"I was looking for some connection between this and Damato."

He thought a moment and nodded.

"A public building. A single killer . . ." she began, trailing off as the list of similarities spent themselves. "Intuition . . ." She hated the term.

"Subconscious thinking," he corrected.

"Maybe I have something to prove," she confessed, lowering her voice as if to further reassure him that this was a purely private consultation.

"Dangerous," he sighed, understanding instantly. "It sometimes interferes with one's strategy for survival."

"You think maybe they'll think I'm an uppity honky broad?"

"They think that anyhow," he smiled. "The power structure doesn't like anyone to stand up in the rowboat." He sighed. "Aside from medicine, this is my particular expertise." His concentration drifted. "It was my wife's fatal flaw. That kind of courage can kill."

"So far I've been a good little girl." She paused, rethinking. "That's bullshit. They think I'm a bumbling bitch. Since that gallery case I'm getting the treatment. You haven't helped. I could have left this room like them. Without doubts."

"So it's a form of vengeance," he said, his smile fading. "Maybe you shouldn't take my speculations so seriously."

She felt on the verge of indignation. It was narrow, small-minded. Clouding one's objectivity sapped one's strength. She went over it in her mind, then concluded that he was partially right.

"Maybe."

"I'm not against it," he said. "But if you're not subtle about it, it can backfire, go against your self-interest." He waited for her reaction. For him, talking in riddles apparently offered a kind of cerebral pleasure. She nodded her understanding. Beneath the facade of amiability were the scarred remains of thwarted ambition. Reaching out, she squeezed his upper arm. It was a distinctly manly gesture.

"I'll be careful," she said.

He removed his bloodstained apron, like the proprietor of a butcher shop closing for the day.

"If I find a connection in my mind, I'll let you know," he said, putting on his jacket. "But I'd be willing to wager that this killing was not political."

"I won't take the bet," she said. There was not a single hard clue to support her own instinct.

The killing of Jorge Perfidio was the banner headline in the *Post*. To his credit, the eggplant had maintained a low profile. But to her horror, as she read the news account, she discovered the chief had stuck his nose into the limelight.

"D.C. Police Chief Roy Howard told reporters that he had called in the FBI, Interpol, the Argentine security agency and other government agencies to investigate the killing. 'We cannot have this in our town,' he said. 'We must all join forces to stem the import of foreign terrorism. If this continues, we will have to develop a capability to combat the menace. This will take some recognition on the part of the Congress, fundwise.' "

There was no reference in the story to the previous killing. It was as though it had been deliberately excised as irrelevant. Not only had the chief taken the heat off the department, he had begun to lobby for more funds.

By evening the story had built. The President held a special press conference to decry terrorism. The Argentines had also gotten into the act. The ambassador was shown before a bank of microphones after carrying a protest message to the Secretary of State. Three days later the story was still simmering.

"Everybody into the sludge," Bruce said, openly envious as he slouched on her sofa, drink in hand. "I need something like that to boost my campaign."

He had come back from New York, discouraged and edgy. Taking the day off, she had devoted the time to preparing a nice dinner for him to chase his blues. He ate little, preferring instead to sip Scotch. To take his mind off his own troubles, she had told him the details of the case, expressing her intuitive doubts.

"They could be wrong," Fiona said. It seemed to spark his interest.

"That doesn't matter. It's the exposure. It's the style, not the substance. Besides, the conclusion is safe. A little killing has just slopped over from Argentina. So what else is new?" His perception came from light miles away and she could tell that his reactions related only to his campaign. Discouragement had also deepened his cynicism. Getting up from the table, he sprawled on the couch. She sat down beside him and gently nudged his head into her lap, massaging his temples.

"It's getting worse, Fi," he said grimly. "I can't seem to rally the troops. My opponent, the spic bastard, calls me irrelevant and there's an undercurrent of Jew stuff just surfacing. The district's changing so fast I just can't relate to it."

"Everything's changing," she said.

"What the hell is your frame of reference?" he said with sudden anger, pushing her away. She did not respond, hoping it would pass.

"If only she wasn't a woman," he said after a pause, his anger vented. "I don't know how to handle it." He let her hands soothe him again. "I just don't know how to handle women."

"Maybe we should come with an instruction kit?"

"No maybes."

"You expect every woman to be like your mommy."

"Now there's insight. You bet your ass. I fear now for all those little boys approaching puberty."

"They'll be tougher. The next generation will know how to handle us girls."

"They won't handle nothing. They'll all be castrated."

"Now that would be a pity." She reached for him there as if to reassure him. In the soft light his eyes glistened moistly.

"I need you, Fi," he whispered. "With me. Always."

"Are you sure it's not just generic? Man needing woman?"

"That, too."

"The vectors have to intersect," she said stupidly. They rarely do, she thought. To him her career was an annoyance, to be disposed of sometime in the future. Was being needed by him enough for her? The question was at the core of her uncertainty. It was incredible how little they understood about each other.

"Do you love me?" he asked gently, disengaging. For the first time in her life she felt the danger of surrender. She wanted to say: Define that, as if she were sweating a witness. Actually, she had resisted the definition ever since she had met him. If it had to do with longing, she did have her moments. And when he was near her, like now, she felt the full power of her sexuality. Could it be sustained for a lifetime? Or was she asking too much of life? She responded by kissing him deeply on the lips.

"I hope you love me, Fi," he said. "Because that's what I need most of all." She felt him pressing her, selling, persuading.

"Take me in," he whispered. "And never let me out. Let's marry."

A part of her was ready for surrender. Its implications frightened her. He was thinking primarily of his own immediate needs and aspirations.

"We'll see," she whispered, unsure of what it meant. "After the campaign."

"Yeah," he drawled. "Maybe then."

XII

REMINGTON SMEARED grease on his burned hand, carefully applied gauze, then wrapped it with surgical tape. The bandage inhibited the mobility of his fingers and he had to utilize one of those clip-on black ties that he detested.

He was showered, shaved, bandaged and ready at the moment the door chimes echoed through the house and his first guests arrived. He had deliberately set the party for that date and time. The guest of honor was the Secretary-General of the OAS, Manuel Ricardo. The cosmic judge would surely enjoy the irony.

A tall man in impeccable tails, the regular butler at his sit-down dinners, opened the door and pointed to Remington, who stood at his regular receiving place in the foyer. The first guests were Senator and Mrs. Harrison from Montana.

"What the hell happened to your hand, Tad?" Harrison asked, after Remington had implanted the obligatory two-cheeker on Mrs. Harrison's heavily rouged cheeks.

"The hammer missed," he said with a grin.

Other guests began to arrive—the Swiss and German ambassadors, the assistant secretary of the Treasury, a titled European and his wife. Remington's small dinner parties were known for their "A" mix, three or four top diplomats, a senator or two, sometimes a member of the Cabinet, a titled couple and, if possible, a cultural figure or someone from the world of high finance, a highly decorated general.

Servants passed drinks and hors d'oeuvres in the big room, dominated by his heroic portrait. In the dining room, hidden by a brocaded screen, white-gloved waiters put the final touches on three tables for eight. Passing from guest to guest, he joked about his bandaged hand.

"You look marvelous," one of the women whispered, the wife of the German ambassador, a Nordic beauty with huge breasts, suitably displayed. She had coquettishly assaulted him on earlier occasions.

"An appellation that doesn't begin to describe you," he said with a wink. "Someday I intend to emulate Hannibal," he added, watching a blush begin below her neck and move downward. He knew she loved the suggestive banter.

"I hope you have a herd of strong elephants."

"I can vouch for their trunks," he whispered in her ear. She giggled with pleasure.

He felt buoyant. High. Deliciously stimulated. His mind seemed fresher, his voice deeper. He had never felt more articulate, more witty and charming.

"Do you expect a plum if the Republicans win, Tad?" General MacIntosh asked. He was a squat yet imposing man, a three-star general.

"I'm keeping a low profile."

"But if something big was offered?" the general persisted.

"That would depend." It was the perfect note, knowing yet noncommittal. "They have to win first."

He moved away, checking his watch. Dinner would begin precisely at nine. The guests of honor, Manuel Ricardo and his wife, had not arrived. It was all part of the preordained plan, the perfect irony. The Pan American Union Building was the showcase of the OAS. His guest list made no allowances for a no-show. Ricardo's presence would be still another validation to be added to the others.

"It was an absolutely ghastly act," someone said, the remark casually flung across the room. He turned to find the knobby face of Countess Faille, looking agitated and already slightly tipsy. "I heard it on the radio as we were coming here."

"What?" someone inquired.

"The shooting." The buzz of conversation lost its momentary rhythm.

"Someone in the Pan American Union," the countess exclaimed, taking another drink from a silver tray.

"It better not come to this country," General MacIntosh asserted.

"What?" Remington asked.

"Terrorists," the general muttered.

"You think that . . ." Remington checked himself and turned away to hide his surprise. Terrorists?

Excusing himself, he stepped behind the screen. The waiters nodded, alert and ready. His experienced eye surveyed each table setting, the flower arrangements, the Waterford crystal, the rare plate, the polished silver. The plate, his mother's pride, had once belonged to Czar Nicholas. Somehow she had managed to get her hands on it before Marjorie Merriwether Post could get to it. The memory was reassuring.

"You'd be proud of me, my darling," he told himself, certain of his mother's presence nearby. "We shall have an exquisite celebration."

At that moment he heard the chimes and rushed to the hall to greet the guests of honor.

The Secretary-General and his wife looked pale and shaken.

"You cannot imagine," Mrs. Ricardo said breathlessly.

"Cold-blooded bastards. They attacked the poor man inside the building."

They, he thought, enjoying their reaction.

"It's frightening. They'll stop at nothing," Mrs. Ricardo said, taking a Scotch from a tray. "I really need this." She took a deep swallow.

"America is no longer safe," the Secretary-General sputtered. "We are no longer immune here."

"Who do you suppose it was?" Remington was all innocence.

"Crazies," Ricardo said, with Latin emotion. "They have no ideology. Destroy for the sake of destruction. The world is going mad."

"We'll have to put a stop to it," General MacIntosh said, as the other guests crowded around the Secretary-General and his wife, eager for details.

The conversation of his guests drifted in and out of his consciousness. Remington listened vaguely, his mind transcending the sense of time and place as he recalled the act, the firing of the pistol, the startled look on the man's face, the surge of ecstasy. He was translating history, illustrating power, recycling his mother's compelling desires. Are you proud of me, mother? he cried within himself. He was certain that she could hear him as he withdrew again into the tunnel of his memoy.

A fall rain had deepened the green of the back lawn of the great house. Puffs of clouds passed over an incredibly blue sky and San Francisco Bay in the distance merged the colors into aqua dotted with foaming whitecaps.

Until then, at the height of his Senate campaign, he had been brave, with an inner invincibility, like hers, that could not be broached. Now the polls showed him losing. He was getting a bad press and words like elitism and dilettante were being used as cruel and deliberate barbs. The prospect of loss came crashing in on him, squeezing out his courage.

"They don't understand," his mother said. "They are fools."

"Whatever they are doesn't matter. I'm losing."

"You will not lose. You'll see."

"Maybe I can't hack it, mother. Maybe I can't realize your expectations?"

"That is unworthy of us, Tad," she said with lofty scorn. "We don't give up."

"I am just facing reality."

"Whose?" she snapped, her blue eyes widening. "They are not going to beat us. Never. And you, my dear, are heading for the White House. It is as simple as that."

"Nothing is as simple as that," he had protested.

"Now, now," she said, smoothing his hair again, forcing him closer, enfolding him in her warmest embrace. She had made a refuge for him out of herself.

The memory was as real as his skin and he felt the familiar tug of pleasure at the center of himself.

The details of the dinner had been impeccably planned. Deliberately, he had not shared the honors with a surrogate hostess. Because it was his mother's celebration as well, he dared not profane it. One of the tables, subtly larger than the others, had been set for nine, and he had inserted himself between the wife of the Secretary-General and the wife of the German ambassador.

"None of us are safe any more," Mrs. Ricardo said.

He wished she would stop harping on that. She drank glass after glass of white wine, ignoring the vichyssoise. Her deep-set brown eyes flitted about, agitated, like those of a trapped bird. He felt mischievous.

"Who was the victim?" he asked, taking the hand of the wife of the German ambassador under the table, as if drawing her into his private conspiracy. The returned pressure on his fingers assured her complicity.

"An Argentinian. Jorge Perfidio. Lovely man. Charming wife. Two small children. It was a hateful act."

"Maybe it was an act of passion," he goaded, watching her empty her glass as her agitation increased.

"Terrorism," she scowled. "They are jealous of us."

"They?"

He was smiling, chiding her, deliberately punishing her for her foolishness. She hadn't the remotest understanding of what had occurred. Was she attempting to trivialize the will of the cosmic force?

"You will have it in this country," she continued passionately. "I guarantee it. You are living in a fool's paradise here."

"Perhaps," he said, but she was not to be daunted. The crab imperial was served and more white wine. He had chosen it carefully, a Chablis grand cru. Later a St. Emilion, 1966, would be poured with the beef Wellington.

He turned to the wife of the German ambassador, whose hand still clung to his, caressing.

"We were talking about terrorism," he said.

"In Germany we have cured that problem."

"Yes," the other woman said, finishing off her wine. "We know all about German cures."

He felt the grip on his hand tighten. The Latin lady's glass was refilled. She was getting drunk now, her pent-up hostility erupting. He enjoyed the spectacle. It was always a public sport in the capital to see someone in the vortex of power lose control.

"Public life is a menace," she lashed out bitterly. "Sop to the unquenchable male ego. Diplomacy is a worthless profession."

"She is getting drunk," the German ambassador's wife whispered, clutching his hand. He listened to the buzz of conversation. Candles flickered. The white-gloved waiters delicately passed the silver plates. The power of this orchestration comforted him. If only they could understand his need, the cosmic pull. It thrilled him to think about it. He wanted to assure them of the necessity of his acts, the glorious inner voltage that electrified his acts. He moved the German ambassador's wife's hand to his erection. She gasped at him, startled. But she did not pull her hand away. Then he turned suddenly to Mrs. Ricardo, bending low, his mouth near her ear.

"Perhaps he needed killing?" The words were designed for her ears only. She turned glazed eyes toward him, her lips trembling, unable to speak. Behind her rouged cheeks her skin went dead white. As he looked at her, there was a brief second of communication, and in that moment he felt the sweetness of confession. The woman abruptly stood up.

"I feel ill." She gagged and cupped her hand over her mouth as she hurried off. The sudden movement at the table forced the German ambassador's wife to remove her hand.

"She drinks too much," she said, apparently disappointed by the interruption.

He had wanted to say: Czolgosz killed him. But that would have been beyond her comprehension.

Fools, the lot of them, he thought. Moths around a candle,

flickering at the edges of power. Only he knew real power, only he had the ability to will events.

When Mrs. Ricardo returned, they had nearly finished dessert. She eyed him warily.

"I hope you are feeling better," he said. She nodded and quickly turned away. He stood up and tapped his glass. All conversation ceased.

"There is no greater joy than breaking bread with friends," he began. "Especially friends so distinguished . . ." The compliments droned on. The Secretary-General was appropriately lauded for his achievements. Remington carefully briefed himself for the toasts, bathing both his honored guest and the others in a warm pool of hyperbole. The response, he knew, would be equally laudatory. Compliments would assail him. But nothing would ever remotely touch what was inside, the secret power.

Still, he could find contentment now in dealing with ironies. There was simply no other way to translate himself to them. Their ignorance was massive, their reality covered by a veneer of self-delusion. They would never know the inner truth of anything, especially of himself. The best he could do was to throw them a bone.

"Few of us has any insight into his own destiny," he told them. He looked beside him at the pale Mrs. Ricardo, barely holding herself together. "We live in perpetual danger. There is a predatory flock of eagles preying upon us, against which we are defenseless lambs. Terrorism, as we have learned tonight, has indeed come to America. Terrorism has torn one of us from the bosom of our loved ones. We cannot, we must not let this occur again." Inside he was laughing at them. One man could easily terrorize a nation. "Perhaps a moment of silence would be appropriate," he said, lowering his head. The guests followed suit. In the silence he thought of his mother. She would have sneered at them all.

XIII

ONE NIGHT in the middle of October, Teddy materialized at the door of Fiona's apartment. He had just come
off duty. Leaning against the doorjamb, he looked sallow and
groggy, and a smell of whiskey clung to his trenchcoat. The
circles under his eyes were deeper.

"What's with you?"

She led him into the apartment and poured him a stiff Scotch.

"She threw me out," he said, sitting down heavily in a chair
and not bothering to unbutton his coat. He took a double swallow of the whiskey.

"Can't blame her." He was wallowing in hurt and self-pity.
She remembered the eggplant's obscene phrase. Pussy-
whipped. "It's not a family game we're in."

"So I'm beginning to understand," she said. "Maybe it's time
to leave. Not worth giving up Gladys and the kids."

"Be a security guard somewhere?" he said. "I don't know any
other life."

"I'm acquainted with the problem."

"Why?" he asked. "What's the magnet? It stinks."

"So why are we in it?"

Once Bruce had suggested that she become an investigator for a government agency like Treasury. A T-person, she had remembered joking. I'm a tit man myself, he had responded, but the humor had merely masked the wish. He couldn't understand what it meant to give up one's badge and the power of arrest.

"It'll pass," she said.

"I agree with her. That's the funny part."

"She's a wife. She should understand."

The remark ricocheted in her mind, finding no resting place. She felt no sense of sisterhood. Her mother's blind loyalty to the "farces" paralleled her feeling for the church. It was simply the glue of her life.

"How would you know, Fiona?"

He said it for her, and she felt a tiny shiver of fright for herself. Bruce's wife, too, would have to understand. It was the nature of the beast.

"Maybe I should give it up?" Teddy said, holding out his glass. She poured. "No future for a white man anymore. Strictly a black club." He paused and sipped. "They got different rules." Something seemed to linger on his tongue and he looked at her as if she was supposed to plead with him to stop. She didn't, feeling this new thing in the air.

"That terrorist stuff is bullshit, Fi."

"What are you talking about?"

He looked around the room with his cop's eyes, checking things out. "They know how to keep it among themselves."

He gulped down the remains of his drink and held the glass out once more. This time she did not pour.

"The ammo of the thirty-two. Old. Like the other."

She understood instantly. "How old?"

"About seventy-five years."

Her mind raced. What had she said to Dr. Benton? A public place. A single killer. Now another thin thread. Old ammo.

"Hadley raised it, but the eggplant beat it in. He's happy letting the Feds and the foreigners chase their asses."

"Who told you this?"

"Hadley. In his cups. It's not even meant for you, Fi."

114

"So why are you telling me?" She knew why.

"I wanted you to know is all."

His tongue was heavy and he was beginning to slur his words. Finally she poured him out a drink and took one for herself.

"You know what you're saying?"

He shrugged. Drunk as he was, he knew exactly what he was saying.

"It won't matter. All the international boys are crawling over town. Soon no one will admit the goof. Everyone will blame the other guy. No one is looking in the right direction anyhow."

"Cover-up!" she blurted. It's wrong, she thought angrily. Standards, too, were another of her burdens. Like compassion. But the latter could be a detriment. The former was essential. It was at the heart of being a cop.

"He ain't so stupid, Fi. He's saving his own ass. A second murder wouldn't have sat so well upstairs. Screw up the tourist business good, reflect on the black mafia that runs things. Look, it could have been worse. They could have screamed attempted robbery and really scared the tourists off."

She began to pace the room, sipping her drink, agitated.

"You had to tell me. You just couldn't wait to tell me." How much shit were these weak men going to deposit on her doorstep, she thought, resenting Bruce as well, an image that only added to her rage. What was she? The great earth mother?

"So what am I supposed to do about it?"

"Hey, Fi. Don't blame the messenger." Teddy closed his eyes, then laid his head on her table. She debated leaving him there. He reminded her of her father, who had used the same device to escape from pressure. "A man needs his cup when things boil over," her mother had said, forcing the same sense of acceptance into her mind. Emulating her mother, she dragged Teddy to the couch.

"We're supposed to catch the bastards," she said angrily and covered him with a blanket. It's not a divine mission. It's only a job, she argued. Besides, there were no other clues. Would revealing the information actually bring them closer to the killer? She doubted that.

Later, tossing in sleepless anger, she continued to argue with herself, an endless harangue about morality, aggravated by the darkness. How dare Teddy draw her into their games? It was as though she were being assigned to rock the boat. Her. The invulnerable double minority. But how? Theoretically, there was only one source of the original leak: Hadley, stiff-lipped, scientific, no-nonsense Hadley, a honky to boot. No one seemed ever to use his first name. If the press got it, he would be frozen out, his career destroyed. They knew how to get their revenge. Maybe if it were one of the brothers instead . . . but her mind finally fogged and she fell into a dull leaden sleep.

Teddy had disappeared by the time she awoke. When her first cup of coffee could not spark alertness, she tried two more. A sour nausea suddenly afflicted her and she debated whether or not to call in sick. She decided that the illness was more emotional than viral, took a long lingering bath, dressed in a pants suit and took the metro to headquarters.

An odd feeling gripped her as she waited for the train. She was contemplating the squared cement indentations of the station's arched inner skin, unaware of the army of silent people who waited for the circles of light on the floor to flicker and signal the arrival of the train. The movement of the people into the train shocked her into awareness.

She was responsible for these people, their protector. Under her jacket hung the weapon of the protector. Her badge, tucked in the jumble of keys, money, lipstick, makeup, aspirin and tissues in her pocketbook, was the holy authority for the enforcement of the rules of society, the symbol of this sacred duty.

These were her charges, her wards, rushing to the open door of the train, oblivious of her, yet depending on her to keep their lives safe from harm. Somewhere, deep inside of her, this must have been her motivation for joining the "farces." Motivation! It was the primal clue to the killer, the primal clue to every human. A wave of self-righteousness swept over her, a divine sense of goodness. Wasn't she the keeper of the flame of order, a soldier in the thin ranks of those who kept the monsters at bay?

But once inside the train, where the brighter lighting individualized their faces, the collective image of humanity splintered. Who among them were the predators, the thieves and killers? She sensed the swirling emotions that lay behind their bland faces, frustration, envy, greed, thwarted dreams, the hidden ritualized horror of ordinary life. Her mission was also to protect them from each other.

Don't you know there is a madman running loose in your city? She wanted to stand up, shout out the words. It wouldn't matter. Few would understand.

I have to care for you, she addressed them silently. It was enough to calm her. Whatever her previous resentment, she knew that somehow Teddy had put the message in the right slot.

That day she and Jefferson finished their paperwork early. As was their pattern now, they were still assigned to routine "naturals," a boring process at best. An accidental car death occupied them most of the morning at Memorial Hospital. They had apparently reached a silent understanding or, as she characterized it to herself, a plateau of indifference. He had toned down his blatant ghetto mockery and she had resisted being baited into head-on confrontations. Somehow they managed to keep the social intercourse on a purely professional level. The relationship wasn't designed to gain any insight into themselves, but they both knew that they were temporarily sentenced to each other.

Yet the very fact that they were outcasts brought them subtly closer. She deliberately drew a curtain around herself, presenting him with the cold visage of a fellow cop, neutered and bloodless. It was never like that with Teddy.

But somewhere she would have to find a meeting ground. In this business, it was impossible to act alone.

"I'd like to take a look at the Pan American Union Building," she said as they drove out of the Memorial Hospital garage onto Washington Circle and into Pennsylvania Avenue. He looked at her archly and reluctantly nudged the accelerator. He appeared in a good mood. By now she knew the obscene implications of what that meant. He had made his point early in their sentence. His life consisted of a nightly round of female conquests, or at least that was the image he encouraged. The big black stud. The Ape. Despite her contempt, she found herself searching for his humanity.

He pulled the car into an illegal parking spot directly across from the Pan American Union Building and, hunching over the wheel, drew a pack of cigarettes from his pocket, punched one up and lit it with the car lighter.

From the car, she observed the Spanish-style building, its green atrium dome glinting in the sunlight. Smoke filled the car and she wound down the window. After ten minutes he reacted.

"Ready to roll? I'm hungry, woman."

By then, he was calling her mama only when angered.

"Why there?"

She had to be cautious. Drawing him in would be a delicate maneuver.

"Good a place as any," he shrugged.

"Why not outside his home? Or on the street? Why inside the lobby? In front of a guard."

"You playing detective games, woman? Who gives a shit? It ain't our gig." She felt his curiosity. "What's in your head?"

"It's bullshit, Jefferson."

"Ain't nothin' but a woid," he said, stamping out his cigarette.

"That was no terrorist attack," she said, turning to face him. The whites of his eyes were scored with red veiny wriggles.

"What's one dead spic?"

"Or white?"

"Plenty of them, too."

"There's more to it."

He seemed suddenly defensive.

"Yeah. I don't wanna know."

"Because he's not black?" she said cautiously. "Not the victim or the killer?"

"That too."

"Don't wanna know what, Jefferson?"

"It ain't our gig," he repeated.

"Suppose I told you . . ." She hesitated. "That this one . . ."

118

She shrugged a shoulder toward the building across the street, "... and the other were connected."

His eyelids fluttered. She could tell he was fighting down his curiosity. Swiftly, in quick bold strokes, she told him about the old ammo.

"Plain and simple. It's a cover-up. The eggplant's in it up to his ass."

"Just you honkies blowin' steam. Old ammo," he sneered. "I didn't hear nothin'."

Suddenly he started the motor and pressed heavily on the accelerator. The car shot forward, coughing.

"I don't know nothin'," he muttered.

"You do now."

"You got fantasies, mama. You should put them to better use."

It was a half-hearted feint and Jefferson apparently knew it. He headed the car along Constitution Avenue, making an illegal left on Fourteenth Street.

"The guy will kill again. It'll only get worse."

"What's one more dead honky?"

She sensed his agitation. Finally he pulled the car over.

"The next one could be black."

"Say what?"

"You heard me."

"What's with you? Leave it alone. They're just itchin' to make us look like dummies. Like we can't run things. They think only white men ..." He emphasized *men* "... can run things right."

"Who the hell is 'they'?" she countered. It was time to take a swipe from another direction. "What about integrity?"

"Sheet. You put it in. You take it out. That's integrity."

Beneath his black mask, she could see the alert street intelligence at work.

"You leave it alone, hear?"

"And if I don't?"

"Sheet."

The anger must have shot through his foot. The car careened forward, moving into the strip, the highest crime district in Washington, Fourteenth Street between K and R. They passed pushers on street corners doing a healthy business in little knots. A few prostitutes in tight skirts and high heels patrolled the streets.

"That's where it's at," he said. "Integrity is stopping that bullsheet. That's real death walkin' around out there. What's one lousy killer? What we got? Five homicides, maybe ten, since that guy got blown away. All black. That's the real war, mama. That's Nam in the U. S. of A."

Something caught his eye and he quickly stopped the car.

"Don't," she warned, grabbing his arm, but it was too late. He was out of the car, running toward a group of furtive loungers. A man with a stocking wrapped around his head looked up suddenly and saw him coming. They broke up quickly and the man in the head-stocking darted into an alley. She had set him off, she knew, and now had no alternative but to follow his lead. She sprinted after him, unbuttoning her holster, her insides lurching, afraid.

When she caught up to him, Jefferson had the man at gun-point in the alley, hands against the wall, his body at a thirty-degree angle. He was searching him roughly, pummeling him in the kidneys, and giving him a running angry lecture. A string of nickel bags of heroin, attached like sausages, were being pulled out of both pockets. Jefferson was just putting on the cuffs when she felt a swift sudden punch behind her knees. She went down, her gun clattering to the pavement. A heavy foot sank into her stomach and she felt cold pressure on her temples. Her own gun, she knew, squinting into the sun.

There were three of them. Trying to squirm free of the man's foot only increased the pressure and she could not restrain a squeal of pain. She felt the humiliation, the shame of it, and her eyes darted to Jefferson's, who shook his head, baring his teeth in a forced smile of defeat.

"Sheet," he said, stepping back. A glint of sunlight bounced off the barrel of his piece, which he kept leveled at the cuffed man, who had turned and watched the fracas, the rigid mask of fear receding. Even as a patrolman Fiona had never experienced such fear and she felt the numbing effect of it. She was trapped and helpless.

"Ease off, man," a male voice said above her. It was the fellow who had the foot on her stomach. She felt the pressure again as she gasped for breath. Her strength was fading. The barrel of her gun was pressed harder into her temple.

"The key," the man said, his fingers beckoning. The pressure increased and she grunted her agony.

"Ah don't care. As soon squeeze her gut," the man said, shouting now.

She could see the forced smile fade and Jefferson turn mouse-gray as he watched her pain. With gun leveled at the men who held her, he dipped into his pocket and one-handed the key with surprising agility. One of the men unlatched the handcuffs. The stocking-capped man rubbed his wrists.

"The piece," he commanded. Jefferson looked at the gun and dropped it to the ground. One of the men picked it up and put it in his belt.

"Git, man," the man with the heavy foot ordered and the others moved swiftly. He took his foot off her belly and lifted her to her feet. He held her in a viselike grip as he backed slowly out of the alley.

Jefferson watched them, his lips clamped in a helpless snarl. Everything was in slow motion. She could feel the man's breath against her cheeks, surprisingly sweet, like Dentyne gum, oddly out of sync with the situation. She still felt the weight of the man's foot and she sucked in her breath in gasps.

Only the sound of their slow grating footsteps reached her. Blinking to clear her eyes of mist, she concentrated on Jefferson's immobile face, sensing his frustration and hatred. As they backed out, she heard the purr of a motor behind her. Her feet hung limply, sliding against the pavement. One heel caught and her shoe came off. Her stocking ripped at the heel and the friction of the pavement bruised the skin. The bright autumn sunlight seemed incongruous and she felt suddenly giddy; it was a slow-motion dance and she was a rag doll, stuffed with straw, without will.

Then, with an uncommon force which shook her insides, she felt the relentless pull of gravity, hitting the pavement like something tossed from a great height. It knocked the breath out of her lungs. She gagged and fought down the bile at the bottom of her throat. For a second, she lost any sense of consciousness. When it returned, she felt the breeze of Jefferson's movement passing her, and caught the glint of sunlight on the barrel of his Magnum as he leveled it with two hands. A moment later, she heard the thump of bullets and the screech of tires.

She felt someone rubbing her back and applying pressure to the base of her skull. Turning, her eyes met Jefferson's.

"Easy," he whispered with surprising gentleness, then, "Fuck off, man," he yelled at the gathering street crowd. The blood that had centered in her stomach surged back into her brain, revitalizing her.

"Just lay there for a minute," he cautioned as she tried to sit up. His solicitousness triggered her anger, and she tamped down her humiliation. Everything was in violation, the method of pursuit, the lack of precaution, the avoidance of radio contact, the Magnum. Everything. She could have the book thrown at him.

"They were big fish," he said, as if to justify his action. "I wasted one muvva."

"You sure?" she gasped.

"I'm sure."

"Well, you made your point, you bastard," she said, climbing up his body as if it were a tree trunk. Standing, she felt dizzy and leaned against him until her head cleared. When she could stand on her own, he moved away and found her shoe, bending and lifting her foot into it.

"Prince Charming," she ridiculed. He let her sneer, his face impassive.

"I needed backup," he said, trying hard to mask the contempt. Finally, he could not resist. "Not fuck-up."

In a way, he had made it seem right.

"First of all, it was not our beat. Second, you moved too fast. On your own. It was wrong and you know it."

She knew her anger was tentative. Nothing could justify her being zapped from behind. It was a raw humiliation.

"I been lookin' for that muvva for months. You saw them kids buyin' nickel bags." He turned his eyes on her, spotlights of blind rage, and she felt their power.

"You worryin' about a couple of honkies getting their guts shot up? This is where it is, woman. Out there is the real war."

His rage checkmated all argument. She could see how far apart they were. Jefferson was a man with a cause. It seemed, somehow, pallid against her own. Her sense of inadequacy galled her.

"I nearly got killed," she said lamely.

He shrugged, but his meaning was clear. It was the woman thing. She was trapped in her biology, unable to provide the backup required for such a mission.

"The street already has it down," he said, getting into the car. Her stomach hurt as she bent and slid in beside him.

"And headquarters?" she asked.

"Forget it."

"And the eggplant? He'll hear about it. You said you got one."

"I said forget it."

Cover-up, she thought. She could not seem to reconcile it with the other. Somehow this one seemed right.

The car moved slowly. On every side of her, she saw the junkies, the prostitutes, the pushers. To Jefferson, they were the real enemy. He seemed to be deliberately flaunting the terrain.

"I get the message," she whispered. "We're not in control here. They bury their own."

"No sheet," he said. The car moved toward Sixteenth Street and a saner world. A thought forced a giggle through her anguish.

"What's so funny?" he asked.

"What's one more dead nigger?" she said, turning, unable to face him.

XIV

BRUCE'S CAMPAIGN headquarters was in an aban-
doned supermarket. His ROSEN FOR CONGRESS banner
hung across the width of the storefront under a sign that posed
a futile possibility: "Will Remodel to Suit."

The location was on the dividing line between the jungle and
civilization. The encroachments had moved in so fast that even
the frozen food display cases in the old supermarket still seemed
cold. Posters hawking junk foods clung to the walls, now
defaced and covered with graffiti.

A large map on a wall told a more scientific story of the
changing demographics. The precincts with the old Jews in
their now gloomy run-down apartment buildings were marked
in orange. "Agent Orange" some critic, with a sense of irony,
had written next to the map key. The minority precincts, meaning blacks and Hispanics, were marked in bilious green, a crescent shape which provided still more grist for the anonymous
commentator. "The fertile crescent," it had been dubbed. The
precincts in between were marked in red. Like an open wound,
Fiona thought.

The headquarters was staffed by eager young men and

women, of every skin color. They seemed universally unshaven, even the women. Fiona had never seen a political campaign in full throttle before. The air crackled with energy as the young people eagerly pursued the most menial jobs. Many of them jabbered away on the telephone in English and Spanish in an unceasing litany of persuasion.

To Fiona, the most disconcerting things about the headquarters was Bruce's face. It was ubiquitous, posted even in the evil-smelling john.

"I don't like you watching me pee," she joked. "It's kinky."

"I'm going to force them to know who I am," he said, ignoring the jest. She pictured every public bathroom in the district with his face posted in front of the toilet.

"You'll be the face that launched a thousand shits." His laughter was hollow. He was preoccupied, operating on the thin edge of rage. His days were filled with "shoe leathering," shaking hands on street corners, making speeches before those groups that still held together in the district, attending an occasional coffee klatch in the dingy apartment of some elderly Jewish woman whose cronies had come mainly to complain about crime and reiterate their fears.

"What can I tell them?" Bruce paced their hotel room, his fingers nervously moving through his gray curls.

She did not enjoy her role, doing odd jobs around headquarters. Sometimes she accompanied him on his endless patrols, trying to convince people that he was indeed their tenuous connection with the mechanics of democracy.

Frequently, he would search out her eyes and smile bravely. He had said he needed her and he meant it. At night he clutched her, enveloped her in a stranglehold of an embrace which kept her up most of the night. His sleep was restless, as if his mind were unreeling some private horror show. Sometimes he woke up screaming, an anguished primitive cry that turned her flesh to goosebumps. But being absorbed in his problems kept her mind away from her own.

After the incident on Fourteenth Street, she had applied for two weeks leave, partly to recover, partly to fulfill her promise to Bruce. To pursue the investigation on her own seemed futile.

To confront the eggplant, like some lily-white avenging female angel, risked more of his wrath. It seemed better to run, to put her indignation on hold. Worse still, she had begun to doubt herself. Perhaps they were right. The "farces" were man's work. Maybe it was time to surrender. Marry Bruce. Her courage somehow could not match her outrage.

In an effort to gain insight into Bruce's anguish, she sought out his opponent at a speech she was giving in a church basement. She was the only white Anglo-Saxon type in the audience, a label that, behind the obvious discomfort, offended her sense of Irishness. Yet she sat doggedly in the sea of darker faces, trying to detach herself from the crowd mind.

The woman, Elena Garcia, was intense, driven by the perceived righteousness of her cause. Her appeal was directly to the blood, and she knew it well. The woman's words hammered away at nebulous forces of repression because of race or origins. Garcia was youngish, attractive. When she talked, flashes of gold showed in her mouth.

She had appeal. She was certainly articulate. Mostly it was the woman's frantic ambition that offended Fiona. How dare she? A pushy spic. My God, she thought, Jefferson's words echoing in her mind, I'm beginning to think like them.

The idea horrified her and she slipped out of the meeting early, suffering their stares and embarrassed by the color of her skin.

"They're asking for a head-on debate," Bruce informed her one evening. They sat in what passed for an elegant restaurant in his district, a whitewashed room decorated with pictures of old Mexico. Latin music was piped in. The food seemed nondescript Spanish and the paella was thick and lumpy. Bruce's campaign "consultant," Herbie Clark, picked away at a reddish concoction of chicken breasts. He was a thin, preppy-looking man in his mid-thirties with round horn-rimmed glasses that could have made him appear smarter than he was.

"No way," Clark said, tomato sauce dribbling down his chin. Bruce and Clark seemed to battle rather than eat their food, chomping away as if they were cannibalizing the enemy.

"He's right," Bruce said. "You can't defend the indefensible."

"He's them. The enemy," Clark said, buttressing his argument. He was, after all, supposed to be Bruce's savior, the hired gun. "It doesn't matter that he voted for all those grab bag money bills."

"It's become their right now," Bruce sighed.

"Garcia is a spellbinder," Fiona volunteered.

"A fear monger," Clark said. "A demagogue. Her solution is to shell out more and more dough."

"Look how it's done," Bruce said with a sweep of his hand. "We've pissed it down a rathole, ruined my fucking district."

"You talk like Republicans," Fiona said, with grim humor. She was growing tired of their hypocrisy. "This is not exactly a silk stocking district."

"Nothing we say will matter anyway," Clark said.

"So why all the wasted energy?"

"Show. Sop to the troops."

It was only in the last few days, up close, that she had observed how deep was Bruce's cynicism. Getting elected was all that counted. Power was all.

"Ideology is manure," Clark said. "This election, like all of them, will be decided on how many lever pullers we get to the box. Pure and simple."

"That's democracy," she said.

"So she's a Girl Scout," Clark said. He was, she decided, insufferably manipulative, and Bruce seemed to be buying it all as if it came from some oracle.

"No," Bruce countered. "Just a cop."

"Just a . . . ?" Fiona said. Beneath the light response was a tug of annoyance.

"Bruce. We got to find the shekels," Clark said. "There's no other way. Never was."

"That's the lousy part." Another double Scotch came and he tossed it back quickly, making a sour face.

"You shouldn't be doing anything else," Clark said. "Transportation alone will cost nearly twenty-five thou. Then we have to keep the kitchen open for a full twelve hours. The whole operation will cost nearly a hundred thou. No kidding."

"I didn't have to do it before. Not on this scale," Bruce protested.

"You wanna win, don't you?" Clark demanded. It reminded her of a promise of a fix to a recently arrested heroin addict. The promise itself was enough to quiet things down.

"I need fifty drivers and at least thirty-four to forty vans for starters. The logistics are a nightmare."

She had looked confused and Bruce felt the need to explain.

"We're going to drive all those old yids to the polls. In groups or one by one. Then we're going to feed them three meals. Make a party out of it. We even have a social director."

"We have eleven locations," Clark said proudly. "It'll be like the Catskills." She looked down at the greasy, lumpy mess on her plate. Somehow it fit the image forming in her mind.

"He's got it figured statistically," Bruce said.

"It can work," Clark said. "It has to work."

The way they addressed her, she felt judgmental, as if they were submitting the plan for her inspection. She felt obliged to voice the obvious.

"How do you know they'll push the right lever?"

"We don't. All we can do is draw pictures. We don't care who else they vote for. Rosen's in a good spot on the ballot. We teach them properly, they'll play the game. We'll put the fear of God in them. Tell them the blacks and spics will do them in. Anything. We'll tell them if they don't pull the right one, no party, no meals. No nothing. Half of them won't know what they're doing anyhow."

"Is this all legal?"

"Perfectly," Clark said.

"Like murder in the first degree," Fiona taunted.

"Yeah," Clark said. "Only if we kill this lady, and get Bruce reelected we get off scot-free."

"It's a buy-out," she said. She watched as Clark's eyes met Bruce's. She wondered if it went against his grain, as well.

"Without the dough, you're finished, Bruce," Clark said.

"I know," Bruce said glumly.

Back in their hotel room, Bruce seemed to be drowning in despair and alcohol.

"You're hitting that pretty hard," she cautioned.

"I know." He had undressed to his jockey shorts and was stretched along the bed, pillows propped, staring into space and sipping straight Scotch.

"A hangover won't help."

She sat down and watched him. He seemed to be bent on transforming himself. He did not look at all like the beautiful man of a few months before.

"Bear with me," he pleaded.

"I'm here, loyal to the end." The remark seemed flippant, but he was too self-absorbed to notice.

"If that's the way the game is played . . ." she began.

"It's finding the money that bothers me."

At first, she thought he was having a moral crisis. To her, he had always been strong and sure, a hero.

"I'll hit Remington. Maybe he can throw me a fundraiser. I've already picked over most of the lobbyists. There's just not enough dough anymore."

"Isn't he a little too far right these days?"

"What the hell has that got to do with it? Remember, he was Kennedy's man. Anyway, people give money for other reasons, not for ideology." He swallowed his drink and reached for the bottle again. She grabbed it.

"Bar's closed," she said.

"That's what I need now. A mommy."

"That's what you got."

"Well then, comfort me. What the hell is a mommy for?"

She did comfort him. He soaked it up like a blotter. At least, he knew his needs. She wasn't so sure about herself.

The next day, she visited her parents in their row house in Brooklyn's Bay Ridge.

"It's Fiona," her mother cried as she embraced her in the tiny vestibule of the now ramshackle house. She wondered if that impression was merely a trick of time. In her arms, her mother seemed smaller, although the smell of her, like strong soap, seemed exactly the same as always.

Paddy Fitz, her father, harrumphed in the living room, where he sat at a bridge table playing solitaire with arthritic hands, watching TV, his morning ritual. A Donald Duck cartoon was playing on the tube. Later, toward evening, he would walk painfully down to the bar and relive old times with other retired cops of his vintage. Old cops like Paddy Fitz died after retirement, a slow death.

His beard rubbed against her face and his faded gray eyes misted as he turned away and coughed. Her mother brought coffee from the perpetually brewing pot on the old gas-fired stove, with its worn enamel.

She suffered the litany of the family chronicle as her mother toted up the lives of her sisters, their children, their husbands, and relatives near and distant. Fiona half-listened, waiting for it to end, knowing by rote when to inquire over some missing name. As her mother talked, her father's eyes drifted toward Donald Duck. She knew she had come for some vague reason, but whatever it was, it seemed unpromising. Perhaps she simply had to get away from the obsessiveness of the campaign, from Bruce and Clark and their endless scheming.

"You stayin' for lunch, Fiona?" her mother asked. She hadn't intended to, but she nodded. In their prime, they had exuded sureness, strength. Or so it seemed. Long ago she had seen through their so-called wisdom. They merely had opinions and, through religion, had always been prepared for the hereafter. It was forever heaven and hell. Nothing in between.

"Pop. I'm thinking of getting out," she said. "Maybe getting married and taking another kind of job."

"Do we know the boy?"

"Hey, pop. I'm thirty-two. I don't go out with boys."

"You're still my little girl."

His genes hung on her like a pall. Was she here looking for his approval, this bigoted shell of a man? Suddenly, it hit him.

"Leave the farces?"

"I think I've had it. I'm fed up. Maybe it's no place for a woman."

130

His eyes narrowed in their wrinkled sacs and he looked at her shrewdly. All their lives they had barely touched. He had orated. She had listened. Once, in a fit of pique at some article he had been reading in the *Daily News,* he had muttered to her from behind the paper.

"Hey, Fiona, they're letting females in the farces."

It was an offhand remark, but it penetrated with the full force of a powerful ancestral urge.

"Would you like that, pop?" she had asked. She had heard an inarticulate sound from behind the paper. She had always wondered if it had meant approval, even though he railed against it when he found out.

"A punk nearly did me in last week," she said. "And my superiors are only worried about their jobs."

"So it's the same there. The punks are always trying to do you in and the superiors are always worried about their jobs."

"They're also corrupt."

"The same," he sighed. He had never been on the take, haranguing others who had. Nor had she ever felt proud of him. Where did it get you? she wanted to ask. She knew the answer. Nowhere.

"Then why?" she asked instead, surprised how easy it was to talk to him in shorthand.

"Somebody has to do the dirty work."

"But why fight them too?"

"You want to give the streets to the animals?"

"Maybe we already have."

It was the closest thing to a conversation she had ever had with him. And it annoyed her to be actually seeking his advice, this man of monumental prejudices. Anger was pushing it out of her.

"I may marry a Jew. He's a politician. A congressman."

"Lord have mercy."

Behind her, she heard the coffee cups rattling on a tray, and she knew her mother had heard.

"He's also divorced. The whole bit."

Her mother held the tray over the bridge table while her father gathered the cards with shaking fingers. After her mother had poured out the coffee she crossed herself.

"It won't do any good," she said firmly.

"And she wants to leave the farces," her father said, blowing on the hot surface of the coffee. He raised his eyes and looked toward her picture on a mahogany table, standing in a gilt frame on a doily. It was a photograph of her in uniform. For the first time, she realized how accessible it was for him to gaze at from his seat at the bridge table.

When she was away from them she could articulate it clearly to herself. There was a childlike purity about them and a well-rutted road one followed. One for men. One for women. One for Irish Catholics. One for others.

"I'm sorry," Fiona said, disappointed. She had strayed from the well-rutted road.

"Who's to say?" her father said, and then firmly: "It's still the greatest calling in the world. No thanks for it. God's work." The old Paddy Fitz.

She wondered if he still believed it.

She finished her coffee but did not stay for lunch.

"I love you both anyway," she said, embracing them. Her father seemed to clutch her tighter than he had ever done before. It was simply too early to surrender. Perhaps that was why she had come home.

XV

IN THE waning days of October, politicians, like desperate schoolboys on the eve of the big game, came to Thaddeus Remington. They came in person. Occasionally they came through high-level emissaries, but always they had a single goal in mind. Money.

He was amused by the subterfuges and strategies they had to work out to gain his attention and his favor. He, too, had developed a strategy for receiving them and set responses to their requests. For those with whom he had some relationship, he laid out a private lunch in the dining alcove overlooking the swimming pool, usually quiche and salad and a bottle of chilled Chablis. For those with whom he had a conversational acquaintance but who had never been invited to his home, he arranged for coffee and cakes in the Rustic Room. Those with whom he had a nodding acquaintance, he invited for cocktails in late afternoon. And, a special few, regardless of his previous relationship, he invited to dinner, a quiet repast of beef and Burgundy in front of a roaring fire.

He had also developed a metaphor for the process. They were the exotic fish in his fishbowl, and he was their only observer.

133

To complete the metaphor, he visualized himself as standing before the lighted tank, arm poised above the waters, a vial of food in his fingers. As the mood struck him, so the vial tipped. Because of federal limits on personal contributions, they invariably asked him to go beyond it, to throw a fundraiser in his home. Sometimes he did, as he had done recently for the Republican presidential candidate.

If there were amusements in his manipulations, they were tempered by the knowledge that he was searching for still another sign. He knew he could not force it. Because of the impending late November deadline, he was getting impatient. It was, he was sure, an inexorable cycle. He must be watchful and alert. The sign would come.

In mid-October, a young senator, Craig Taylor, came to him for financial help. Remington had mixed the martinis and settled into a wing chair opposite the supplicant. He remembered the rush of publicity that had greeted the man when he was elected from the State of Washington six years ago. The man had an attractive wife, two pretty children. A golden family. Central casting could not have done better.

The senator's blond hair had not yet begun to gray. It was perfectly trimmed. He wore a matching moustache as well and cufflinks stamped with the seal of his state. There was, Remington observed, a crispness about him, a cleanliness that reminded him of himself. He saw the man's persona clearly, the fragile but effective facade, the obsessive yearning.

"I'm thirty-seven," Taylor said. He had just catalogued his desperation. He was two hundred thousand short. He couldn't understand what was happening. He had worked hard for his constituents. Remington studied him. Perhaps he had started out too assured, too certain, too cocky. Remington's eyes darted to the portrait of himself above the mantel.

"If I lose, it won't be the end of the world," Taylor said. Then, after a long pause, he drained his martini. "Will it?" Remington watched the senator's eyes search the room, then glitter like hot coals. He rose and refilled his glass.

"Depends on how you see your world." Remington watched him shrewdly, feeling the spur of pursuit.

"They didn't much like my vote on the Panama Canal," he said. "Hell. A junior senator hasn't much power." He sipped his drink. "I need this win. I learned a hell of a lot. I've made my mistakes."

"And if you had the two hundred thousand, could you win?" The man looked up. A light flush rouged his cheeks.

"I think I can," he said earnestly. "I come over well on the tube. My record is respectable."

"And the polls?"

"That's why I need the money. I'm down."

"And then?" Remington prodded, the vial of fish food tipping, teasing.

"Then? I'll win."

"How can you be sure?" Remington asked softly.

The man shifted in the chair.

"I want to serve."

"Serve whom?"

Obviously, the man hated the role of supplicant. Remington wondered how far he would have to go to destroy the man's facade.

"The country," Taylor said firmly. Did he really believe that? Remington knew the force of it, the power of wanting; the agony of being lost in the black tunnel of ambition. To disguise his agitation, he got up and mixed another batch of martinis. Refilling Taylor's glass, his fingers shook and a drop of the liquid spilled on the man's lap.

"You've been politically defeated. You know what it means." Taylor pleaded.

"I do know." He could see that the senator did not have the inner reserves to withstand defeat.

"I really need your help," the senator implored.

"Why come to me?" Remington asked, enjoying the malice. He enjoyed seeing them dangle. Some were less vulnerable than others. Some would never buckle, no matter what defeat they sustained. He was interested only in the weak ones. Like Taylor.

"You know the score," Taylor said. "You know where I'm coming from."

"It's late in the game," Remington said.

"I know I can pull it out."

Taylor emptied his glass again. There had been no talk of ideology. No talk of party. The level of the man's appeal was even more basic. Remington sensed it. Did it signal a coming sign?

Standing up, he stepped close to the senator's chair and tipped the pitcher once again. With his free hand, the senator reached for Remington's waist.

"I know you understand," he said. He looked down, meeting the man's tortured gaze. Remington felt the pull of it, frightened. Had he been looking for this? Surely not this. The man's touch became a caress. He felt the blood surge, the center of him respond. Before the man could touch him there, he had moved back. Taylor flushed and downed his drink quickly.

"You're a fucking fag!" Remington shouted. He felt his legs tremble. Deep in his pants, his erection twitched. "It's disgusting."

"You're wrong," the senator pleaded. "It's a complete misinterpretation."

"Get out of my house!"

"You've misinterpreted . . ." Taylor began. His voice, high-pitched, was on the verge of hysteria. Remington would not turn, would not look at the man's face.

"At least . . ." The words began as a sob, then, tremulous: ". . . let's keep it in this room. Whatever it is you think."

The senator's footsteps receded. He heard the door close and sought out a mirror to see his image. His skin was pale, like alabaster. A film of sweat covered his face. Had the other man seen it, sensed it?

In the steamroom, he turned the cold taps on full blast, hoping to clear his head. An errant memory had snaked its way into his thoughts. Perhaps the cold would strangle it. Receding, it still clung, like smoke smell to the edge of memory. Then he shut the taps and put the steam on full blast, feeling the surge of heat singe his skin and chase the cold.

He brought himself to a nebula of consciousness, that moment when the mind clouded over and anxiety faltered. Feeling faint, he shut the steam taps and let the cold drench him again. Revival came slowly, then quickened as the adrenalin surged up again and he was able to stand without dizziness.

He wrapped himself in a towel, groped for the bed, and staring at the eagle's beak, which reassuringly hovered above him, let himself sink into a deathlike sleep.

In the distance he heard the door chimes. Opening his eyes, he listened for voices. Remembering, he cast off the chilled towel and with a dry one rubbed himself alert. A buzzer sounded and he flipped the intercom switch.

"Congressman Rosen, sir," Mrs. Ramirez said.

"*Sí.*"

He dressed quickly. His skin still glowed from his heat-cold shock treatment. He took a tiny gold scissors from his dresser, clipped off a white carnation from a bunch in the tapered Meissen vase and stuck it in the buttonhole of his charcoal gray jacket.

Surveying himself in the mirror, he brushed his damp hair, checked the part, the knot in his tie, the position of his belt, the knife edge of his pants, the loops of his shoelaces, alternating his gaze to the different mirrors, catching himself at various angles. He was pleased with himself; he was well girded. Who was it downstairs? Another supplicant? He waited patiently for recall, knowing that he had deadened the past. As he reached the upper step and began his descent, he remembered. Of course, Bruce Rosen. He felt the first cutting edge of exhilaration as the sign, the true sign, began to emerge in his mind.

"Bruce." He held out his hand.

"Tad." Their eyes met. He watched the inside of the man's hazel field, observing the yellow-flecked center, until they shifted nervously. He understood instantly, the animal alertness. Fight or flee. All exits were closed to this beast. He smiled with delight.

"What will it be?"

"Scotch, please."

His eyes searched the forest of bottles on the glistening bar cart. He picked up a pinch bottle, displaying it.

"The good stuff. You look as if you need it. It's been getting better for twenty years."

"I wish I could say the same," Bruce said.

"I can," Remington replied, holding up a glass and pouring it half full. He reached for the ice and Bruce nodded. He poured one for himself.

Remington lifted his glass, "To victory."

"I'll drink to that."

They settled into chairs opposite each other. From somewhere in the house two clocks chimed at once. It was precisely eight o'clock. Remington checked his watch, which was always perfectly timed, then studied Rosen again. He had never really looked at him before, although they had bantered scores of times at Washington social rituals, yet revealing nothing to each other. The man had style, he observed, in a dark brooding Semitic way. The graying curly top and deep-set eyes gave him a theatrical air that he had obviously turned into an asset. Also, he could hide behind his cheekbones, as he was doing now, trying unsuccessfully to mask his desperation.

"Winning isn't everything," Remington purred, determined to tear off the mask immediately. No sense in wasting time, he thought. Rosen shifted in his chair and put his glass down. He had, Remington was sure, decided to keep a clear head.

"Yes, it is," Bruce said. "They changed the battle plan. While I wasn't looking. The traditional liberal is as dead as Kelsey's nuts. They want raw meat at the lower depths. The limousine liberals are stepping on the brakes. The Kennedy aura went south with the Pepsi generation."

Rosen had obviously strung the new clichés on a necklace of cynicism, hoping to find the right appeal. Remington chuckled to himself.

"It's a new ballgame," Bruce continued, unwinding a tight spring. "My district's falling into the slime. I'm wrong for it, the wrong sex, the wrong color, the wrong antecedents, the wrong voice, the wrong party. I look wrong. I sound wrong." He bent over and stuck a finger in his chest. "I think wrong."

"You're hard on yourself, Bruce," Remington said.

"We're both wrong," Bruce said. So he's also shrewd, Remington thought, feeling the thrust at his innards. "The Oswald bullet made us both obsolete." Remington felt his pulse quicken. "Only it's taking me longer to die."

There it was. The sign. A bullet can change history. He wanted to stand up and cheer.

"I'm looking for resurrection, Tad," Bruce said after a long pause. He had picked up his drink and finally drained it. Remington had resisted getting up for a refill, not wanting to break the spell. "Maybe you as well."

"Me?"

"You can't be comfortable with throwing in with those aging Boy Scouts with their sash of merit badges flapping over their chests. Jack was our man. He's always going to be our man."

"He got caught in the wrong rhythm of history," Remington said cautiously. Would Rosen understand?

"You believe that old wheeze about them dying in office every twenty years?

"They do. Facts are facts," Remington said, elated.

He wanted to explain about the cosmic force. Instead he said:

"When the natural order fails, providence intervenes. In 1860, Lincoln. In 1880, Garfield. In 1900, McKinley. In 1960, Kennedy. Do you think these all happened by accident?"

"Who the hell knows?" Bruce said irritably. He got up and poured himself a refill.

I know, Remington wanted to tell him.

"It will undoubtedly happen again," he said instead.

Bruce was obviously confused by the tack the conversation had taken.

"We don't understand history's lessons. Someone has to point them out. Keep pointing them out. There is a cosmic force, a divine rhythm . . ." He checked himself, still unsure. He wanted to scream it out. I am the instrument; you are the sign.

Sensing that he was losing control, he stood up quickly and strode out of the room. In the corridor he paused, leaning against a wall to catch his breath. Suddenly he felt their eyes staring down at him from the pictures hung along the walls, Garfield, McKinley, Lincoln, Kennedy. They were randomly placed, seemingly without design, scattered among other historical memorabilia. But there was no escaping them. They anchored the corners, reaching out, reminding him what he must do. Perspiration ran down the sides of his chest. Recovering, he came back into the room.

"How much do you need?" he asked abruptly.

"A hundred thousand," Bruce said, startled. "To . . ."

"Never mind for what. I'll get it for you."

"You will?" Bruce's jaw had dropped but his eyes continued to probe Remington as if seeking confirmation.

"I'll sign a note and be responsible for raising the money."

"My God, Tad. I can't tell you how grateful I am."

"Want to kiss my ring?"

They moved, laughing, into the dining room, where the corner of the long table had been set for two. As they came in, Mrs. Ramirez stood aside, greeting them with a shy smile.

If he wins, I will know for sure, Remington thought, reaching for the bottle of Burgundy, jabbing the corkscrew point into the cork. *For sure.* He poured the ruby liquid into his glass for the first taste.

XVI

D R. BENTON'S hands were surprisingly smooth for his age. Fiona had often observed them during his autopsies. She saw them now, as he handed her a pony of sherry with the same delicate grace that probed dead tissue as if it were alive. They were seated in the living room of his modest house in a quiet neighborhood in northeast Washington, one of the few that had somehow escaped the ravages of urban change. The city was sprinkled with these surprising oases of black gentility.

On the wall beside his book-lined shelves were citations, photographs, memorabilia of a life of achievement. His wife had been a lawyer, one of the first black women lawyers in Washington, a dubious honor, he would comment ruefully, for which she paid "bitter dues." Dr. Benton was a second-generation medical man.

"My father's fee was occasionally turnips, sometimes collard greens and squirrel. Have you ever eaten squirrel, Fiona?"

"Never on Fridays," she bantered.

She had taken the Eastern shuttle back to Washington earlier in the day. Bruce was busy making plans with Clark for the big "hegira," as they had begun to call their election day ploy.

Remington's money had buoyed Bruce's spirit and the need for her had measurably lessened. She wasn't sure whether she ought to be relieved or disappointed.

"No sense me hanging around," she had told Bruce. She had been on the verge of asking for more leave, staying until election eve. It was a question of the lesser evil. She chose to go home.

Bruce was disappointed, but now that the scent of victory was in his nostrils he felt more secure. Besides, she found herself surprisingly uninvolved, an appendage. The candidate's girl friend.

"You've been wonderful," Bruce told her, insisting on driving her to LaGuardia. "That's what loving is all about. When you need me, I'll be there, Fi." He squeezed her hand and burrowed it against his thigh.

"I know," she said, not wholly convinced.

"These bouts of insecurity and paranoia every two years make us all crazy. At least, in the Senate you can space out the agony."

As he drove, she looked at him in profile, the handsome face pointed at the road. Occasionally he shot her a seductive look, his eyes flashing, offering a wink of charm and reassurance. It was little gestures like that that titillated her.

"Do you love me?" He asked this, always at odd moments, catching her off guard. The question had become a litany, yet the random repetition, like a sultry love song on a scratchy record at breakfast, sounded hollow.

"Don't be ridiculous," she would reply at these off moments. Maybe it meant something different to her. When you're "in love" you're supposed to know it beyond the shadow of a doubt. But when it counted, when his embrace was urgent, and the joy of it engulfed her, when the question came in gusts of passion, her response was immediate, emphatic, without doubts.

"Yes. I love you. Yes. I love you."

In the afterglow, when it was as good as it could be, he invariably told her, like a comment on a college term paper for high achievement:

"Perfect pitch, Fiona."

142

Was that love?

There were times, many times, when she missed his closeness. Alone in her bed, she felt an enormous void. The depression of loss was awesome. She wondered how she had survived aloneness all these years. There had been other men. Not many. She detested both the catalogue and the comparison. None of it had ever really moved her in a purely physical sense. Not until Bruce.

When she had seen him faltering, she had intellectualized her emotion. She wished she hadn't seen him so vulnerable.

Once, during an investigation, she had had to poke around a male locker room. It seemed permeated with maleness, the residue of sweat and striving, torn jockey shorts, a discarded jock strap under a bench. In the adjoining bathroom, the line of urinals added a touch of militant arrogance to their exclusivity.

It wasn't the physical difference that affected her. More like a psychic difference. Aggressiveness, ambition, violence. It was raw, mindless. Like the involuntary gorging of their penises, a mysterious primitive demand for maleness.

"You've seen me at my worst," he told her as she stepped out of the car, the tender good-byes completed. "Break a leg," she had said, adding, "just keep the rest the way it is."

As his car sped away from the airport curb, she felt an immediate sense of loss and, contradictorily, an unburdening. Perhaps, she wondered, deliberately searching for some humor to tide her over, she should hire Dr. Benton to dissect his primal urges and cut away those she detested.

She had planned to clean her apartment but the effort to assuage her sense of loss had once again opened the door to her outrage. She wondered if it were all connected. Not wanting to be alone with her uncertainty, she called Dr. Benton.

"I'm looking for tea and sympathy," she told him now, as she settled herself in his living room.

"Sherry is better," he said. "As for sympathy, I'm sorry. You don't look in dire need."

"I'm just confused," she admitted. "I've had a double helping of politics. Professional and personal."

"Life is politics," he shrugged. She told him first what Bruce's campaign was going to do. In the telling, it didn't seem as devious.

"So what else is new?" Dr. Benton said. "The winning is all."

"Whatever happened to integrity?" she asked. She felt his eyes searching her. Turning away, she looked around the book-lined room. In books people worshiped integrity. Life was different.

"I think you're making harsh judgments," he said. "Much too rigid."

"Then where's the standard?" she asked.

"Is integrity a requirement of society?"

"You can't answer a question with a question."

"You can if you want to avoid the answer."

"Now there's a strategy for survival."

"You should heed those words, Fiona."

"I know," she agreed.

"She was like you," Dr. Benton sighed, looking at his wife's picture. A calm dark woman with soft eyes peered back at them. "Integrity came first." Instantly, she felt the sisterly bond. Had he seen through her? She realized suddenly that she had come for more than tea and sympathy, more than sherry. She told him about the so-called cover-up; she added "so-called" only out of respect to his caution.

"Saying it seems such a small thing. Why is it so big in my mind? So against the grain?" She thought of Bruce, also against the grain.

She watched his eyes shift. It was a subtle move but enough to show that his guard was up.

"Honesty," he said, smiling. "It will get you every time."

"I can't screen it out," she confessed.

"You'll learn. It doesn't always equate with survival."

"But there's a killer loose. He's already wasted two people."

"You can't pin that on yourself."

"But he's trying to evade our responsibility to find him. I feel like an alien."

"Now there's a subject I can empathize with," he said.

"You people always think with your skin."

144

She had blurted it out without thinking. The eggplant's trigger response rang in her mind: *And you always think with your pussy.* If he hadn't said it, he surely meant it.

"Conditioning," Dr. Benton said. For a moment, he seemed disconnected, lost in thought. "Whoever it is, he'll do it again. You have to learn patience. If he does it in our jurisdiction, you'll have your vindication." It wasn't the advice she had wanted to hear.

"What about human life?"

"Compassion," Benton sighed. "The curse of police work."

"It's like waiting for the other shoe to drop."

"Exactly. More sherry?" She downed her drink and he refilled her glass. She noted that his hands shook, uncommon for him. He settled back in silence. She let him ponder, knowing that he was searching to fill the vacuum.

"Aside from your captain's motives, survival is his only real goal; the fact is that the revelation would make people uncomfortable. Not only the powers that be. But ordinary people on a tourist holiday. Visiting the seat of government. More tourists are killed in automobile accidents."

"It's still wrong."

"That it is. Ethically. Professionally. It'll all come out in the wash. It always does."

"I keep thinking about that innocent guy out there waiting to get his."

His lashes fluttered and his eyes opened wide. "That's too heavy a burden for you, Fiona." He shook his head, challenged finally in his gut. "The man's obviously a psychopath. No one can be responsible for that."

"But if we don't do our best to find him, we're not earning our keep."

"My God, woman," he blurted. "You take too much on yourself." His gaze drifted again to the photograph of the dark woman. "Like her. It ate her alive. This is no well-ordered paradise."

"I guess I'm in the wrong business."

With his smooth polished hands he reached out and touched her arm.

"We're both in the wrong business, Fiona. I started out to be a healer."

She tossed in bed all night. Then got up, took two aspirins and spent the rest of the night tossing on her couch. In the morning, she was groggy, her thoughts wispy and untidy.

Jefferson welcomed her back with uncommon concern.

"You okay, woman?"

She hadn't turned him in. For that, she hoped, he might be grateful.

"Integrity sucks," she muttered, hoping it confused him.

"Say what?"

Well, she sighed, they were back on the old track. They spent the day investigating a suicide, which seemed a tiny leg up from the perpetual naturals that they were assigned. The victim was a young man of twenty. His mother was ill and hospitalized and, in despair, the boy had tried to hang himself. But he couldn't seem to manage it. Then he stabbed himself in the gut with a kitchen knife, but miraculously missed all the vital organs. Finally, he swallowed a full bottle of gout pills. They did the trick.

"Now that's determination," Jefferson said.

"At least he had the courage of his convictions."

Jefferson looked at her and shrugged. She felt transparent and brittle, helpless, feminine. You've lost your *cojones*, Fitz, she railed at herself later that night, sitting alone in her apartment, slowly sipping straight gin. After four gulps, it made her nauseous and she put it aside.

Bruce called her at midnight.

"Tomorrow is V-Day," he exulted.

"For vote or victory?" she asked, masking her mood of despair.

"We've got the logistics down to the last gallon of gas. This guy Clark is a genius. If the weather is good, we could hustle out maybe five or six thousand more votes."

"Enough to win?"

"Pray to the Madonna . . ." She could picture him sitting alone at his desk at campaign headquarters surrounded by debris, discarded Styrofoam containers, half-eaten burgers, soft drink bottles, mildewed newspapers; the sour stench of human aspirations. She had detected this strange effluvium emanating from him in those last days she had spent with him, something oozing out of him along with the usual juices. She could almost detect it through the telephone.

". . . I need every edge I can get. The iron lady, I hear, is frantic. She's yelling foul all over the place. I'll say this for the broad. She's tough. She'll be a shoo-in two years from now." He hesitated. Still, he wouldn't totally give in to optimism. "If she doesn't make it now. She could, you know. Something could fuck up." There was a long pause. "You love me?"

"You have to ask me that?"

"Yes."

"Of course I do." Integrity does suck, she thought bitterly.

"It was wonderful, your coming up. It helped a lot. I wish you were here now. But I'm glad you're not. I have an assignment for you."

"For me?"

"I promised Remington you'd be at his place tomorrow night. He's having a big election party. I owe that man a lot."

"Must I?"

"I need a cheerleader. Hold his hand. I'll need him for the Senate run."

A long sigh came down the line. "I think I'm his surrogate. He's living vicariously through me and the others he's helping. Poor bastard. Always a bridesmaid, never a bride. You go and keep things warm for me." She could hear his breathing, forced and hard. "I better beat that broad."

His vulnerability crackled over the wires along with that musty odor.

"I'll do my duty," she groaned. Always a bridesmaid, never a bride. Maybe it was destined to be her fate as well.

"You love me?" he asked.

"I told you," she said evasively.

There was another long pause. She could hear his breathing.

"Put the phone there," he commanded. Damned if I will, she thought, but said nothing.

147

"Feel me?"

"Yes," she lied.

"Good?"

"Yes."

"Love me," he said after a while. She did not wait to hear the click of the phone.

All the fireplaces were lit in Remington's house and every light burned brightly. Three big television sets blared in the drawing rooms. In the dining room, under the polished crystal chandelier, the long table was covered with an elaborate buffet. Remington wore a red velvet jacket with a black collar and red paisley slippers. Fiona recognized many of the faces from her previous visit, mostly diplomats, and a scattering of politicians.

She had arrived at seven. The crowd was noticeably subdued, like a birthday party after the candles had been lit.

"NBC already picked my man," Remington said, kissing her on both cheeks. "The computers have taken the suspense out of everything." His blue eyes glistened in the light. "Now we have to sweat out your boy."

"We'll know soon. The polls closed at seven," she said.

He looked at his watch. "I've got one helluva investment in your man."

"So I'm told."

He was fiercely energized, a trifle breathless, as he moved about the room, the perfect host, chirping one liners to his guests. Occasionally, a light cheer went up as a group huddled around one of the sets tried to squeeze some excitement out of the results.

"There's a new day a-coming," someone said.

"A goddamned revolution."

"Be careful what you say," someone said near her. "Dobrynin is over there." She looked toward the smiling, unflappable Russian ambassador. She missed Bruce's running commentary on who was who, the tart gossip. Wandering from room to room, she paused occasionally to study the scrimshaw, the portraits of Presidents, the historical letters. In the large Rustic Room, with its huge stuffed animal heads, her eyes wandered over the gun cases.

"Interested?" It was Remington's voice, startling her.

"Professionally, yes." She turned away from his probing eyes, toward the guns. He began to explain their origins.

"They played an important part in our history," he said.

"I'm sure," she turned around to face him. "Why do you suppose people collect these?" There was a tone of derision that she had not intended. He seemed to ignore it.

"I can't speak for other people."

"All right. Then for yourself."

"It gets one close to history," he said thoughtfully. "Touching yesterday. These little machines have had a lot to do with creating our past. And some will direct our future."

"They also kill needlessly."

"Not them. They're only instruments."

"They kill people."

"People kill people."

He seemed to grow distant. "Sometimes, there is a need to kill."

"A need! That's crazy."

"People have motives," he said.

"These little buggers make it easy to give in to them."

"Exactly, they're only instruments." He smiled charmingly. "In Caesar's time, they used the blade."

"Guns are easier. Quicker, less messy."

"Dead is dead, however it's done."

"You should be in my line of work," Fiona said. "The bullet is very popular."

"Then without guns, you might be out of work," he laughed, moving away. She took a glass of white wine from a silver tray and moved to the other end of the room. His remarks had disturbed her and her thoughts chased back to the two still unsolved murders. What was the killer's need? she wondered. A shiver went through her. Sitting alone, she let the time pass, avoiding conversation, feeling uncomfortable and out of place.

"Meez FitzGerald," someone said from behind her. It was Remington's Spanish maid. "You come."

She followed her up the winding staircase to a small paneled study. Remington sat at an antique desk and held a telephone. He was smiling broadly, red puffs rouging his cheeks.

"You tell her," he said into the phone, handing her the instrument.

"I did it." It was Bruce. In the background she heard shouting and music. He was screaming into the phone. "We creamed the bitch."

"Wonderful, Bruce." She was surprised at her lack of elation.

"You can't ever give up in this business," he shouted. He lowered his voice. "You love me?"

"I told you." Again, she found herself strangely evasive.

"I'll be home tomorrow. We're going to celebrate. And Fi. I want you to kiss that son-of-a-bitch Remington for me. A real deep one. We owe him. Got to go. Love me." She heard the click and replaced the instrument in its cradle. Remington was watching her, his face still flushed. She stood up and moved toward him. Fiona always does her duty, she thought.

"He says I should give you a kiss."

He opened his arms and drew her in, pressing his lips against hers, forcing her mouth open. His urgency startled her and she felt his body press against her, his hardness clearly defined. My God, she thought, struggling against him. He held her in an unbreakable grip. Suddenly she sensed something that made her go limp for a moment. Some odd similarity to Bruce. She sniffed. Was that it, she wondered, the smell of them? Finally, he released her. He was panting and beads of moisture sprouted on his forehead.

"It was only supposed to be a kiss," she said, when she had recovered her breath.

Would it have mattered to Bruce if she had gone further? She walked out of the room. Never, she thought. The man repelled her.

XVII

T HE FACT that November 22 fell on a Saturday was another sure sign of the rightness of his mission. It was a force of gravity, relentless, irrevocable.

Mrs. Ramirez left for the weekend on Friday night. Before she had gone she made him a dinner of cold salmon and fresh fruit and uncorked a bottle of white wine.

"It's all right," he told her. "No need to wait around. I'll eat later."

She looked at him with her shrewd eyes, shrugged, and soon he heard the front door close behind her. It begins, he told himself, feeling the latent exhilaration. Hadn't he set impossible goals for himself? Rosen's chances were almost nil when he came to his rescue. And hadn't the first two "events" left him completely unscarred by suspicion? Such things meant something. They were signposts, urging him forward.

There were still many obstacles ahead. But he did not dwell on them. Everything would happen in due course. First one revelation. Then another. The cosmic eye was clever, its judgment infallible.

In the garage, he climbed up the ladder to a spot near the

rafters where he had hidden the Mannlicher-Carcano 6.5. It lay in its grease-filled oilskin sack, a blanket wrapped around it. It had not been disturbed for five years. He had bought it from a secondhand dealer in Boston, not yet knowing the full implications of his purchase. How could he know that a sure hand was guiding him, even then?

Cradling the gun lovingly, he brought it up to his bedroom, along with a pile of rags. He stripped down to his shorts, spread papers on the floor and slipped the greased rifle out of its oilskin sheaf. For the next hour he rubbed it clean, dismantled it, then reassembled it. All its mechanisms worked perfectly. From a box of bullets, also wrapped in the blanket, he took out three cartridges and balanced them next to the silver comb and brush set on his dresser. Then he burned all the excess rags and newspapers in the fireplace, setting aside the oilskin sheath and the blanket for future use. All his weapons had been scrupulously preserved. Someday they would be permanently displayed, complete with descriptions recounting how he had used them.

Back in the bedroom, he attached a Japanese-made telescopic sight, and tested the effectiveness by pointing it at his neighbor's house. A light was on, and he adjusted the scope to catch a remarkable view of a television screen. He pulled the trigger, heard the click, certain the bullet would have gone dead center into the set.

Then he posed naked with the gun in the myriad of mirrors. He felt like an ancient warrior with a modern weapon. He pointed the gun at his image and pulled the trigger. Moving it waist-high, he pulled it again, then lowered it, the flat of the stock against his erection. He pulled it again and again. He jumped on the bed, rifle in firing position, his erection rubbing against the smooth stock. Again and again he pulled the trigger.

After a while, he picked up the telephone, asked for information and got the number of the Russian Embassy.

"I want Marina," he said to the embassy operator. He was barely able to control his laughter.

"Who?"

"Marina," he repeated. Then he hung up and dialed the Cuban Mission.

"This is A. H. Hiddel," he said.

"Who?" said a Spanish-accented voice.

"A. H. Hiddel," he shouted into the phone, repeating the name until the voice at the other end hung up. Surely the cosmic force would not deny him these sly little joys. He could not remember when he had been so happy.

"Look at me, mama," he shouted at his image in the mirror. He held the gun in one hand and his erection in the other. "See me, mama. I know you can see me through that mirror. Your little boy. Watch it come out." He moved closer to the mirror and, hand working feverishly, ejaculated on its surface. "Watch it, mama. See it, mama."

He calmed down slowly. His heartbeat decelerated, his breathing normalized. He slipped between the sheets of his bed, put the gun beside him and wrapped his legs around it. The metal barrel began to warm. He grew drowsy and soon fell into a deep dreamless sleep.

Waking up, he was instantly alert. He shaved, took a hot shower, toweled himself dry and traced the name, O. H. Lee, in the mist of the mirror.

Unzipping a garment bag, he removed brown chino pants, a T-shirt and a blue reversible jacket. How long had they been hanging there? He was not certain. He had little memory of time. From the dresser drawer he withdrew a small container and took out $13.87. He counted out the change carefully, making sure of the amount. It was all there, as he had left it.

He taped the gun to his flank; it was awkward, but necessary. He drew on his pants and tested his walk, then checked his appearance in the mirrors. His left leg had stiffened but he could bend his right leg at the knee, which would enable him to drive. He took the three bullets, still balanced on top of the dresser, and put them in his pants pocket. Then, he drew out a pair of gloves and placed them in the pocket of his blue jacket.

He limped down the stairs, made himself a mug of instant coffee, and drank it quickly. From the closet where he had stored the other weapons he took a .38 Smith and Wesson Victory revolver with a sawed-off barrel, checked to be sure it was fully loaded, then stuck it in his belt.

It was impossible to drive the Volkswagen with his stiffened left leg; he had to take the Bentley, which he maneuvered smoothly out of the garage. He was calm, fully alert. He felt no sense of danger or anxiety. Because it was Saturday, the traffic was light on Connecticut Avenue. Yet he deliberately drove slowly. He had plenty of time. The car swept past the Mint, below an underpass, then swung into the Southwest Freeway.

The plan was like a precircuited matrix in his mind and he drove ahead without the slightest hesitation. He took the exit marked "U.S. Capitol," then turned right and moved the car into the front parking rim of the Jefferson Building at the Library of Congress. He had no permit, nor did the question of tempting fate give him the slightest sense of insecurity. Besides, it was Saturday and most of the staff was off. The force would provide.

A black guard paid little attention as he signed his name at the door. A. H. Hiddell. It was all routine. No ID required. He smiled pleasantly.

He limped up the staircase to his left. He had been through the Library of Congress only once before, a tour by the chief librarian, who had been a guest at his house. He remembered having suffered through the entire tour. The chief librarian relished every moment of it, explaining, lecturing, citing the library's eminent history. His only interest was to find the way to an upper window.

Now he moved up the stairs, gripping the banister, to the top floor, limping through the corridors. He opened a door, discovered a small alcove office with one window overlooking First Street, which he had remembered from his tour. Across the park he could see the Capitol rotunda, looking like molded ice on this cloudy day. The Capitol parking lot was only half filled.

Locking the office door from the inside, he untaped the rifle. Then, pointing the gun in the direction of the Capitol, he looked through the telescopic sight. He stroked the trigger, listened as the mechanism moved in perfect sync. Satisfied, he lay the rifle against the wall and opened the window.

He looked at his watch. It was 12:15. Still fifteen minutes to go. He inserted the three bullets in the rifle, put on his gloves and knelt in front of the window, the rifle butt down on the floor beside him. His mind was clear, his thoughts calm. Lee, inside of him, was surely watching with approval, equally calm and self-assured. Anxieties had disappeared. How wonderful to have been chosen, he thought, grateful, humbled.

At the proper time, he knew that his mind would register the hubbub, the cacophony of noise, the hum of motorcycles, as the motorcade moved ceremoniously through the streets, bearing the Golden God. He waited, listened. His body tensed, the adrenalin charging, Lee's voice calmly commanding. Steady, the voice said, as he looked again at his watch.

It was 12:25. Slowly he lifted the gun into the window, the barrel steadied against the sill. He placed his chin against the stock, knowing that in a few minutes the god would flash across the scope, the person meant to be sacrificed, the necessary symbol. I will be worthy, Lee, he whispered. We are the chosen ones. We must obey the command.

Time froze. Visions burst in his mind, like the pieces of a broken mirror suddenly made whole again. He saw his mother's face, watching him in the mirror of time.

"It is your destiny, son," he heard. "Your divine destiny. I can feel it." He was touched with her gentle truth. She held him in her arms. Them. Lee and him. As she had also embraced the others. Soon she would also embrace John, sweet handsome John.

He squinted down the barrel. His finger tensed. The moment was coming. He could hear the sounds, the motorcade. A car moved slowly. An open window, a man's elbow leaning out. Beside him, a woman's smiling profile. Sandy hair. A sure sign. It was him. Guide me, Lee, he cried, and steadied the gun, the scope searching for the spot behind the ear. Then it was there, frozen. The car seemed to stop, inviting him to act. Rifle tightly braced against the sill, he squeezed the trigger. The man slumped. He squeezed again, and the man jerked sideways. He could see the woman lean over and he pulled the trigger one more time. Then silence.

Working swiftly, he retaped the rifle to his flank. He had intended to recover the spent cartridges but he could not bend properly; he had to leave them there. Wasn't that meant to be, as well? He opened the office door and moved down the corridor, his hand groping for the pistol in his belt. There was one more thing he had to do—Lee would remind him that the act had an encore. He dared not incur Lee's wrath.

He moved down the stairs with surprising ease, slowing as he reached the lobby. A few people milled about, looking at the exhibits. Pausing before the guard, he nodded and smiled. The guard's eyes, however, were busy elsewhere, watching some activity occurring across the street.

"What is it?" Remington asked.

"An accident."

"I thought I heard something," he said.

"Backfire probably," the guard shrugged.

He heard a siren in the distance. He retrieved his Bentley from the parking lot and drove it into First Street. Police cars began to gather. The traffic slowed, and a policeman got out of his car to direct traffic. That one? He gripped the pistol. No. He turned into the Southwest Freeway, put the pistol in his lap and turned off on Twelfth Street, heading northwest. He looked at his watch. It was nearly one.

He parked the car in an alley just below Thomas Circle, untaped the gun, placed it on the floor behind the front seat and began walking north, crossing the circle, passing in front of the International Hotel. He held the revolver in the side pocket of his jacket, his eyes searching the semi-deserted streets. Few pedestrians were visible. Suddenly he saw the blue uniform walking away from him east on N Street, lumbering along aimlessly.

He walked quickly, hearing only the tap of his shoes along the pavement. He caught up with the figure, a big man. He looked at his watch. It was nearly 1:15. The policeman had nearly reached the intersection. A few cars passed. An old woman carrying a paper bag was coming toward them.

"Officer!" He was surprised at the sound of his voice. The policeman turned. A black face. He was momentarily startled, but it was too late. He saw the man's mouth open in a vague response. Drawing his gun, he pumped four shots in the vicinity of the man's heart.

"Poor dumb cop," he said, or heard himself say, knowing now it was not his voice.

He did not run. There was nothing to fear. Slowly he walked south. He saw a movie marquee, a string of lights, shining brightly, beckoning. Soon he was standing in front of the ticket seller.

"One," he said, holding up a finger. From his roll he peeled off five ones and entered the darkened theater. A porno film was playing. The slithering bodies, the strange gyrations on the screen hardly aroused him, and he watched them blankly for more than an hour. Men came and went, shadowy figures, concentrating on the action on the screen. Finally, he got up and left.

The Bentley was exactly where he had left it. Before he got in, he checked the rifle on the rear floor.

I am invulnerable, Lee, he whispered after he had settled into the car. He headed south again. He made a right turn on K Street, then right again on Connecticut Avenue.

"Three done. One to go," he said, regarding himself in the mirror. His eyes. It was his voice now. Waiting, he knew her answer would come.

"You can do anything you want to do, Tad."

He felt her presence in the car. The warmth of her aura gushed through him. He pulled into a side street, cut the motor and, overcome with an ecstatic happiness he had never known, cried tears of joy.

XVIII

JEFFERSON SAT beside her, silent and morose. She had sensed the welling of emotion in him at the church and she had deliberately taken the wheel for the slow ride to Arlington Cemetery. Officer Temple had served with Jefferson in Vietnam and his senseless murder had moved him to a rare show of feeling. He had actually cried in church; the incongruity with his usual macho bluster tore the mask off his vulnerability. The Department had determined to make a big show in Arlington Cemetery to underscore Temple's service to his country and the community. The killing of a cop always united the disparate elements of the police fraternity. Intrigue and politics were suspended. All infighting was postponed. The family had been attacked.

Fiona felt it too. Hadn't the same thing happened to Old Fitz, her grandfather? Officer Temple had been a ten-year veteran with a family of five. Not a world beater, his record was, nevertheless, a good one, achieving sudden new heights by this brutal killing. Temple's wife worked as a secretary in the Census Bureau and he moonlighted as a cabdriver, sometimes going with less than four hours sleep. It was a not uncommon occurrence. There was quiet heroism in that.

The newspaper stories made much of his selflessness, his family life, with a self-conscious determination to create a hero out of the black cop. Representatives of police departments from as far west as Chicago were in the funeral procession.

"Damn," Jefferson said beside her, wiping his tears, "the poor bastard. Another dead nigger."

"What the hell has that got to do with it?"

"Everything," he muttered. She let it pass. For some reason, she thought of the other man who had also died that day. She wondered whether there was an outpouring of grief for him, at that other funeral in a Methodist church in Prince George's County. A white man also struck down by an unknown killer. Probably only a handful of relatives were present, bewildered by the popping flashes, the strangers in attendance, their eyes watchful and suspicious. There wasn't a shred of evidence to connect the killings. And yet . . . she shrugged away the possibility.

The dead white man was a used car salesman. He was, according to the woman customer with him, taking the Chevy Impala in which he was killed on a test drive. She had insisted, she told the police, that he drive a minimum of twenty-five miles and he had come all the way down from Lanham, driving around Capitol Hill in aimless patterns to show her how the car handled in city traffic. The only common thread of the killings was the fact that both men seemed to have no compelling reason to have been wasted.

Fiona had read the woman's verbatim statement. Her dress was splattered with blood, a detail noted in parentheses. She was a waitress with a salty tongue, reddish hair, blousy, cynical, wary, much used and abused. "I was driving," she told them. "But the car was a piece of shit inside. They had made it all shiny and new-smelling and I told him to drive the damn thing himself once we got into the city. He had just taken the wheel and was saying: 'See . . . smooth.' He was going slow, just rolling. It wasn't smooth. No way. And the brakes were too tight. I also didn't believe it only had fifty thousand miles on it. That was bullshit, too." They had grilled her. She was a hard broad and despite the horror, the humor trivialized it. USED CAR SALESMAN KILLED BY SNIPER the headlines read in the *Post*, as if the headline writer, immune to the endless saga of news terror, could not resist the absurdity.

They had tried to connect the lady romantically to the dead man and she had really given them a piece of her tongue.

"Him," the transcript read. The interrogator was obviously speculating. The invective came out like a stream of consciousness. If she had been Queen Victoria, she couldn't have been more indignant. Unfortunately she was white trash in their eyes, and they had really leaned on her, searching for motives.

As for the dead man, he was the other side of the coin. A red-neck con man from West Virginia. Mathew Luther Pringle, a ridiculous name. His police sheet was the catalogue of a drifter's rage, barroom brawls, nights in the tank. He had beaten up his wife in Charlestown. They had reconciled. He beat her up again and then left their squalid nest. "Did he have enemies?" Someone had surely asked this of his estranged wife. "I would have pulled the trigger myself," she might have responded.

Worse, the whole litany spilled across the front page of the *Post*, like ketchup stain. They couldn't find a picture of Pringle anywhere, not even from his high school yearbook. He had opted out after the first year to join the army. Why, Fiona wondered, couldn't they have written something else instead of Used Car Salesman? At least Officer Temple had gotten his picture in the paper and a headline reference as a "Hero Cop."

The connection still nagged her. For a few hours it had nagged at everyone, including the eggplant. But the autopsies denied the connection. Pringle had his head blown away by a rifle and Temple had his heart exploded by bullets from a .38 revolver.

"Coincidence," the eggplant had concluded. He had pulled the troops together in the lineup room. The chief was there as well, looking somber, as he listened to various reports. Everybody at homicide was present, even those who stumbled in from sick call. They had two crazies, a wacko sniper and a cop killer, but it was clearly the cop killer who had their attention.

"I want that muvva," the eggplant shouted after he had outlined the details. He had, of course, been gilding the lily. For him the death of Officer Temple was a minor miracle, like a piece of flotsam that nudges a drowning man to shore. He was holding on for dear life. By the time the meeting broke up, he had them believeing that Temple's killer was the Antichrist, while the sniper was some dumb deranged kid playing with matches.

They had found the three empty cartridges on the top floor of the Library of Congress. So the shots had come from a public building. The connection seemed studiously avoided.

Without attempting to resurrect the contentious circumstances of the two previous killings, Fiona quickly ascertained that the ammunition had been of comparatively recent vintage, made less than twenty years ago, exploding further her own nagging suspicions. A connection, therefore, could only remain in her mind, a lingering intuitive burr.

The sniper's vantage was easy to calculate. As for motivation, despite their intensive grilling of the hapless waitress, it seemed an example of random selection. The victim had simply appeared in the killer's sights at the right moment.

Watching the eggplant rage during the meeting, her thoughts coalesced around a discordant theme, like an irritating off-key musical phrase in a classical piece. Try as she could to screen it out, it was impossible. Worse, it nudged her funny bone and she had to bite her lips to keep herself from laughing out loud.

"Who benefits?" It was the investigative axiom around which every criminal investigation whirled. In this case, the immediate beneficiary of Temple's killing was none other than the eggplant. It was almost as if he had heard about the sniper killing, realized its damaging potential and went out with a gun to drill down the black cop. In her mind, he might even have invented the victim or, at the least, exchanged the bodies. Who gave a shit about a drifter, a no-good used car salesman, who also happened to be white? If she had a conspiratorial mind, she might have also put the headline writer in league with the eggplant. And Officer Temple himself, the gallant upwardly mobile self-sacrificing hero-cop. And the keeper of the personnel records who had created heroic police exploits for Temple as well. And the Argentinian junta.

It was bizarre because what it boiled down to was a conspiracy against her, blocking her from getting even a shred of help for what they would all say was an intuitive compulsion by a pushy cunt. Still, she knew she was preparing herself for that moment of confrontation. Be patient, Dr. Benton had said. Not that the role of gadfly tantalized her. She wondered if she would be able to muster the courage or stand the pain when the time came. Sooner or later, it would have to come.

To complicate matters, Bruce had returned to Washington like a man fully cured from a debilitating illness. He had become his old self or, at least, her old image of him, strong, loving, beautiful. At Tiberio's, where he took her to celebrate his homecoming, she had searched his face for any signs of residual trauma, and found none at first. But midway through the meal, she caught it, a faint rumble like the distant sound of an oncoming train.

"The bitch wouldn't call me to concede," he said, caressing the rim of his wine glass. He had been holding her hand under the table and she felt the knuckles harden.

"Maybe she didn't like the way you won."

"You win any way you can," he said. "Would you have rather I lost?"

She felt his attempt to make her guilty. Anger rose in her like a geyser.

"It's like cheating."

"So was she."

"How so?" she snapped.

"She wasn't one of them either. Educated. Aggressive. She had broken out. It was only a stepping stone. Besides, she was taking advantage of her femaleness and the color of her skin, darker than mine. Actually, we were two of a kind. She had a white lover."

"What's so terrible about that? So have you."

"Hers was a woman."

"How noble then to have ignored it."

"We weren't sure. Clark had paid for the information. It could have backfired. Besides, we were thinking ahead. The gay vote is not to be ignored in a statewide election. As a front runner, I don't want to get anybody mad. Not yet."

"No. You wouldn't want that." He looked at her archly.

"I won. That's the bottom line." His fingers tightened around hers. "You're getting self-righteous in your old age," he said gently.

"Can that be all?"

"Come on, Fi. It happens that way in business every day. It's accepted. The law of evolution. The strong eat the weak. The smart eat the dumb. It just hangs out more in politics. The media put the wash on the line, stains and all. I'm not saying I like it. I just hold my nose, close my eyes and take the dose. Who am I to change the rules? Especially if I want to continue playing. You think the cops are any different?"

He finished his drink, like a winded athlete who had worked up a good thirst, and ordered another.

"Don't confuse the issues," he said quietly, turning to kiss her neck. "I love you and I hope you love me. Don't look for perfect. Better a winner. A survivor, Fi. There's nothing worse than a loser."

"No," she said sadly. "I guess not."

"Believe me, I can imagine how she must have felt," he said. "Anyway, you'll be happy to know that I called her."

"How gracious." She could not quite get the edge off her anger.

"Butter would melt," he said. "Why not? I told her it was hers next time around. She knows where I want to go. Be a good little girl and stand in line, I told her. I could feel her ambition sweating through the phone."

"Could she feel yours?"

"Of course she could. Takes one to know one."

She pondered this a moment, wondering why she wasn't sharing his enthusiasm. Something about him frightened her.

"So where do you want to go?" she asked, feeling foolish because she knew the answer. Why couldn't she leave it alone?

"Fiona's a strange one." Her father's words came back in a rush. Perhaps all that original sin shit had encrusted itself on her reason. She was thinking so hard she had barely heard him say "Up." But she made him repeat it.

"Up," he said again. "Maybe President. *Numero uno.*"

"That far?"

"Why not?"

The heat in his fingers rose. Turning, she saw his eyes glisten. A vein palpitated in his neck. She imagined he was salivating.

"What good is living without striving for an impossible dream?" he said, puffed up with pride. "The bigger the better."

She saw him clearly now. What he was offering was company, not real sharing. Perhaps it did not exist. The shock of revelation sobered her and she projected a lifetime of loneliness for herself. Without her realizing it, he had moved closer, his thigh touching hers.

"Let's change the subject," she said. She had better start making compromises, she told herself firmly, and pointed to her glass for another drink.

They watched the body of Officer Temple lowered to its Arlington grave. Observing the somber faces, she sensed the pull of unity, and the pervasive power of comradeship. At that moment they were one mind, a unit beyond race or class or gender. She wished she could cry. But then the first shovelful of dirt was cast into the open grave and she felt the guilt of the living reality. Nothing had changed.

"It was a damned shame," she said later, after they had returned to their car. His big, hamlike hands gripped the rim of the automobile wheel as he eased the car out of the parking lot in fits and starts. The car always seemed to react to his inner moods.

"Just another dead nigger," he growled.

"You're being unfair," she said.

"We should be out there, lookin' for that dude." It was enough to telescope the message of his discontent. It was a good time to fix blame.

"Hell, Jefferson, we're in Siberia together," she countered.

"It wasn't me that asked for this. Let's just accept things for the time being. The eggplant's the enemy. Not me."

"I should be out there in the street," he said. "I knew him. I knew his family. His kids." She could see the sinews in his neck force a swallow. "I should be out there, finding the muvva who wasted him." He turned to her. "You just don't know."

"You think so?"

"How could you . . . damned bitch," he mumbled. He was, she sensed, reaching for something deep inside of him. She admitted to some brief speculation about his history, but he had been so off-putting and offensive that she had deliberately let it pass, convincing herself instead that he had been hatched from a big black egg, whole and mean. What she knew about him was shorthand. He was a Ranger in Vietnam. He lived alone. He chased women.

"You know why bad is good in ghetto talk?"

She shrugged, stringing along.

"Because good is bad . . ." His voice trembled and she turned away. "You wear this skin, you know. My old man . . ." he swallowed quickly. "He was bad . . . You know what it is to drag yourself out of that shit? You know how many bodies you have to walk over? My mother wouldn't eat so's I could become . . . a person. You know who the real enemy is. Not you honkies. You're all just turd, subhuman. The real enemy is those niggers, killers, junkies, robbers . . ." His voice trailed off. She wanted to reach out, to comfort him. I feel your agony. She wanted him to know that.

But suddenly the car was speeding up Canal Road, along the Potomac. The speedometer climbed as they crossed the border into Maryland. Still she said nothing.

When the car turned off into a side dirt road, she became uneasy and began to finger her piece, hanging in its holster.

"Calm down, Frank," she said gently, as she had been taught to handle people caught in the whirlpool of rage. "We're out of our jurisdiction."

Ignoring her, he drove the car to the end of the bumpy road. She sensed that he had been here before. The dirt road ended at the edge of a clump of evergreens, through which she could see a narrow trial. Abruptly, he stopped the car and rushed out, heading into the woods. For a moment the illogic of his action stunned her and she sat in the car, uncomprehending and confused.

The vaguely familiar sound, like the boom of a bass drum, roused her.

"No, Jefferson!" Her voice was stuck somewhere in the base of her throat. She ran into the woods drawing her revolver. As she ran, she heard the boom again, alleviating her panic. At least he hadn't shot himself.

He was standing on the bank of the river, firing the Magnum in a rhythmical beat at a spot on the Virginia side. The target was a small clump of saplings, each splitting apart as his deadly shots ripped at them.

He stood stiffly, showing no emotion, his feet planted firmly, his body braced against the recoil. He fired round after round until the saplings were totally destroyed. Calmly he observed the wreckage for a few moments, then slipped the Magnum back into his holster.

"Feel better?"

He grunted and they got back into the car. "That's one way to throw away your career," she said after a while. The car seemed to slow down and she could sense that he was, at last, mastering his rage.

"You're not the only one with feelings around here. You haven't got a patent on anger. It's my career, too." When he didn't respond, she felt her own emotions take hold. "It's not worth it. You've worked too hard." She reached out and touched his arm. When he didn't flinch, she increased the pressure. He did not talk for a long time. Finally he turned and looked at her.

"I got to work to get it under control," he said calmly.

"I know."

"Do you?" he snapped, lips curling.

"Maybe you should put that energy to better use."

"Like what?" He looked at her and she saw the old lasciviousness.

"Like what I told you about." She paused, wondering if he

understood. She had thrown the pebble in the pond.

"You mean about the others?" She could see the ripples begin.

"They could be all connected." His silence encouraged her and she continued.

"The MO. Random selection. The killer just upped and pumped the bullets in at close range. Temple was a desk cop. He had no enemies. Hadn't made an arrest in years."

"The ammo doesn't tally," he said flatly, his attitude suddenly professional. "The gun was a thirty-eight Special. S. and W. Victory model. The barrel was sawed down. The ammo recent vintage, maybe fifteen years."

"Not bad for a guy not working on the case. It also wasn't connected with a public building. Temple was shot in the street." She was reversing roles now, drawing in the hook.

"But the time frame. I drove it last night. About half an hour. They were thirty-five minutes apart." Strangely, the ghetto inflections had disappeared.

"And all four with different weapons," she pressed.

He shrugged. "Maybe there's four of them out there."

"Maybe."

"Four white men. It's a white man's crime, Jefferson." She watched him flinch again.

It was, she knew, statistically right. Blacks weren't good at mass killings. They got caught too early. And the motivation was different. Usually money. Addiction. Domestic anger. Transparent rage. This was more complex, beyond explanation. All she had to go on was intuition. She wouldn't dare mention that.

"White killer. Black victim. That turn you on, Jefferson?"

The car lurched, heading east on the Beltway.

"We got a natural to investigate," he said, and remained silent until the car turned again, going south on Connecticut Avenue.

"If it connects," he said, "I gotta see more."

"Suppose I force it?"

"I gotta see more," he repeated.

The car moved in fits through traffic.

"You're one hell of a shot, Jefferson," she said, strangely elated. "A real killer."

XIX

ECAUSE THOSE who attended the inaugural balls were always disappointed, Remington kept open house from ten o'clock on. Engraved invitations were sent to various ambassadors and politicians who were certain to troop in with horror stories about crowds and traffic. He had gone to the Kennedy ball at the Armory in a snowstorm, but he had the box next to the Kennedys and Jack had waved and Jackie blown a kiss. Even the old man had punched him in the arm. Remington had loved it, but after the assassination it was never the same again. He went to the first Nixon ball, came home disgusted, and never went again.

Three liquor bars were placed strategically around the house and in addition to the usual buffet, he had set up a special bar with three professional omelet makers on continuous duty. This was, after all, to be a gala celebration in more ways than one.

The past two months had been euphoric. Nothing could ruffle his calm. He slept like a baby. Eagerly, he had read the accounts of the police investigation, until they faded from the papers. It was amusing, too, to see how the newspapers had concentrated more on the killing of the policeman than on the sniper. The fools. They had missed the main point. Poor Officer Temple. A tiny footnote to history. How could he have been more obvious, leaving them three spent cartridges from a 6.5 millimeter Mannlicher-Carcano, manufactured by the Western Cartridge Company of East Alton, Illinois. More proof of their ignorance.

He also regretted not getting the angle right, although the ninety-yard distance was reasonably close. But the car wasn't open on top and he couldn't quite fire from behind, although he would have loved to have read the autopsy report to find out how close he had come. The fools. It should be as plain as the noses on their faces. What it proved was that we were a country without any sense of history. That's why we were doomed. That's why he could never have been President. His sense of history was too profound.

"It is preordained," his mother had assured him. "Meant to be." But the divine forces had changed their minds at the last moment, saving him for what would come later. He would show them all how vulnerable we had become as a nation. How our leadership would grow weaker. How the Presidency would fail! It was his mission to reverse this decline.

He waited now for the last signs to come, the ultimate signals. Every sensor in his being was tuned in to pick them up. They would come of their own accord, as the others had come. Yet, they had merely been dress rehearsals for the main event.

During the swearing-in ceremonies, he had sat a number of rows behind the President on the Capitol steps, a reward for his fundraising efforts. He was probably visible in the photographs, another footnote to history, and archivists would one day pore over them with a magnifying glass looking for his face. This is the man that saved America, they would say.

Before he dressed, he studied the photograph of Lincoln's swearing-in. It was the first photograph ever taken of that event. Lincoln and the crowd behind him looked blurred, but an astute eye could see that the tall man in the stovepipe hat, looking wan and tired, was marked for death. Hadn't Wilkes himself been in that crowd?

It was appropriate that the cosmic presence had urged him to do Lincoln last. Wasn't he the last great leader, the Emancipator, the one who preserved the American nation as God had meant it to be? Were we one day doomed to be a splintered nation again, torn apart irrevocably by decadence, alien creeds, indifference, selfishness, greed? The nation craved the historical reminders he was being ordained to recreate.

Each mission accomplished had brought him one step closer. The day would come when the world would understand what he had achieved. I am tolling the bells, he told his images in the mirrors. There was one spot in the room where bits of his reflected image could be seen on every mirror at once. They were like people, seeing him differently. Only one had ever truly seen him whole.

"Mother! See me." He stood, as he always did in that spot, naked, revealing himself to her. He watched that part of him grow, pulsate with life, the blood surge. "My young god," she had told him. He had watched her eyes, lashes fluttering, felt her sweet soft touch gently on his flesh, the ecstasy so moving that the joy of it, the residual wonder of it, would stay with him for a lifetime. Even now, he felt it; could recall it at will.

"You mustn't ever," she had told him. He had stood before her, contrite, humiliated, ashamed. The gardener's boy. She had seen them at it. The boy was pretty, with large sad eyes that would stare out with longing as he helped his father trim the hedges, rake the flower beds around their pool.

Young Tad, as he referred to himself even then, had invited the boy for a swim. It was, he knew, even then a powerful unnatural force, leaving him without will. It was dusk, the sun glowing golden in a display of California spring and he had told the boy that there was no need of bathing suits, not then with darkness coming. Hadn't he shown him by removing his own clothes? The boy had hesitated, turning shyly as he removed his shirt and pants, his pink skin glittering in the golden glow, a fleshed reed swaying gently in the warm breeze.

"It's all right," he had whispered, still not diving, showing himself, watching the boy's grow and lift. Time had only deepened the imagery. The boy had come closer, hesitant, moving silently. He had by then grown to his fullest. Young Tad as well. They had simply moved toward each other. The dusk was tardy that night. It was the first time in his life that he had understood the sign. The divine will had simply stopped time so that his mother could see.

On the balcony above the pool, backlit by her dressing mirror, which had caught the last golden spears of the hesitant sunlight, she had seen them. What had brought her to the balcony at exactly that moment? Since it was the first sign, he had naturally puzzled over it. Why had she deliberately waited?

He had seen her only when he had turned; he, a bitch dog in heat, on his hands and knees on the trimmed grass, the gardener's boy doing him like a giant mastiff, grunting, sweating. By then, neither of them could stop. The gardener's boy was too busy with his pleasure. It came, young Tad was certain, at exactly that point that he had seen his mother, had met her eyes and seen in them the terror. Young Tad knew, too, that he could never live with that look of terror, that it had to be erased for all time.

She had quickly disappeared inside her room. The darkness had descended like a dropping stone and he seemed at once to be faced with only two alternatives. To throw himself in the pool or go up to her and erase that terror. He chose the latter.

She was sitting quietly, looking into her mirror, staring through tears. He was certain that all she was seeing was the two boys, in their animal squirming, their obscene coupling. In his panic, he had not bothered to put on his bathing suit and he kneeled against her, naked and miserable, a supplicant.

"Forgive me, mama," he cried, flooding her peignoir. He reached upward, hungering for her embrace. She turned toward him after a while, her cheeks moist, her lips trembling. Briefly, she studied young Tad's ravaged face, then grasped him to her soft, soothing, billowing breasts. Below her peignoir, she, too, was naked and, surely by divine design, a snowy breast revealed itself and he kissed the hard nipple.

She held him there for a long moment, then lifted him, stretching her arms before his nakedness.

"You mustn't ever," she said gently. By then, her peignoir was fully opened.

"My darling boy," she whispered, her lips touching him. He watched the rising of himself again, not obscene now, pure, cleansing. She lifted her breasts, which formed their own warm caress, around him.

"A man," she said, looking clearly at him. His hands caressed her soft blond hair. "My man. You must be a man."

Standing there, wrapped in her flesh, he felt the floodgates open and the obscenity, the unnatural evil, spill out of him. In its place was his gratitude, his love.

"Oh, mama," he cried as she held him. Tears of joy came then. He felt the sweet touch of her, her goodness and purity. She stood up and removed her peignoir, showing him her full body in the soft light, the curved womanly form.

"Look at me." She turned in a complete circle. Then she walked toward her bed, leading him by the hand. She lay back, watching him.

"I am woman," she said. Her voice was a song. She opened her body to him and, for the first time, he saw what a woman was.

"My baby," she purred. He hesitated, wanting to stand there forever. He stared at the darkness between her legs until she reached out to touch him and bring him to her.

"Mama. Mama."

He heard it again. Now! How many times had he said it when she was alive?

"You are a man. My man," she had cried out.

He heard the words again, gasping out of her, proving his manhood.

"Mama, mama."

He shuddered, feeling waves of pure joy, the intensity of which would mark him forever. But he knew the pact was made at that moment.

Moving from that spot which replicated his full mirror image, he carefully laid out his tuxedo, his jade studs, his patent leather shoes with the bows, his diaphanous bikini undershorts, lingering over the smooth silky fabric, then laying it neatly on the bed. A long shower calmed him and by the time his guests arrived, he could greet them with complete confidence: with his carefully cultivated charm, the shy self-effacing smile to put them at their ease, the humorous jibe, offering the intimate bonding of peers.

He knew exactly how it was done, the admiring glance for the ladies, the discreet flap of his lashes, the meassured pressure of the handclasp, the brief intensity of serious conversational exchange, revealing a bit of personal, informed knowledge that flattered and reassured them.

"Soon you will be playing ping-pong with computers on your television sets," he told the Chinese ambassador who arrived, as always with his interpreter and his inscrutable smile.

To a defeated congressman already connected to a major defense contractor, he said: "By the end of the year, you'll be screaming for tax shelters." And to his wife, he whispered: "Put it in diamonds. They're still a girl's best friend."

"That's what I need most," she agreed with pleasure.

Most of the guests arrived red faced and agitated by the traffic, the crowds and congestion of the various Inaugural balls. When one bar got too crowded, he showed people to the others.

"The President looks marvelous. It's a wonder he can still smile in that flesh crush," a senator said, between bits of cheese puffs.

"He must show himself as superior to the discomfort," Remington said seriously. "A true leader knows what to do."

"Your house is the only place to be, Tad." It was the wife of the German ambassador, showing her usual expanse of bosomy flesh, itching as always for a flirtation, and he chose not to discourage her. There was currency in flirtation as well. Everything depended on appearances, mystique that hinted of vast potential gain.

He had invited people new to Washington, politicians and administrators swept in by the winds of change, their eager faces unable to mask their ambition as they wallowed in the trough of power. They came to town in waves, grasping at the coattails of the ultimate manifestation of it, the Presidency.

"It was wonderful. Wonderful." A newly appointed cabinet minister exulted. "I love it."

"That's because you're one of the stars," Remington said. The man flushed with happiness and dipped into a glass of champagne.

"We may not be able to get things done. But we'll sure as hell have fun."

He had invited members of the press as well, although cameras were strictly forbidden. To a lady from "W," he was charmingly firm.

"He can come in and drink, but he'll have to check his camera at the door." A number of photographers had gathered shivering in the cold, their puffy faces lost in icy vapors. They were like a herd of cattle, magnets to the trappings of power.

"We must remember to feed the animals," he told the caterer.

"We have an outdoor coffee van for the chauffeurs," the caterer assured him.

"Those as well," he said, pointing to the growing knot of reporters and photographers. The caterer scurried off.

"Fantastic as always, Tad." The voice was familiar and Remington turned to face Bruce Rosen and his girl friend. He shook his hand and embraced his upper arm, then gave Fiona a two-cheeker.

"This guy is going places," he told her.

"Thanks to you, Tad." Bruce lowered his voice. "I'm very grateful." He felt Fiona's uneasy stare.

"I've got a clear shot . . ."

It was Bruce speaking, but Remington's mind had drifted. A spear of panic jogged him. Shot? He remembered suddenly what kind of work she did. Another sign! Had she worked on any of the cases?

" . . . at the Senate seat," Bruce continued.

"We'll make it," he murmured, nodding, turning to the girl. Was she probing? Was it his imagination? He shook off the strange sensation, determined to speak with her later.

"Maybe even higher some day. The President," he said, watching the policewoman's face.

"Why would anyone want that job?" Fiona asked.

"Because it's there," Remington quipped.

"There's not a man in this room wouldn't give his right nut for the job," Bruce said, upending his Scotch.

"Soon maybe the left as well," Remington showed his teeth, masking the sting. There was a sign in this somewhere, he told himself, certain the woman would respond. The odd tension between them quickened his interest.

"What's a woman to give?" she asked.

"The matter hasn't come up," Bruce said, grinning stupidly. A slight thickening of his speech revealed that he had taken one drink too many.

"It will," she said firmly.

"A good woman can work wonders," Remington said.

"You mean an ambitious woman," Fiona responded quickly. Remington wondered whom she was really addressing.

"Behind every great man is a woman," Bruce said, clasping her arm. "I hope this one will go the route."

"You could do worse," Remington said.

"I have," Bruce giggled.

A female guest distracted him suddenly, tapping his shoulder. He turned and grimaced. It was Louise Padgett. She hadn't been invited and he was surprised to see her. "We'll talk later," he said smoothly. It was meant for Fiona and he was certain that she understood.

"I came anyway," Louise said, obviously drunk. Her makeup was smeared, her face puffed and distorted.

"I read about your party in the papers."

"You look wonderful, Louise," he said, determined to placate her. He had discarded her, never answering her calls. She had only been an instrument. Didn't she know that?

Louise took a glass of champagne from a silver tray, tossed it off and took another one.

"You threw me away like a piece of meat."

"Not here."

"Where then?" she sneered.

Guests crowded in. The noise level increased. Remington nodded, shaking hands.

"Prince Charming," Louise snickered, spilling some champagne on her gown.

She finished her champagne and leaned on the wall for support. He took the glass from her, grasped her arm and led her through the crowd, smiling as he maneuvered her through the corridors, into the kitchen.

"A bit under the weather," he whispered to Mrs. Ramirez. "I'll help."

He signaled her away.

"It's all right," he said, dragging her along. He managed to get her to the back stairs and, half-lifting her, steered her into his bedroom, locked the door and pushed her on the bed. She fell with a half bounce and lay there like a discarded puppet.

Her eyes were open. She looked at the carved eagle and dissolved into hysterical laughter.

"Drunken slut." He hadn't expected her to comprehend, but she turned her bloated face toward him, squinting, struggling to focus her eyes.

"Gimme a drink," she blurted, her lips dribbling saliva. He felt a wave of nausea.

"I'll get somebody to drive you home."

"Drink," she cried. "Fuggin' bastard. Use people. All alike. Like him. Somebitch. Stick it in, then spit on me. I'm a human been, you fuggin' bastard."

She tried to rise on one elbow, fell, then, grabbing a bedpost, lifted herself.

"Ish not fair," she whimpered.

"All right," he said, flashing a forced smile, moving toward her, touching her cheek. His hand recoiled. "Just stay quiet."

He ran down the stairs, found a glass and took a bottle of champagne from an ice bucket and brought it back to the bedroom. She was still sitting where he had left her.

"See." He held up the bottle of champagne. "Nothing but the best." She took the glass he offered her with a shaking hand, she drank unsteadily, the liquid slopping down her chin. He poured more.

"Drink up." He tipped the glass for her, watching her swallow repeatedly. Her eyes glazed over and she dropped the glass on her lap. The stain spread over the satin material of her gown and she looked at him dumbly, barely able to raise her head. Pushing her gently, he laid her on her side. She had passed out.

Relieved, he let himself out, locking the door from the outside. Breathing deeply, composing himself, he walked slowly downstairs into the crowd and made his host's rounds.

The drunken woman was a brief annoyance. After she slept it off, she would be mortified and embarrassed. Now, he sensed, the true tests were coming. Would he measure up? He would be given doubts to overcome. He would be rendered vulnerable. He would have to be alert. All his inner resources would be questioned. His courage as well. Obstacles would be placed in his path. He would have to take risks.

At that moment he saw Bruce's girl friend. She was sitting alone on the floor of his Rustic Room, eating from a plate balanced on her lap. One of a group clustered around a television set, she watched the election night activities. The President was getting out of his limousine, waving to a crowd, making an appearance at the last Inaugural ball, one of ten. The announcer was commenting on his ebullience, his lack of fatigue after such a frenetic day. In the camera's eye, the President plunged into the crowd, shaking hands, wearing his well-honed grin. The phalanx of Secret Servicemen were obviously having a difficult time, jostled by the surging crowd. But the President was undaunted, displaying himself, an offering for their adoration. He was the President, the American leader, the father.

"Isn't it dangerous?" someone asked. Remington saw the picture through a film of mist. Below him, he heard Fiona say:

"Yes, it's dangerous. Any crackpot with a weapon can do him in."

"Then why expose himself?" another man asked. He was a lobbyist for an important arms manufacturer, a heavy-set man with a plate piled high with food.

"He is the President," Remington said with passion.

"We've had enough dead Presidents," the man said. "That's not his job."

"A child also needs a father," Remington said sharply.

"I agree," Fiona said. "He wants the job. He takes his chances. Anyone with the will could do him in."

"Or with a gun," Remington said. Again the words came in a rush, without prior warning. He knew that he was merely a spokesman, a conduit.

"They'd have to be crazy. A psychopath."

"Not necessarily," Remington said. Again by rote. The woman turned to him and eyed him curiously. He felt her careful observation, the sense of exhibitionism in himself. See me, he commanded silently. Can you really see me?

"Nobody in their right mind could possibly want to shoot the President of the United States."

"Right is relative," he said. She was silent for a moment, turning back to watch the television screen. The President was moving through the crowds. The Secret Service had reorganized its phalanx and the President and his wife were moving toward the stage, still waving, still smiling.

"I suppose," she said, "a person could construct his own logical motivation, even though it may be logical only to himself. I've seen it a number of times in my work."

With a struggle, the lobbyist mumbled something and got to his feet, moving away. Remington squatted beside her.

"Seen what?" he asked.

"A murderer who will calmly explain his crime in terms of either its necessity to himself or to the victim. There is very little remorse in such a perpetrator."

"Remorse?"

"Like there was no human connection between the murderer and his victim. Strangers coming together to illustrate a point."

"But suppose the point is essential?"

"Oh, they all believe that."

"Does it happen often?"

"Frequently."

Her answers did not miss a beat. Nor did his questions. This, too, is necessary, he thought. The risk. The test. He moved closer to the woman. Her fork played with her food.

"But if there's no connection? How do you apprehend the killer?"

The woman laid her fork on the plate. He knew he had engaged her. That was essential to the test.

"We don't. Sometimes we have to wait until the pattern reemerges. The MO, modus operandi. Or the killer makes a mistake."

"And suppose he doesn't make a mistake?"

The woman shrugged. There was a long pause. Her thoughts seemed to have turned inward. That sniper case, he wanted to say. But he held off, feeling the pulsating energy of the question between them, trying to will it out of her.

"There are always open cases like that in my business," she said. The trembling began deep inside of him.

"I read something recently," he said, barely able to form the words. "A sniper."

Her eyelids fluttered and a tiny tremor showed in her cheek.

"As the English say . . . a baffling mystery."

"How so?"

"No apparent motive." He felt her hesitation. "He seemed to have worked it out with some careful logic. The Library of Congress. Why there? And he left three cartridge cases."

"From what kind of gun?" He paused, his hand sweeping toward his gun cases. "I know guns."

She looked at him strangely, following the arc of his gesture.

"Italian, I think. Man something."

"Mannlicher-Carcano. Very common."

"They always are."

He could not detect the slightest hesitation. The age gap seemed like a deep ravine, impassable. Seventeen years ago she must have been in her middle teens. Time had blunted the real meaning. Again, the message was clear, the necessity of his mission underlined. They must not forget. Never! Her ignorance was appalling. It was all there for them to find. He had provided them with a road map.

"Someday, I suppose you'll find your assassin," he said, standing up.

179

"Someday," she said, but her expression showed no conviction.

He left her there watching the President present the obligatory clichés to the ball crowd. In a little while, those guests who had attended this last ball would roll in. The house was crowded almost beyond its capacity, the noise level deafening. He decided to check out the food situation in the kitchen.

"We have enough, Mrs. Ramirez?"

"Plenty."

"Good."

"And the lady?" She reminded him.

He decided he had best look in on her. He found the right key and opened the door. He had left a small light on in a corner of the room. It was still on, offering a puddle of yellow illumination, bathing the rest of the room in shadows. Below the swooping eagle the ruffled bed was empty. He looked around the floor. Nothing. Then, he saw that the bathroom door was closed.

He put his ear to the door, heard sounds, but they were hard to distinguish. A kind of hoarse breathing, he decided, hesitating briefly. He rapped on the door with his knuckles.

"Louise," he called discreetly. There was no answer. Louder. "Louise!" He listened, then rapped again. He tried the knob. It was locked from the inside.

"This is nonsense, Louise. If you don't open up, I'm going to break the door down."

There was no answer. Moving back, he tensed his legs and rushed the door with the flat of his shoed foot, hitting it squarely above the knob. The jamb cracked and the door swung open.

In the shadowy yellow light, he saw her body on the floor. At first, he thought she was asleep. Animal-like sounds came from her throat. But when he switched on the light, he saw the blood. She lay in a pool of it, and it spread under his shoes, over the tiles. He knelt beside her and some of her blood smeared his white shirtfront. Locked in one hand was his silver-plated revolver. He pushed her inert body away as if it were rancid with disease and would contaminate him.

XX

FIONA LISTENED to the presidential platitudes with feigned interest. She had no desire for conversation or Washington small talk. Bruce rolled in it like a pig in swill. The whole scene, she decided, was like a giant convention even if the name tags were invisible.

Also, she was OD'd on people asking her: "And what do you do?"

"Eat chocolates," she sometimes said, covering the put-down with a smile. "No, seriously," the interrogator would respond. Sometimes she said: "I'm Congressman Rosen's broad."

"I guess you can't type then," was an occasional rejoinder.

"You've got to learn to mix," Bruce would admonish, catching her bored look as she pretended to study a painting or a book or, like now, stared blankly at the television tube. She saw him approach, bracing herself for another rebuke. But before he reached her, another image caught her eye. Remington was motioning her from one end of the huge room, darting in and out of the shadows like a jack-in-the-box.

"Me?" she mimed, then sensed Remington's urgency. Bruce followed her.

"Where are . . ." Bruce began, then stopped short at the pale figure of Remington. They followed him as he raced up the back stairs. Remington did not look back, hesitating only as he opened a bedroom door.

Once they were inside, Remington locked the door, partially shutting out the cacophony below. She had barely time to assess the jumble of images, the many mirrors, the huge bed with the spread-winged carved eagle hovering above, the bloody footsteps along the carpet. In the bathroom, her investigatory eye took over. The woman groaned. She was still alive. Inspecting the body, Fiona discovered the large open wound in the woman's upper left arm. The shot had been oblique, making a deep furrow in the flesh.

"Lucky bitch," she said, looking up at the pale, anxious faces.

"A belt," she ordered. Remington produced a leather belt, which she wrapped around the flabby upper arm above the wound, pulling it tightly. Blood gushed over her gown. Ignoring it, she tore a towel from the rack and applied pressure directly to the wound. The woman, obviously a novice at the suicide game, had shot herself in the upper arm. She probably had had no serious intent. She opened the woman's fingers and shook the gun to the floor.

Bending over, she listened to the woman's heart and felt the pulse of the uninjured arm. From her color it was apparent that she had lost a lot of blood.

"Don't touch anything," she commanded. Bruce turned away with a dry heave and Remington backed out into the bedroom, his shoes leaving additional bloody footprints on the carpet. Neither of them said anything.

She worked over the prostrate form for nearly half an hour, loosening and tightening the tourniquet periodically and keeping the wound staunched with the towel. She could hear low voices in the other room.

"Is the ambulance here yet?" she called. She watched the woman's face. She made a pillow with another towel, and placed the woman's head gently on it. Then she stood up.

"Will she be all right?" Bruce asked. He stood back in the bedroom, looking queasy.

"She needs to be stitched up, but I think we caught her in time." She glanced at her watch, bent down and loosened the tourniquet again. The blood still oozed from the wound, but it had slowed. She tightened the tourniquet again.

"She may also need a transfusion. Maybe there's a doctor downstairs?"

"Are you crazy?" Bruce looked at her as if he meant it.

"Crazy?"

"We can't tell people about this." Then, more gently: "I don't have to explain, do I, Fi?" He came close to her and grabbed her shoulders.

"You see, don't you? The media would suck it up like a sponge. If it's not necessary . . . I mean, can we somehow avoid it?" His eyes pleaded, a look she knew well. "I don't want to hurt the woman." He looked at Remington, who was white as a sheet. "If we can possibly avoid it, Fi."

"You mean not report it, as well? A gunshot wound? I can't do that," she said firmly. "I'm a cop. I'm here at the scene of an attempted suicide. This is a gunshot. It should be reported."

"Dammit, Fi. You know how to fix it. If the woman's okay, then what's the harm?"

"She has a mouth," Fiona said.

"She was drunk." His eyes continued to plead. "We owe this to Tad." Remington watched them impassively; his normally pink glow had turned to chilling gray. She wondered if he was in shock.

"If you could . . ." he began meekly, hesitant as he studied her.

"Why put him through the mud? And me, as well? And everybody downstairs? In a way, we're lucky she didn't do the job right."

"Would you have asked me then?"

"Of course not. You know me better than that."

"Do I?"

"What's the harm? If it doesn't hurt her."

To avoid a decision, she went back to minister to the woman, loosening the tourniquet again. The blood was coagulating, oozing gently now and the woman's color had improved. When she touched her, the woman opened her eyes and groaned.

"It's all right," Fiona said, brushing the hair back from the woman's forehead. Tears spilled out of the edges of her eyelids.

"Poor bitch," Fiona muttered. "Us both."

She saw Bruce's face in the mirror, his eyes begging, frightened.

"It's not like I'm asking you to rob a church," he pleaded again. "It's hardly more than a little white lie."

"She really has to be sewn up. It could open up again." Being pragmatic helped postpone her decision. He came closer and opened his arms in a wide embrace, clasping her.

"We don't need this kind of problem, Fi." His arms soothed her. "Why be a purist? What harm would it do?"

"She needs a doctor," Fiona said, insinuating herself out of his embrace. "Whoever he is, he has to report it as well." It felt better to shift the responsibility.

"I owe him this, Fi," he said firmly, shooting a glance at Remington, who remained silent.

"You want me to get the doctor?"

"You know how these things work. It's not my line."

"You know what you're asking?"

"For crying out loud, Fi. What does it matter? It's not a lifetime career."

She wanted to protest, but the woman's groans grew louder. She felt cornered, beyond choice. Remington's eyes probed her. She saw something sardonic in them and wondered why he was not pleading his own cause. How clever, she thought. He owned Bruce now.

"Come on, Fi. Please." Bruce said, in panic.

The groans grew louder and she ran into the bathroom again. The woman was struggling at the edge of consciousness, feeling the pain now, the drunken stupor fading.

"Just lie still," Fiona ordered. She felt contempt for the woman for putting her in this position. Lifting her arm gently, she looked beneath the towel again. The blood still oozed, but lightly now.

"You want to die?" She shot the words into the woman's ear.

"No."

"Then for crying out loud, lie still."

"Please." It was Bruce's voice again, persistent, whining. Fiona went to the bedroom telephone and with shaking fingers dialed Dr. Benton's number.

After three rings Dr. Benton answered, his voice hoarse and smoky, filled with sleep.

"I have no right to ask you . . ." she began.

He was at the back door in less than half an hour. She led him up the back stairs. Bruce had stayed with the woman while Remington rejoined his guests. Many were now saying their farewells. When she arrived with Benton, the woman was still on the bathroom floor. They had thrown a blanket over her. The room was a mess with bloodstained footprints crisscrossing the carpet.

"In here," she directed as Bruce stepped aside. Benton immediately began checking the wound after surveying the woman's vital signs. He took her pulse, listened to her heartbeat and checked her blood pressure. Without a word, he removed the toweling from the wound, looked at it, removed the belt, loosened now, and disinfected the wound. Then he stuck a hypodermic needle in her arm. The woman grimaced but did not scream. Deftly he closed the wound, using ten stitches in tiny loops. He loaded another hypodermic needle and punched it into the uninjured arm.

"Sedative," he said. He was impassive, businesslike. She was not used to seeing him with a live patient.

"I'm sorry I dragged you into this," Fiona said as he repacked his surgical instruments.

"So am I," he muttered. He had pointedly ignored Bruce, as if he sensed the source of his involvement.

"I'm not going to report this," Fiona said, her throat rasping.

"I know." Dr. Benton kneeled beside the woman, felt her pulse again and inspected the closed wound. "She'll be weak, but I think she'll be fine. You'd best get her into the bed."

"I can't tell you . . ." Bruce began.

"Then don't," Dr. Benton said.

"Thank you," Fiona said and helped him on with his coat.

"No more words," the doctor said. "Maybe I needed it as

185

well." He seemed to be speaking to someone offstage. "She said I didn't have the courage to take risks." He kissed her on the cheek. "I know, Fiona. I know."

She and Bruce lifted the woman onto the bed. Her gown had risen up, revealing a black garter belt ringed with ruffles, above a thick curly black patch of pubic hair. The sight inflamed Fiona, as if, somehow, they were both participating in a form of rape.

"The presidential box," Bruce smirked. "Poor lady."

"We are all poor ladies," Fiona snapped. She pulled the woman's gown over her nakedness and covered her with a satin comforter that lay folded at the foot of the large bed. She felt the same sense of violation.

"She'll be fine," Bruce said. "Come on, Fiona." She shrugged him away. "That's what this town is built on. Little favors."

"Must you?"

He was silent after that and they went about the business of cleaning up. She dropped the bloodied towels in the hamper.

"It's not like we've committed a murder," he said. "You're flagellating yourself needlessly, darling," he said, after they had straightened the room. The bloodstains on the carpet had turned brown. "You're taking it too seriously."

"I'm just like the rest of you."

Remington came back into the room. The color had returned to his face. He looked at the woman in the bed with distaste.

"She'll be fine," Bruce said. His debt had been paid in full. Remington looked at Fiona and smiled with obvious gratitude. She turned away disgusted.

"You never know when people will do wild things," Remington said. "On the outside they appear normal, like you and me. Then poof. Something sets them off and everyone around them becomes . . ." He groped for words. "Innocent victims."

"I think you can skip the lectures," Fiona said. She was tight-lipped and edgy.

"Even the innocent victims have a right to try and save themselves," Bruce said, having regained his authority. "The news hens would have pecked away at everybody in this house."

"Amazing, isn't it?" Remington had turned to view the sleeping figure in his bed. "How the will of the assassin continues to play out its power? Like a fishing line with a hook buried in some monstrous fish who refuses to surrender." She caught a note of admiration in his voice, a bizarre injection of another mood. His previous panic had disappeared. He seemed reflective now.

She also sensed the complete absence of compassion in the room. Perhaps at that precise moment, an hour or so ago, the woman had confronted her total insignificance, the weightlessness of her existence. A single, inadvertent puff of wind had given her life the only momentum it had ever had. The rest was apparently as passive and uninteresting as a blob of unformed clay.

She dared not wonder why the woman had decided to shoot herself in Remington's house. Perhaps it was the inauguration, the recall of an earlier one, the memory of the one golden President standing hatless in the cold. In some respects, the house was an appropriate place, garnished as it was with memorabilia of the dead President. It was the most appropriate place of all.

Understanding the woman's motive did not identify her own. Why the hell had she taken such an absurd risk and drawn Dr. Benton in as well? Bruce's motives were clear as air. In his politician's eyes, ambition powered a kind of brute force. She could taste it, feel it, smell it in him, and she hated and loved it at the same time. Did it inspire a sexual power as well? The image of a piston, oiled and pounding in perpetual movement, flashed across her mind. The symbolism was unnerving and a tingling shiver passed through her. She had been deliberately manipulated by her lover.

Was it possible she could be so slavish? Was it love, really, or some other compelling fascination, the loss of which could derange her like the poor anguished woman in Remington's bed?

"I want to go home," she said, turning, moving down the stairs. A few guests still lingered. The caterers were cleaning up. A drunk was asleep on a couch and the air was heavy with the smell of stale smoke, alcohol and overdone food still simmering in its silver trays. She found her coat on the rack and crossed the large living room to a still open but unattended bar, filling a tumbler with Scotch, which she half-emptied before Bruce joined her. She carried it with her to his car.

Traffic on the streets of Washington was light; the last inaugural stragglers were headed homeward. They had ushered in another presidency.

"Quite a night." Bruce drove with one hand on her thigh. She wanted to push it aside, but her will failed her. The sense of surrender was too powerful to resist. She finished her tumbler of Scotch and tossed the glass onto the back seat.

"You were wonderful," he said. "An unsung heroine. Really, Fi, you helped us through a bad time. I'm so damned proud of you." He gripped her thigh harder, but she did not respond; the alcohol was taking hold. "I'll make it up to you somehow, darling. And you can be sure Remington won't forget it. More than anything you saved his ass. If that ever leaked out, his place would be *verboten*. " He was silent for a long time, although his hand continued to stroke her. His possession. "You are quite a lady." He turned toward her. "And I think it's about time we got married." She remained silent.

"It's time," he insisted. "We've got lots to do." She heard his words, felt the pressure of his hand, caressing now, sensing her predictable response. Oddly, her mind was racing, as if the alcohol had stimulated rather than dulled it. Something was nagging at the back of her consciousness, something inchoate, half-formed. She groped for it.

At the intersection of Seventeenth Street and Pennsylvania Avenue, she looked past his profile to the White House, partially obscured by the deserted reviewing stand.

"First night," Bruce whispered. His eyes glistened, caught momentarily in the glare of a street lamp. "Must be fantastic. I'll bet they're in the sack now. Doing it. What a moment!"

"You'd give anything to be there now."

"God, yes. The bedroom's up there," he pointed. The car picked up speed as it moved past the antique-spired Post Office Building. In the distance, the Capitol dome was a mound of white light, like a scoop of vanilla ice cream.

"It looks so clean," she said.

"Beautiful."

Reaching out, he took her hand and put it where she could feel the hardness. She did not remove it. The connection was mysterious, abstract and incomprehensible. The idea seemed to cleave her in two. Can the genders ever really know each other? Perhaps being alone in a male world had alienated, denatured her. She felt suddenly besieged, frightened, helpless.

In her apartment, he embraced her against the door, then led her to the couch. She knew her body was opening, magnetized by the urgent force of his masculinity while her mind continued to explore its reasons, investigating, as if that other part of her were outside of herself watching, trying to understand. She felt engulfed by some animalistic, evolutionary force that defied resistance, forcing its possession on her. Some special knowledge seemed to be reaching out to her beyond time, impaled now on a force of maleness that transcended categories. He could have been a horse, or a dog, or a lion. It didn't matter. The masculine imperative was pressing, driven, and even in the powerful whirlpool of her pleasure, she knew that a force inside of her was demanding to tame it, capture its essence. All men, it seemed, were victims of its inner compulsions, with women doomed to be the anvil on which the force was hammered out. Yet she was certain that the anvil would always out-endure the hammer.

The insight softened her and she let him linger in the embrace, until natural fatigue made him uncouple. Leading him into the bedroom, she undressed him like a child and lay down naked beside him, her back and buttocks nestled against his warmth.

Unable to sleep, she continued to explore the thing that was nagging at her.

It gnawed away, and she tried not to lose the thread. Something Remington had said. She was certain that a spear of inner light would uncover the source of her mystification. Something simple. She played a game of hot and cold with herself, determined to find its cause. She grew drowsy. Her eyes closed. She entered a world of half-dream, half-reality. An image of the golden President intruded. She saw how he had looked then, on that day, when she, a teenager, had been glued to the TV set along with her family, an electronic wake. They even took their meals in front of the set. A whole generation had absorbed the images. How had they been changed by them? Remington's voice superimposed itself.

"Amazing how the will of the assassin continues to play out its power."

The words arranged themselves in counterpoint to the remembered fuzzy images of the tube, filtered through more than seventeen years, a vision that could not, would not die, until her whole generation was wiped away by time. Then she found what she had been searching for. It came in a gush, accompanied by a hissing sound, like a cold wind leaking through the hairline crack of a wall.

"Someday, I suppose you'll find your assassin."

He had not said killer.

Before she slept, she made sure the words were engraved in her mind.

XXI

W HEN SHE left the Martin Luther King Library, the sharp winter sun burned her eyes, already sore from hours of reading. She had crawled out of the warm bed at first light. Bruce was sprawled beside her, his mouth open, gulping air in a deep sleep. The events of the last evening had faded in her mind, larded over with this new excitement. She had slept fitfully, then at the crack of dawn had wakened with a start, as if fearful that further sleep would diminish the memory that needed to stick in her mind.

She reached for the handiest clothes that she could find, a jogging suit that hung on a hook in her closet and a pair of sneakers. In the bathroom, she looked at her reflection with bloodshot eyes, splashed cold water on her face and brushed her hair in quick strokes. On her desk she found a spiral notebook, mostly blank pages. Fearful of waking Bruce, of having to explain herself or plunge into a postmortem of last night's events, she silently closed the apartment door and arrived at the library ten minutes before it opened.

Shivering in the cold morning, she bought a container of coffee and gulped it down. It burned her throat, but she was determined to get it down. She wanted to be at the library the minute it opened.

The card file on the Kennedy assassination was extensive and shuffling through it quickly, she found the file numbers of the *Report of the Warren Commission,* and soon had a dog-eared hardcover copy. The binding was broken and some of the pages were loose; it had been read over and over. Her hands shook as she turned the pages in a frenzy. Time passed. Her concentration was intense and before she realized it, her notes had filled nearly half of her spiral notebook.

"My God." The words became a periodic exclamation in the large quiet reading room. Each time she said them, the librarian lifted her head and frowned, until Fiona mimed an apology. Vaguely familiar names filtered back in memory, Lee Harvey Oswald, Jack Ruby, Officer Tippet. The latter name was barely a memory, an inconsequential footnote. It shamed her not to have remembered.

One would think, she reflected, that such a traumatic national event, so heavily covered at the time, would have lingered in the mind with every detail intact, a permanent matrix. It was true that she was only fourteen at the time, but like everybody within eyeshot of a television set, she had been glued to it, thrilled and repelled by its repetitive horrors. What she realized now was that she remembered little. Not even the date and year, only that it seemed to have happened before her eyes, in her parents' living room, with her father's curses, like a Greek chorus, in her memory.

From the extent of the card file and the dates of the various books, the event had taken on a life of its own, and even the most recent Congressional exercise seemed somehow outside the mainstream of national life. Time, indeed, marched on. The flames of passion had cooled although the mass of reading matter attested to a hard-core group of aficionados, like birdwatchers being turned on by a newly sighted species.

With mounting excitement, she filled her notebook, then extrapolated a list of especially pertinent data. She felt the thrill of Columbus seeing land for the first time, of Edison discovering the perfect filament, of Einstein balancing the equation that proved his theory. Nothing like this had ever happened in her life. It was the ultimate insight.

She was suddenly grateful to Remington for having kept his obsession alive, proving that for some the world had stopped spinning at the moment of the bullet's impact. Like the poor woman last night who had made a half-hearted attempt to join the golden President. It saddened her when she discovered that she could not even remember the woman's name. Like Officer Tippet. Footnotes!

She finished the Warren report just as the slanting rays of the sun began to throw lengthening shadows across the polished tables. A stomach growl reminded her that she hadn't eaten all day and when she stood up her joints ached. Smiling, she returned the book to the librarian's desk.

"A term paper?"

She nodded, but the reflex was a kind of warning. She had no doubt about the enormity of what she had uncovered. The question was, how was she going to disseminate it? But even before that, she would have to confirm what was barely a theory. Her mind raced through possibilities, but all she had were unproved coincidences. The notebook in her hand suddenly felt heavy; her fingers were trembling.

Outside, she breathed deeply, but the cold air only made her light-headed; she couldn't think through the muddle. Perhaps the best course of action was to take it right to the eggplant, confront him with her theory, throw it on his desk as a kind of personal vindication. That was what the old Fiona might have done. But this new Fiona, having passed through the events of last night, knew better. The new Fiona lived in the real world, the last vestige of naiveté and idealism squeezed out of her. This was her territory now and she had to protect it. She owed it to herself, to her sex. She had to keep them from taking it away from her. The glory boys.

She felt like a fly, too fearful to alight in any one place. But no place seemed secure. Except one. Dr. Benton, for inexplicable reasons of his own, had answered one call. He was there when she needed him, although she could only make out the vaguest outlines of his motives, something to do with his dead wife. Had she the right to do it to him a second time? Out of sheer panic she began to run.

The rush hour had started in earnest. The bureaucrats were heading home, like a giant wave, the headlights of their cars probing the darkness. The city was a giant brain with millions of electronic circuits administering an unwieldly government, each, like herself, a breathing, living entity with its own motives and aspirations. As she ran, moving inexorably in the direction of Dr. Benton's house, she contemplated how confronting the world's vastness and indifference could stunt the emotional growth of a man like Lee Harvey Oswald. What secret conflagrations had maddened him, exploding his anger at that precise moment when the leader of the country would come into view? Her compassion annoyed her, inhibiting her perspective. It was, she told herself with brutal candor, her fatal flaw. Understanding the killer was different from feeling his pain. It was better, she knew, to excise all emotion.

By the time she reached Benton's house, she was sweating through her jogging clothes. Thankfully, the lights were on and as she bounded onto his porch she could see him alone at his dining table, a book propped in front of him, eating his supper.

"I'm sorry," she blurted, after he let her in.

"The woman?" he asked. She could see his brief flash of terror.

"Something else." She realized that her condition and dress must have startled him. She followed him inside. The place smelled of fish, and she noted two small fried trout on his plate, one of them carefully dissected, its bones neatly placed near a baked potato.

"I've got some soup left."

He started toward the kitchen. "And you'd better get out of those clothes. You'll catch pneumonia. There's a robe hanging on a hook in the bathroom."

Quickly she dried herself, put on his robe and returned to the table. She was ravenous and slurped the soup with four slices of bread. Between bites of his fish he watched her. She could detect an undercurrent of anxiety. She had placed the notebook

on the table beside her. She pushed the bowl away and opened
it.

"The Pringle killing. The sniper job from an upper floor of
the Library of Congress. Do you remember?"

"That's the cause of all this excitement?" She could tell he
was relieved. "No complications with the woman?"

"I don't know. I doubt it." It was an evasion. She hadn't
checked. He put down his knife and fork and studied her.

"Are you all right?"

"Very much so. Do you remember Pringle?"

He was thoughtful for a moment. "All my files are in the
office." He put on his glasses, got up and looked at a calendar
over his kitchen telephone, rubbing his chin.

"Pringle? The sniper?" she repeated.

"Yes," he said, turning and looking at her over his glasses.
"Extensive brain damage. Yes. It was a Saturday. I remember.
They called me at home. There were two cases that day. The
policeman. Officer Temple." He looked at his calendar again.
"November twenty-second."

"Right. Does that day mean anything?"

"Saturday. Just another day," he sighed, hinting at his loneliness.

"That's all it means?"

He struggled to remember, his eyes narrowing. Finally he
shrugged in defeat.

"John F. Kennedy," she said.

"Ah, yes," he nodded. "Nineteen sixty-two."

"Sixty-three."

His eyes focused on her. She knew she had his attention.

"The killer left three cartridges on the site. I could swear they
were made by the Western Cartridge Company. And the rifle.
I stake my life on it, it was a Mannlicher-Carcano, Italian Army.
The cartridges, without my checking, would be 6.5 M, American made." Her words tumbled out. "There was also a bullet
that pierced his neck. Right?"

"Yes. I remember that. But it was all in the report."

"I never saw the report," she said.

He straightened in his chair, turning slightly, as if cocking an ear. She didn't wait for a response. "I'll even tell you the exact time the shots were fired. Pringle at twelve-thirty P.M. Temple at one-fifteen P.M."

"I remember. It was quite a day. I had just finished lunch."

"Temple took four bullets directly in the heart? Just like Tippet." She patted the notebook. "It's all in here."

"You mean the two killings are related? The weapons were different. One was a revolver, if I'm not mistaken."

"A thirty-eight. Oswald had gone back to his boarding house to get it."

"Incredible."

"Texas Book Depository, remember? Library of Congress. Books."

He stood up and paced the room. She turned a page in her notebook.

"I'll bet he signed A.J. Hiddel in the security man's book when he walked into the Library of Congress. That was the alias Oswald used when he bought the rifle from a mail order house. There's more. Much more. But these will do for starters."

"You sure it's not just unrelated coincidences?"

"I'm hoping you will confirm that it isn't. If I start poking around . . . He's down on me as it is. And I won't confront him with this unless I'm dead sure. Even then, I'm going to have to think about it."

"I'm not sure I understand."

"He has a way of brushing things under the rug."

"But why? You could make him a hero."

"A thousand reasons. It's an open case. It's coincidental and speculative. It can stir things up and leave him in the exhaust fumes. There's such a thing as being too big. He can look stupid by not picking up the similarities earlier. Or he could overreact for fear that I'd go to the press. I could go, of course, but that would blow my career . . . if there's any career to begin with, considering how they treat women. Not to mention the color of my skin."

She didn't give him time to react. "Then there's other possibilities. Speculation about the Kennedy assassination is endless. The government has spent millions tracking down every theory that's been advanced. People have made fortunes on the speculation. It's an industry in itself. There's the other gun theory. Maybe this is the other gun. There's the Russian agent theory; that the man who shot the President was not Oswald at all. Then there's what Big Jim Garrison of New Orleans, remember him, tried to prove years ago. In short, Dr. Benton, any way you look at it . . . it's too hot to handle." What it boiled down to was that she believed the eggplant would be frightened by its magnitude.

"How did you get on to it?"

She hesitated. Dr. Benton sat composed, serious, concerned.

"Last night." She wanted to explain it without alarming him. She plunged on.

"That woman. She was one of Kennedy's mistresses. And our host, Thaddeus Remington. He was a friend of Kennedy, an old loyalist. His assassination affected both of them, probably thousands of others." Including Bruce as well, she thought, and now herself. "To them, he became more than a memory. An obsession. Everything they do seems to relate to that one traumatic moment."

"You knew that? About the woman?"

She studied her hands, ashamed to face him.

"I'm sorry. It could have been a real mess. Far more than you bargained for. I probably abused your kindness. I'm doing it again right now."

"You're certainly having an impact on what I thought would be a tranquil late middle age."

"At least, you've got that far," she said. He leaned over and patted her shoulder.

"She would have been proud of me," he murmured, his eyes drifting to the picture of his wife. "She used to rebuke me for being afraid to take chances. She took them, but it ate her up alive. Maybe I see something of her in you. Maybe that's it."

"I had to tell someone," Fiona said, pressing his hand. His flesh felt warm, restful, soothing. "We're an odd couple."

"Not so odd," he said softly.

197

"I'm still hungry," she said. He went into the kitchen, battered up some eggs and poured them into the frying pan.

"So what's your theory?" he asked.

"I was afraid you'd ask that. One thing is clear. This is not your ordinary screwball. And there's always the possibility that he just might be the other gunman, tired of anonymity, sending us signals. Actually, I haven't got that far yet. First, I've got to confirm what I strongly suspect."

"And you want me to help confirm it without rocking the boat?"

"You can, Dr. Benton. I know you can."

Up-ending the frying pan, he dumped the eggs onto a plate and added toast and bacon.

"Used to be a short order cook," he chuckled.

She wolfed down her eggs, talking with a full mouth.

"The Warren Commission thought they tied everything up in a neat little knot. They thought they were being fair. There's a long section on disproved rumors, witnesses that came to other conclusions. You could drive tanks through the holes they created. Officer Tippet, for example, is accused of knowing Oswald, of disobeying orders and being in the part of Dallas where Oswald's boarding house was located. He didn't radio for help when he knew he was being apprehended. He knew full well that the suspect was an armed and dangerous killer. Even riding alone in his squad car is suspect, despite all the explanations. The police generally came out like fools. They actually looked as if they were setting Oswald up for Jack Ruby's bullet." Her mind raced back over the events recounted in the Warren Commission report. She was certain that the clue, the case-busting clue, was buried in the event. The idea suddenly penetrated that she was actually probing a murder that took place seventeen years before.

"Maybe it wasn't Oswald at all. Maybe this guy who wasted that used car salesman was Kennedy's real killer." She shivered.

"I think you're being carried away, Fiona."

"That's what worries me," she said. "They won't take me seriously. And if they do, they'll take it away . . . Forgive me. I'm hyper. I feel like I'm sitting on a keg of dynamite."

"You are," Dr. Benton agreed.

"And I'll bet you're sorry you've got mixed up with me."

Suddenly he smiled, a big warm sunny compassionate smile.

"I've learned never to come to any conclusions until the autopsy is complete," he chuckled.

"I'm not sure I'm happy with the comparison."

"Even if it all does check out. What then? There's still the bottom line."

"That word again."

"Sooner or later, you'll have to present your theory to the eggplant. The big question in his mind, after the smoke clears, will be: All right now, will this get me the killer? That's what gets the brownie points. Have you figured that out yet?"

"No." She paused and looked steadily at him. "But I will."

XXII

SHE HAD hoped the day would be sunny. She always found greater courage in the sunlight. Instead the day broke overcast and gloomy and a light snow had begun. Outside the homicide office the world looked half-made. The snow hadn't yet covered the streets. Sitting at her desk, typing to keep busy, she watched the eggplant's office. Detectives moved in and out.

What she was typing made no sense. Ostensibly, for whatever prying eyes were around, she was doing another of their interminable natural death reports. She hoped this would be the last day of that assignment. Maybe the last day of everything. She glanced at Jefferson, who lifted his eyes from his desk, squinting over the smoke from the cigarette that dangled from his lips. Was she waiting for exactly the right moment? Or was she simply too frightened to act?

She heard high-pitched throaty laughter. A detective came out of the eggplant's office smiling and shaking his head. He was alone now. She clutched her files and stood up, feeling dizzy and slightly nauseous. A telephone rang in his office and she could hear his booming cajoling voice. She sat down, relieved, and glanced at Jefferson again. He nodded understanding and encouragement. Once more, she reviewed her presentation. Everything had checked out exactly as she knew it would. Dr. Benton had been exceedingly thorough and his known bent for caution aroused little suspicion. The fact was that, although the case was officially listed as open, it was in actual fact a dead issue. No clues. No viable suspects. As the eggplant must have wished, it had simply gone away. Other murders had occurred to push the case into limbo. A prominent physician had been stabbed by one of his patients. The case was quickly solved. The physician had had numerous lovers, and since his clientele was prominent, the papers were able to be mildly salacious. Even Teddy had a resurrection of sorts by breaking the case of an overeager jogger who had plugged one of his victims, then left a line of clues that brought the police to his door within forty-eight hours. The cases were now set for trial. Convictions seemed certain.

The new administration had, predictably, created a heady atmosphere in Washington, spreading optimism like molasses. It was the honeymoon period. Everybody, including the press, seemed to have temporarily put away their weapons. In a little while something would set things off and everything in the city would turn nasty again. Like life, Fiona thought. Bruce was busy organizing his Senate campaign and still pressing her for a decision.

"I've got something hot going," she told him. "Let me just get it behind me."

He was busy with the jockeying that came at the beginning of each Congressional session, and it helped ease the pressure, leaving her free to pursue her private investigation.

Dr. Benton, even as he provided information that seemed to fit her theory perfectly, became a devil's advocate. Perhaps it was merely skepticism or maturity or else he was simply bent on slowing her runaway enthusiasm. They jousted over endless cups of coffee at Sherry's.

"Hadley can't be absolutely certain about the rifle," he pointed out. All his information came through what others thought was innocent inquiry. She was not quite ready to show her hand. "The cartridge fits. But there are other rifles that could have fired them. A Mauser, for example."

"That's what they thought originally," she said. She was determined to counter his arguments as quickly as he made them. "Even the thirty-eight could have come from another type of revolver. It's really not airtight."

"The case file confirms everything else. Times. Date. Symbolic vantage. Your report on cause of death. Considering the conditions, it was similar enough to the Kennedy killing. The exact angle and anatomical target would be hard to replicate at any rate."

"Almost impossible."

She lowered her voice and looked around the restaurant. The dirty windows were steamed and the air was heavy with the smell of boiled cabbage. Friday, she thought, automatically remembering her childhood.

"The case file had a Xerox of the library write-in sheet. A. J. Hiddel, just as I predicted. An anonymous name, no record anywhere. The investigating officer actually checked more than fifty cities before he gave up." She laughed. "I could have told him that." She snapped her fingers for more coffee and the fat proprietress ambled over to them in her dirty apron, poured, then moved away.

"I even measured the distance from the room at the library to the street where Pringle got it. Eighty-seven yards. Three yards short of the real thing. He may not be the original, but he sure makes a good copy."

She watched his reactions. He was being reflective, searching for flaws.

"What about witnesses?" he asked.

"The guard was a blank. He could remember only color. White. There's a moral in there somewhere. No tall or short, fat or thin. The file has him quoted verbatim. He thought he remembered a man with a blue jacket and a limp."

"A limp?"

"How else would the man bring in the rifle undetected?"

"Not bad," Dr. Benton admitted. "But what is the significance of the blue jacket?"

202

"Oswald wore a blue jacket. Later, in his room, he changed to a khaki one. The old woman who witnessed Temple's killing remembered only a man in a khaki jacket, further embellishing the two-man idea. But you see, Oswald had gone back to his boarding house to change and pick up the revolver that was to kill poor old Officer Tippet. Here again rumors run rampant. The timeframe between the site of the assassination and the killing of Tippet is questionable. Oswald apparently took a bus and taxi to get to another part of town, a feat he made in incredibly short time. Our man obviously took poetic license and used his own car. But he made the timeframe exactly. Temple simply materialized on demand. It was as if he had participated willingly in the scenario."

The words tumbled out like coal down a chute, but she could see that Dr. Benton was following it, tracking her as she recited the events of the Kennedy assassination.

"It gives me the creeps, all these coincidences. But you've got to admit that I've got it down fairly tight. It's a reenactment." She slapped the table and the coffee cups clattered in their saucers. "There's someone around loose that thinks he's Lee Harvey Oswald."

"So it would appear."

"But why?"

Dr. Benton stroked his chin and played with doughnut crumbs, trying to make them into a ball.

"I've been thinking about that. Part of his delusionary system. Maybe he's sending us some kind of message we can't quite decipher. A warning. Maybe he is the suspected second gunman. Maybe, considering the mythology that has grown up around it, he is the real gunman. Maybe, as you speculated, Oswald didn't fire the weapon. Who knows?"

"Grist for the mill," she shrugged. "The case is open in name only. It's obvious he wants to forget it. No need to wake the sleeping dogs. Same for the Temple case. Nobody wants to push a case that has only the slimmest possibility of going to closing. Even a cop killing. There's been nothing but dead ends."

"So why pursue it?"

"Because it's there." She remembered Remington's words

about pursuing the presidency. Remington again. He seemed to hover over the case like an impatient vulture.

Confiding in Jefferson had been a necessary evil. Since her objective was now to be put on the case full time, she didn't want to raise a fuss within the department. A breakup of partners in the fifty-man homicide branch always created a stir. Another reason was purely personal, probably vindictive, although she tried to convince herself that she was above such pettiness. She wanted to make him part of her conspiracy. If he was so damned concerned about pursuing the death of Officer Temple, she would give him his opportunity. She invited him up to her apartment during a lunch break. Strictly business, she told him, sensing his stimulated libido. If he harbored any illusions, they were quickly dispelled when he saw her apartment. The walls were a mass of Scotch-taped charts that included a blowup of the killer's probable Washington route, side by side with Oswald's Dallas trail. There were also magic marker charts entitled "Weapons," "Timeframe," "Fatal Wounds," "Motives."

Munching cheese sandwiches, Jefferson listened to her presentation, his face immobile as she searched it for a reaction. Feigning impassivity was one of his special skills.

"Sheet," he said when she had finished, slapping his thigh, his lips breaking into a sardonic smile.

"You buy it?"

"Say what?"

"Cut the ghetto shit. Do you buy it?"

"You mean this dude just upped and pumped four bullets into Temple for no fuckin' reason?" He got up and without asking poured himself half a tumbler of Vodka.

"It was all part of the script, the next move after wasting Pringle. Or doesn't your interest extend to white men?" He ignored the sarcasm.

"That dirty son of a bitch. Just upped and blasted away. No warning. Nothin'. Poor bastard."

"Got your furies up?" she asked smugly. He finished his Vodka and slammed the glass on the table.

"Bet your ass."

She watched him with satisfaction as he paced the room.

"Want to get on the train?"

"Suppose the chief says no?"

"I'm going to make him an offer he can't refuse. If you're in it, you're in it. You can't check out once I make my pitch. It can hurt you. I give you fair warning." She knew that he had already calculated that.

"A man who would do that is a fuckin' animal."

"And white," she added. He nodded, showing his big toothy predatory grin.

Finally, the eggplant hung up the phone. It had seemed an eternity. She stood up, files clutched in her hand and with a final knowing glance at Jefferson, went into his office and closed the door behind her. He was surprisingly placid. She had stayed out of his line of sight for months.

"I'd like you to hold your calls," she said in a tremulous voice.

Her legs shook as she undid her papers and Scotch-taped them to the wall. When she turned, he had a supercilious grin patched across his face.

The telephone rang. He reached for the instrument then hesitated. After the third ring, she put her hand on it.

"I mean it," she said, her lips tight, her eyes narrowing and intense. Shrugging, he let it ring itself out, then leaned back in his chair, lighting a cigarette, blowing out the first smoke ring, a signal of his sufferance. I'll listen to you, bitch, he seemed to say. She began to talk.

She proceeded haltingly, avoiding his face, determined to wait out his reaction. She pointed out the killer's route from the Library of Congress to the vicinity of the International Hotel. Deliberately, she held back certain facts, like her theory that after Temple was shot, he had probably ducked into the nearest movie house, which happened to be showing a porno flick, on Fourteenth Street. Oswald had gone into a movie theater after wasting Officer Tippet. It was in the movie house that he was captured. If she had told them that, she would have been marked down as a smartass. Above all, she didn't want them to think of her as arrogant and superior.

The eggplant shifted in his seat, moved forward slightly, reacting, fighting not to absorb what she was telling him. When she completed her presentation, she turned to face him squarely. His face was hidden in a cloud of cigarette smoke.

"Well?" There was a long pause.

"It's . . . it's an interesting theory."

"That all?"

"You want me to stand up and applaud?"

"Maybe." She was sure his mind was turning over possibilities, searching for holes, weighing everything against his own motives.

She controlled her impatience, using the time to gather up her presentation and return the papers to her briefcase.

"So what am I supposed to do?" he said finally.

"I want to work it out. Jefferson and me. He knows."

He frowned and blew smoke.

"If it flies, it's only an MO. It doesn't nail us a killer. Might even make us look stupid for not seeing it earlier."

She had expected that. He was appealing to her loyalty now, blatant and clumsy. She knew he was frightened.

"The big boys will come down on us like hound dogs. The FBI, the Secret Service, the fucking politicians."

"So what? There's no place to hide."

"Easy for you to say. What the hell have you got to lose?"

He was letting his fear talk now. And his bias. She remained silent, letting him boil up a full head of steam, work it out. He stood up and began to pace the room. A lieutenant knocked and came in. He started to say something, ignoring her.

"Will you get the fuck out of here?" the eggplant shouted. Swallowing his words, the lieutenant quickly turned, slamming the door on his way out.

". . . and if I don't, you'll scream cover-up to the press."

"I didn't before," she said. He stopped pacing.

"I know about the old ammo," she said. "I could have done something then." The words came out calmly. But the implied threat hit him in the midsection. He seemed to cave in physically, groping for his seat. He lit a cigarette, puffing deeply.

"You don't know what it means to be leaned on. I was saving

everybody's ass. You don't know what it means. There's vested interests. Somebody's got to protect us." He rubbed his temples, a gesture of martyrdom.

"No one else will know," she said.

"It slops over. It's obvious there are no secrets around here."

"All I want is a chance to pursue it, a quiet investigation. Just Jefferson and me. Who knows, we may close it."

"Fat chance. The man's a psycho. There are no fucking clues. At least, the dumb bastards haven't found any. And stirring up the Kennedy thing will put us under a spotlight."

"I thought you liked spotlights."

"This one's too hot."

"We might get lucky."

"Lucky?" He looked at her with bloodshot eyes, thick with despair.

"Anyway, you have no choice." She snapped her briefcase shut. The sound of it seemed to explode in the room.

"Sit down," he groaned, pointing to the chair in front of his desk. He waved a black finger in front of her nose. "No leaks. No press. Nothing in the files. And if we close, we share."

"Deal," she said, restraining a smile.

"You tell that to that big black bastard."

"Done."

"And you keep me in the picture." He hesitated, suddenly deflated. "I was a goddamned good homicide cop. Ninety percent closings. Seventy percent convictions."

She stood up and started to walk to the door. His muffled voice stopped her.

"Do you think the others are connected too?"

The possibility had nagged at her, but she hadn't pursued it. But something in his voice prodded her.

"Maybe," she said, half-believing it.

"I was afraid of that."

"Intuition?"

She could not resist it. Without waiting for an answer, she walked into the drab gloomy interior of the homicide office.

XXIII

REMINGTON STOOD on the receiving line under the glittering chandelier in the rotunda of the White House. Ahead of him, the President, his wife, and their honored guests, the Italian President and his wife, greeted the people as they filed past. The chief of protocol, responding to a marine officer who asked each guest for his or her name, made the formal introductions to the President.

The line moved slowly. Many of the guests were already known to the President. They were a mixture of cabinet officers, senators, congressmen, ambassadors, businessmen, actors and actresses, and those who, like Remington, had helped in the campaign. Remington's date, Cordelia Blaine, a stately woman magazine editor from New York, could not quite conceal her nervousness, despite her frozen air of nonchalance. For most of the guests the ambiance was awesome. This was the pinnacle of social success. A state dinner. Guests had flown in from all parts of the country and their names would appear in many of the nation's papers tomorrow morning.

"What should I say?" the Blaine woman whispered.

"Tell him how nice it is to be here," Remington soothed.

Most people were tongue-tied in the imposing presence. He was, after all, the President. The man.

"I mean something substantive. Something important."

"Say something about his being right about the Russians?"

"Not that important."

The line moved. They were getting closer to the President. He noted that most of the guests tried to hide their fawning. But it was futile. They knew where they were.

All doubts had been dissipated. All tests passed. He had, he was certain, run the gauntlet. The events of his inaugural party were proof positive. Providence again had intervened. The cosmic force had manipulated events, strewn his path with dangers. The Padgett woman. Congressman Rosen and his detective girl friend. A suicide in his home and the resultant scandal-mongering in the press would have been a clear signal to abort his plans. And he had practically confessed or, at the very least, broadly hinted to the woman detective. Now she, too, had become further proof of his divine protection.

The Padgett woman had been embarrassed and contrite, and he had sent her home the next morning. Once again, she had served a useful purpose. Nothing on earth could stop him now. Even the invitation to this state dinner had offered him confirmation. It was happening according to a preconceived plan. All he had to do was to keep his senses open for each fresh signal.

He had been in the White House many times before, especially in those halcyon days of the golden President. The image of that office had been badly tarnished since then.

Suddenly the President's blue eyes focused on him. His slightly crooked smile flashed as he grabbed Remington's upper arm.

"I won't forget what you did for me, Tad." The President turned to his wife. "This man helped me out during the campaign," he said. "I owe him."

"I believed in you," Remington said as the President continued to pump his hand. He felt the strong grip, the connection of the living flesh, the transfer of energy between them.

"And I won't let you down."

Insincere platitudes. Detestable locker room braggadocio. Jock talk. It was another hint of the decline of standards, another of his mother's predictions come true.

"A flint-hard decision must come out of a highly civilized sensibility. We need another Thomas Jefferson. You could be that man, Tad." Her later theme would always be "serves them right."

They moved into the state dining room, dominated by a huge fireplace over which hung a giant portrait of Abraham Lincoln. The tables had a fruit theme, a social secretary's idea to usher in the spring. It was, Remington observed wryly, the first day of that season. March 20. Another special day was irrevocably approaching. Less than four weeks. The final addition to the American quartet. He looked at the face of the reflective Lincoln. Their eyes met. Soon, he nodded.

He was seated between a television star and a newly elected senator's wife. The senator had been swept into office on the President's landslide.

"Somehow I expected more," the television star whispered. He shared his conversation between the two ladies, although concentrated on watching the President, who sat two tables from him, in the democratic fashion of eschewing a head table. The man was animated, charming, every inch the President, certain of the glow of power that radiated from within him, splashing its illumination over the others. Surely he was well aware that he was the center of this universe, the absolute apogee of mortal man. At the thought, Remington's stomach curdled and he quietly laid down his fork beside his half-eaten filet mignon.

"Why does everybody seem so ordinary?" the television star asked.

"Reality is never any match for fantasy."

"Who should know that better than me?" she said coquettishly.

"This is my first one," the senator's wife said, unable to hide her childlike wonder. Her husband sat across the table. He was from Idaho and had the unfinished look of a state politician.

"Think you would enjoy the role?" he asked the senator's wife.

"Who wouldn't? Wouldn't you?" He was taken off guard. It wasn't simply rhetorical. She was waiting for an answer.

"For this"—his hand flashed out in a sweeping gesture—"I'd kill." It was entirely spontaneous. The words had gushed out. The woman seemed mildly stunned.

"Kill who?" the television lady asked, misunderstanding.

"A figure of speech," he quickly replied.

"Not me," the television lady shot back. "Look at all those people watching." She nodded toward the cadre of Secret Servicemen who ringed the room, little colored buttons on their lapels, tiny microphones in their ears. "All that security. The poor man has no privacy." She bent over and put her lips close to his ear. He caught a sour whiff of alcohol. "Anyone of us could get him if we wanted to."

He felt the heat of a rising flush. For a moment, he wondered if he was throwing off vibrations.

"But how many of us really want to?"

The tinkle of glass aborted his train of thought and suddenly the President was standing, holding his champagne glass, making a toast to his honored guest, the Italian President. His words floated in the air, mellifluous, reassuring.

"Civilization owes so much to your peninsula. Our friendship is not simply one of convenience. It is part of our heritage. The sons and daughters you have sent us have helped build America . . ." The meaning faded. Only the sounds filtered through his consciousness. It didn't matter what he said. The mere utterance gave the words a touch of the oracle; every syllable would be recorded, preserved, permanently engraved in this historical record of their time. Perhaps hundreds of years from now someone would have the means to connect with this man, simply because he was the President.

And he, Thaddeus Remington . . . what legacy would he leave for future generations to ponder? Who would know that he too had lived a life, thought thoughts, dreamed dreams? For a moment, his courage flagged. He needed another sign, needed it

211

badly. He began to sweat and when he lifted his water glass, his hands shook and a few drops spilled on the table.

"There is no point in ever being second," his mother had said.

"Everybody goes to the same place," he had countered. It was a theme of his then, to ward off the pressure of her frustration.

"No, they don't," she had said firmly.

"They'll remember me, mama. Us." The toasts were over. The guests moved toward the East Room for the entertainment.

Cordelia Blaine took his arm as he moved. He passed the President, who winked a greeting.

"I must say, Tad. I'm damned impressed." She squeezed his arm. "I think it makes you very sexy."

The implied promise revolted him. She was there only because she was attractive, youngish and appropriate for the evening. An interchangeable face and body. This immersion in the warm bath of reflected power could titillate, stimulate desire. That was not real power. He knew real power.

A small stage had been prepared in the East Room and the guests sat about in a semicircle of folding chairs. Somehow, he found himself two rows behind the President, who sat with his wife and honored guests in the first row. Remington opened the program. They would be presenting *Hands Across the Sea*, one of three works by Noel Coward always presented as *Tonight at Eight-Thirty*. He had seen it years ago and remembered reading that it was now in rehearsal for a revival at the Kennedy Center.

Of course. There it was, he told himself, feeling his mounting excitement as the players began to recite Coward's lines. Coward! The name itself had its own intrinsic message. Waves of laughter reverberated in the room. The President chuckled. The message was pristine. He was not a "coward." The lines from *My American Cousin* rolled across his memory, those fatal lines that masked the shot:

"Well, I guess I know enough to turn you inside out, old gal, you sock-dologizing old man trap. Heh. Heh. Heh."

He watched the President's head bob back and forth with laughter, concentrating on that vulnerable spot behind the left ear destined to offer itself in replication.

Hands Across the Sea.

Like *My American Cousin*, the play presented on that fateful night, the setting was England, both authors English. The humorous character foil was also a colonial. How wonderfully it all fit together. He was transfixed, searching now for moment of laughter that could mask his own shot.

The character of Piggie says: "How's your daughter?" Mrs. Wadhurst responds: "She's a little better, thank you." Piggie retorts: "Oh. Has she been ill? I'm so sorry." Mrs. Wadhurst replies: "She's been ill for five years." The audience roars. In his mind, he could see the shot enter the President's skull, clean, not a trace of blood.

"Wilkes," Remington whispered.

"What?" Cordelia said beside him, as the laughs subsided.

"Nothing." He avoided her eyes. He was Wilkes now, the handsome poseur, obsessed beyond endurance, determined, whatever the consequences, to meet his rendezvous with destiny.

The applause thundered through the East Room. The actors took repeated bows. The President's wife blew them kisses. Then the President stepped up to the stage and shook hands with the principal actors. With a gesture, he hushed the audience.

"Let no man say that the influence of the British is not as profound as ever," he said. "You know, I used to do what these folks do. And I promise you this. My wife and I will be at the theater to see the rest of it."

The audience responded with more applause. Remington slapped his hands together with special enthusiasm. The road ahead was clearly marked.

XXIV

S HE WAITED for him in Tiberio's taproom, ignoring the bartender who had mixed her martini and had tried to strike up a conversation. No, she had told Julio, she didn't want to be seated just yet, not until the congressman arrived. The truth was that crowded rooms made her feel claustrophobic. She was also a mass of new sensations, edgy, nervous, unable to sleep.

"What's with you?"

Bruce asked the question repeatedly. Her evasions were growing less creative. Her mind as well. Her brain seemed unable to absorb another piece of information. Jefferson, too, was showing the strain.

At first, they had carefully examined the scene of the sniping. It told them nothing they had not previously deduced. They traced the original investigation, burrowed into Pringle's background, again interviewed the lady who was with him in the car at the time. Surprisingly, the original investigatory team had done a superb job. They carefully sifted through everything that they could learn about Officer Temple. They interviewed his wife, his children, the one eyewitness. It was pure drudgery, but both she and Jefferson agreed that it had to be done, had to be discounted irrevocably. Finally, they conceded the point to their full satisfaction. They were both random victims.

As she had promised, she kept the eggplant informed in a series of whispered, clandestine meetings in empty corridors, police cars and street corners. The duty roster had them still checking out naturals, but even the slowest of their colleagues were beginning to sense that they were working on something unusual. It had been the eggplant himself who decided against meeting in his office. It was out of character to have too many meetings with her. Everyone knew that their relationship drew sparks.

They continued to comb through the archives. Under the Freedom of Information Act, all information and evidence about the Kennedy assassination was open to the public. The material was infinite, and the evidence itself, the bullets that killed, the Mannlicher-Carcano rifle and 38 S. and W. Victory revolver were slowly being destroyed by use. From the condition of the material, one would have thought it had long ago given up its secrets.

She had asked Bruce to get her materials from the Library of Congress. Cartons of books were delivered to her apartment as well as reams of bound testimony.

"What is it all for?" he asked. "They think my office is investigating the Kennedy assassination."

"I can't say. Please. Don't press."

It only piqued his curiosity.

"Some new evidence?"

"Please."

The material kept coming. Stacks of books lay helter-skelter over her apartment. She had to clear a path from her front door to the kitchen and bedroom.

"The answer is in there somewhere," she told Jefferson.

She read until her eyes burned. Everything fit and nothing fit. Millions had been spent on investigations that spawned more and more theories. The army of private investigations had multiplied geometrically. A list of inquiries into the archive materials had reached the multi-thousands. Scholars, students, housewives, ex-cops, lawyers, doctors, from almost every country of the world, had sifted through the material. What were they all looking for?

Had she stumbled upon something that would, once and for all, put the matter to rest? One could, she decided as she pored over the material, make a reasonable case for Oswald not being the killer of Kennedy. In custody, he had denied it vehemently. Ruby had killed him in front of millions of TV viewers. The testimony at the Ruby trial left the motives unclear. Why did Ruby kill Oswald?

Then there was the trial of Clay L. Shaw, accused of fostering a conspiracy that was not even remotely proven by his accuser, Big Jim Garrison, the New Orleans district attorney. He was looking for his own piece of immortality. It seemed that everyone who touched the case, however remotely, was looking for that.

Pursuing the information, she felt like a dog running perpetually one length behind the mechanical rabbit. It was maddening. Soon she could hardly distinguish between history and the present. Who was she pursuing? Kennedy's killer or Pringle's? It bedeviled her.

She could see how others had gotten swept up. Theories piled on theories and not a single year had passed since the assassination that did not bring forth new theories, new books, new demands for investigations, new authoritative sources.

"I can't compete with this," Bruce told her one night. He had stopped by after a long session of the House, looking tired and drawn. As usual, she was combing through the material. He grabbed a volume of the Warren Commission report which she had been reading and flung it across the room.

"You're killing yourself. And it's not fair to me."

Obviously, all was not going well for him. She sensed that in passing. But it did not move her. Nothing moved her. He kicked over a pile of books.

"I'd like to know where we're going."

"I'm involved in something big, Bruce."

"So am I. This Senate thing is not as sure a shot as I figured. I've got lots of competition."

"You'll figure out a way, Bruce. You always do."

Her encouragement was perfunctory. She just wasn't interested.

"How long do I have to wait for your attention?"

"I wish I knew," she said in an abstracted voice.

"Maybe we should split?"

"Maybe. I'm just wound up in this. A little patience. Please."

He sat down heavily on the couch, pushing aside a pile of books.

"I've tried to be supportive, Fi. But you've got to admit this is beyond the pale."

"I know."

Still she wasn't moved. But she sat next to him anyway and stroked his arm distractedly. "I've got this tiger by the tail . . ."

"What about this tail?" he said, as he put her hand there. She had been neglectful of that as well. Somehow it triggered a programmed sense of duty and she opened his pants and began her ministrations. It was, she admitted, purely mechanical.

"I love you, dammit," he whispered.

"I know."

"What do I have to do to flag you down?"

She had to search herself for a reaction; it alarmed her when she could not find it. Her body, too, held back. She forced it, feeling pain as she pressed her weight, straddling him as he sat there.

"I wish you'd join me," he whispered, responding. His breath came in short gasps as she pumped him to climax.

"Even when it's bad, it's good." He felt used, manipulated.

"I'm not myself," she said lamely.

"You could at least try to share it."

She shrugged, her mind elsewhere.

"This is Bruce here," he pressed. "We're supposed to be lovers. We're supposed to share secrets. Nobody does what you're doing without one helluva reason," he argued, waving his hand around the room.

She forced herself to comprehend.

"Maybe I've exaggerated it out of all proportion?"

"Now that's no exaggeration."

"Shit," she said, getting up. "Look at this. It's an earthquake of uncertainty. There's a whole army out there, still looking for Kennedy's killer."

"And you?"

"I'm beginning to believe I've found him."

Saying it out loud gave the comment a credibility it didn't deserve. She quickly qualified it. The dam of restraint broke.

"It nags at you as you press on . . . and on and on. Did Oswald kill Kennedy? And did he do it alone? The evidence is there. But pieces of the logic are missing, and nothing wraps it up with a ribbon. That's why it continues forever. All the elements for doubt are present. A stay in the Soviet Union. A Russian wife. A tough-moving target. How many bullets? How many shots? How many guns? Why does Tippet . . ."

"Who?"

"That poor bastard. Nobody remembers." Even Tippet, Temple's counterpart, sparked mysteries. "Why was his car in the area of Oswald's boarding house? Why did he try to make the arrest alone? Why didn't he radio for help when he saw the suspect, supposedly a vicious desperate killer? Why? Why?"

Her agitation alarmed him. "Take it easy. You're all in a lather."

"See," she said. "The secret of perpetual motion. That's why so many people are hooked. Why couldn't our Library of Congress Killer have been an ordinary sniper?"

"So that's it?"

She avoided a direct answer. She had not wanted to tell him, but having got it out she suddenly felt better.

"The fellow has got a delusional system that beats all . . . or . . ." She hesitated. "He's screaming some kind of a message."

"Like what?" He was interested now.

"You think I know?" She hesitated, feeling his hand on her arm. "We have here a nut using the same gun, the same basic scenario, the same timeframe, the same bullets. Even killing a police officer in the same sequence. See why I'm going bananas?"

He let out a low whistle.

"So that's my competition?"

"I know I'm overreacting. Worse, everything I've read only increases my suspicion."

"About what?"

"About who killed Kennedy."

"You think this sniper . . . ?"

"I don't know. And yet I discount most of the theories. They're all flawed. Seems to be strictly a money-making or notoriety-creating situation. In all this . . ." She waved her hand again over the reams of material. "There's only two crazy things I've picked up. Only two . . ." She had not dared to tell them to Jefferson or Dr. Benton. They were already telling her to go easy. She knew she was straying from the bottom line. She caught Bruce's frozen attention. See, she wanted to shout, how it hooks you. His silence made her rush on.

"In the archives. This testimony. Oswald was a member of a hunting club outside Minsk where he lived. He was the worst shot of the group. Members who didn't bag anything were ridiculed. It was simply bad form not to bag something. Oswald couldn't hit the side of a barn, his sharpshooter status in the Marine Corps notwithstanding. Don't forget: military equipment is better. And the conditions of the range are ideal for a fixed shot. Anyway, on one outing no member was allowed to go home unless he got a kill. It was getting late and one of Oswald's companions was growing impatient with Oswald's inefficiency. Finally, after Oswald missed shot after shot, the companion bagged a rabbit and gave it to Oswald. 'Here, Oswald. You can go home now.' Tell me, how can a man who can't shoot that well put three bullets into a moving target from ninety yards with a $12.38 rifle, using a cheap telescopic sight? No way."

"Did your sniper do it, the fellow in the Library of Congress?"

"Precisely the point."

"And the other?" Bruce asked.

"Jack Ruby. Remember. Stay with it for a while. The cast of characters can get really real." She laughed, breaking her own tension. "Really, real. Anyway, at the exact moment of the assassination, the exact moment, twelve-thirty P.M., Jack Ruby was sitting alone at the window of the *Dallas Daily News* office. Alone! He had gone there ostensibly to place an ad for his nightclubs, a business that could have been done in minutes. But he seemed to have stalled and lingered. For no apparent reason. The window afforded the only clear unobstructed view of the assassination."

"Well?"

"Well what? Just two unrelated circumstances." She felt too tired to continue, and slumped against his chest. He held her close and kissed her cheek.

"What's in it for you, Fi?"

"I wish I knew. It's the icing but not the cake."

"And what's the cake?"

"Finding this lunatic with a rifle."

She sighed and turned toward him, feeling the first real tingle of sensuality. Reaching out, she brought his head down and kissed him deeply on the lips. This time it was his response that was muted, his concentration elsewhere.

"I've really had it, Fi. I think I'm a burned-out case. I better get home. The kids expect me tonight." She was reluctant to let him go, but her touch confirmed his disinterest.

"That, too," she mumbled, thinking of Oswald again. "That night before the assassination, he couldn't make it with his wife, Marina." That allegation diminished the other theories. It was easy to scream sexual compensation. In fact, it was Marina's most damning revelation.

"It happens sometimes," he said, moving her aside.

"Are you going to shoot the President?" she asked facetiously.

"I don't even intend to think about him," he said.

She felt bad about spilling the story to Bruce. Even the eggplant's tongue-whipping a week later could not chase her guilt. The son of a bitch had trusted her. The next day he had met her in the corridor, deliberately stalking her to a candy vending machine, a frequent meeting place, located in a setback of the corridor.

"Ten weeks," he scowled. "Sooner or later we have to fish or cut bait."

"You mean cut bait. Then let it sink to the bottom." Up to then, she had withheld her suspicions. Finally, she tested them on Jefferson and Dr. Benton. Their reactions were harbingers of what she might expect from the eggplant. You're getting in too deep, Fiona. Quicksand! Better keep all that under your hat. Catch the sniper. That's all he gives a shit about.

"You're gonna put my ass in a sling." The eggplant told her. "They'll crap all over me if they know I've been doing this on my own."

"I need a little more time," she lied. There was no end in sight.

They had also not found any connection with the previous two killings. She had, perhaps deliberately, raised impossible expectations in the eggplant's mind. Besides, there were only the two of them and all the old leads were ice cold. But the theory was still tantalizing, too tantalizing. The problem was that, so far, it had led nowhere.

"It can't go on forever," he said.

"We're trying," she said lamely.

"The chief finds out, I'm dead as Kelsy's." His bloodshot eyes were pleading. "It's one thing to hate my guts, FitzGerald. And another to cut my balls off. Somebody is going to find out about this." He appeared on the edge of exasperation. The full force of her guilt surfaced. She had, she knew, betrayed him. She had talked too much to Bruce. We have no secrets, he had said.

Oh, yes, we have, she thought angrily.

"We've been careful," she said, hoping to placate him.

"People know you've been poking around," he said. "It's the Kennedy connection that's got to be kept under wraps."

"I promise you. It's separate."

"It better be." He strode off unhappily. Poor bastard, she thought. As if for spite, she put money in the machine and pulled the lever on Milky Way. Nothing came out. She banged the machine. The eggplant turned around and shook his head sadly.

She made a gesture of futility. It conveyed the meaning of both situations.

It was also wearing down Jefferson. Essentially a man of action, he had left the research to her. But when it brought forth no new leads, he became rebellious.

"But we're no nearer to the dude," he pointed out. Surprisingly, he had been gentle and cooperative as they went over all the old ground. Now he was getting antsy.

"It's there, somewhere," she told him, flogging herself to continue.

Her date with Bruce at Tiberio's had all the trappings of an important "event." It was, after all, the scene of their first date, and they had gone there only on their most festive occasions. Unlike then, he had begged her to come. "I need you to be there," he had pleaded.

She wondered about his urgency. Was the moment of truth at hand? Fish or cut bait? She wasn't mentally prepared to make any lifetime commitments at that moment. Why couldn't he just leave her alone?

His lips were cold when he kissed her. A blast of icy air had come surging out of Canada and the papers had begun to express concern for the cherry blossoms. She smelled his shaving lotion, the brand she liked. He had shaved at the office and changed his shirt. Please, Bruce, don't force any decisions now, she wanted to cry out. She followed Julio to the table under the floral paintings, a burst of bright yellow and reds that matched the table flowers.

Sitting beside him, he gripped her hand under the table, lifted it to his lips, kissed it, then continued to hold it. He ordered a double Scotch and she asked for a martini.

"I'm living dangerously," she said. "I'll get smashed."

"Good. It will take the edge off."

"You think so?"

"I hope so."

It was, of course, the banter of courtship, the bright repartee that had punctuated those early moments together. He was deliberately playing recall. Coming up, she was sure, was the moment she dreaded.

Their drinks came and he lifted his glass.

"To us," he said, kissing her on her neck. His lips had warmed. His touch was soothing. She could not deny the feel of it, the sweetness of it. If only she could be more mindless, more instinctive.

"When are we going to get off the merry-go-round?" The question seemed more teasing than imperative and she let herself drift along. Squeezing her hand, he moved it along his thigh, touching hers as well.

"This is my woman," he whispered.

"Maybe my priorities are all screwed up," she said.

"The pot calls the kettle. What the hell is driving us, Fiona? Why don't we give it up? Fifty years from now who will give a damn?"

She sipped her martini. Her tongue was growing heavy.

"Maybe we're afraid to stop striving," he continued. "Afraid of the boredom. Sometimes I think boredom is the real enemy, worse than defeat. I mean, what would I do with my life if I didn't have this?" He shrugged, letting the question hang in the air. "I don't know which is worse. Boredom or loneliness.

"This business of politics. It takes you right up the road to meglomania. So I won't make senator. So what? It's not the end of the world. As much as I tell myself that it doesn't make a difference . . . I want it so badly . . ."

At least he knew what he was, she thought with growing irritation.

"Like you, Fi. We're driven people."

Like me! It was a view of herself she resented.

They were interrupted by Julio, who rattled off pleasantries in his rapid Italian accent. He started to offer culinary suggestions.

"Whatever you think," Bruce said. Fiona nodded. With a courtly bow, he moved away, flashing hand signals like a traffic cop.

"See," she said, "everybody's striving."

223

"I had an idea, Fi," he said.

She braced herself. Perhaps it *was* time for surrender. Don't throw love away, she warned herself. When this obsession passed what would be left? Save yourself. Loneliness would come again. Who cared who killed whom? What was so important about Kennedy's killer? Or Pringle's? Or anybody's? Let society fend for itself? Enough overbearing self-righteousness? Out moral flame? She was sick of dealing with death. The thought made her smile and she squeezed his hand. Ask me now, she begged in her heart. I'm ready.

"I need something so big, so overpowering, that everyone will have to stand up and take notice."

"What?" she was confused.

"They're out there like jackals, Fi. Everyone is jockeying for position. I've got to outfox them now. Take the initiative."

"What the hell are you talking about?"

"This Kennedy thing. It has an infallible aura about it. A mystique. I doubt if I could get a budget for it. But it's got a kind of pizzazz. This whole crime thing is heating up again. It hooks right in. And maybe you can make a breakthrough. Who knows?"

The waiter brought pasta for starters and he quickly began to eat.

"You mean publicity?"

"It would play well, Fiona. It always has."

"I told you all that in confidence."

"I'm not betraying it. I trust my people."

"Your people?"

"Crime sells, baby. And what's going on in the Big Apple alone is scary. Murders up fifty percent. They're really frightened out there. Don't you see how the Kennedy thing ties in? It's a springboard. A headline grabber. Not a year goes by that some publisher doesn't try to set off an explosion. The idea is to use it with deftness."

He looked at her and held up his hand, as if to stem her growing anger.

"Fiona, really! They're not going to let you use it. They'll take it away from you. Hell. I've got a shot at a Senate seat. And you can come along. That's the whole point of the exercise."

"I can hook right in . . ." she mimicked.

"Damned straight . . ." he hesitated.

"I'm not saying you have to quit your job. Hell. Now that would be a plus . . ." His voice droned on, impervious, self-obsessed.

". . . the timing has to be perfect. Connected somehow with some terrible crime. Some humiliating travesty for all of us. What we're looking for is something that engraves itself on the public mind. Clark says . . ."

"You told him as well?"

He looked at her strangely.

"If I can't trust Clark, then the ballgame's over."

'Do you trust me, Bruce?" Her head had fully cleared now.

"You, Fiona?"

"Me."

"How could I love you if I didn't trust you?" he said with indignation.

"Don't," she said emphatically.

He looked at her strangely. She barely missed a beat.

". . . because if I hear one single word about this from anybody . . . anybody . . . you included . . . I will personally, publicly, tell the world. Every outlet I can find. About our little cover-up at Remington's house. The whole sordid little story. Grist for the mill, you called it. The mill would love it."

The blood drained from his face, "You're serious?"

"Dead. As dead as your career will be."

"What about yours?"

"Mine? Since when does that matter?"

"I think you've misinterpreted this. Fiona. I love you. I wouldn't do anything to hurt that . . ."

She stood up and the plate of pasta splashed to the floor. Eyes turned toward them. Julio came running forward.

"It's nothing. Nothing." He snapped an order to the waiter, who scurried off to the kitchen.

Pushing the table aside, she slid out into the aisle and stormed out of the restaurant.

XXV

REMINGTON HEFTED the little brass Derringer in his palm. It felt smooth and cold and good. A gun dealer in Arizona had sold it to him, complete with balls and caps. All he would need was one of each. For years, he had kept the Derringer in its velvet-lined case in the drawer of his bedroom chest.

For this mission, he knew, he would be allowed poetic license. He would not be jumping onto any stage, or wearing spurs, as Wilkes had. In his belt he would carry a long dagger, emulating Wilkes, although that would be more for historical accuracy than for action. If someone tried to thwart him, however, he would not hesitate to use it.

He would carry the Derringer in the hip pocket of his tuxedo pants, the right pocket, ready for action at that crucial moment when laughter would be rolling through the theater. He would have ample time to aim and fire the ball into the President's brain. To be certain that the message of similarity would sink in, he planned to shout out the words: Sic Semper Tyrannis! Someone would surely hear them.

There would be other parallels to Wilkes's act. He hoped the time of the shooting would match. Lincoln had been shot precisely at 10:15. Naturally, he hoped he would be apprehended alive. It would give him a wider forum, a pulpit for a greater expression of his views. In the letter addressed to the editor of the *Washington Post*, he had laid out in clear terms the reasons ordained upon him by the cosmic force.

"Right or wrong, God judge me, not man," the letter began, just as Wilkes had done. Written in his own hand, Remington had set forth the simple caveat: "We can no longer suffer the consequences of less-than-great presidential leadership. Some way must be found to provide the conduit for the best qualified, absolutely the best, to step forward and stand for this high office. We no longer have the luxury to be led by second-rate men." He had agonized over the addition of "women" and finally had succumbed. He needed the broadest possible base of empathy. "Men and women," he had written finally.

"What I have done, I have done solely to establish that point for all future generations. History, I know, will vindicate me." In another paragraph, he confessed the three previous killings, although he did not attempt to offer reasons. The investigations would tell their own stories. Surely, his acts would set off a chain reaction that could easily span the entire millenium. Perhaps beyond that. The name of Thaddeus Remington III would forever be engraved on the public consciousness. Coming generations, once the enmity of the moment disappeared, would surely understand the divinely inspired logic of his acts.

"Mama. You will be proud," he said to the split mirror images. He knew she was watching. She had always been watching. Nothing could possibly go wrong now. Every detail would fall into place for the final climax, the crowning act. Hadn't they done so in the past?

His deep research into the history of Lincoln's assassination had convinced him of this long before the signs had emerged, proving the existence of the grand design. Tiny details, like a routine mix-up in ticket sales at the Ford Theater, four weeks prior to the fatal day. It was the policy of the theater to move patrons to more favorable empty seats further forward at the end of the first act. Four ticket holders had arrived at the beginning of act two to discover that other patrons had taken their seats. The ticket seller, determined to placate the irate patrons, led them to the box seats above the stage. He discovered that the boxes were locked and with a swift kick broke the lock clasp and opened the door. The lock was never repaired, providing what could only be deemed divine access, assuring Wilkes's success.

Then there was the case of Lincoln's guard, John F. Parker. He was supposed to be sitting on a chair outside the President's box. He was an unreliable fellow, also a bit of a drunkard. As soon as the Lincolns were ensconced in their box, the bodyguard left his post to have drinks in the tavern next door. Without these two circumstances, Wilkes could never have accomplished his purpose. Surely, a master puppeteer was at work.

All four of the people in Lincoln's box when the shot was fired faced doom. Mrs. Lincoln went mad. Major Rathbone, who was stabbed trying to apprehend Wilkes, attended his fiancée, Clara Harrison. They later married, but years later, the major murdered his wife and spent his last years in an insane asylum.

If Garfield had appointed Guiteau minister to Paris or, for that matter, to anything, his death, too, might not have occurred. And McKinley. His meeting with the public had been an afterthought. Kennedy was reluctant to go to Dallas.

Remington knew that these assassinations were irrevocable. Once the machinery was set in motion, the final act was preordained. Nothing could stop them. Just as nothing could stop him. Nothing!

Through his friends at the Kennedy Center, he had reserved the box next to the presidential one for the entire run of *Tonight at 8:30*. Also, through these friends, he was going to ascertain what night the President had chosen to go. He would know this on the day of the performance. How could he possibly arouse suspicion? Wasn't he known to the President? The Secret Service would ignore him as a threat.

He would invite others to join him for that performance, all in formal evening wear. He knew exactly where he was going to sit, where the President would sit. It was completely worked out in his mind. All previous tests had been passed. The signs were unmistakable. He was the instrument.

"They will rue the day," his mother had said after his Senate defeat. "You must make them pay for their ignorance."

He spent the first week in April walking around the city, observing details he had never stopped to notice before. He visited the National Gallery, that very spot where he had achieved his first "breakthrough," lovingly viewing the pictures that had served as the backdrop for this historical act. At the Pan American Union, he strolled through the atrium, looking up to see the dome of light that fed the plants around the fountain. He walked from the White House following the route of the inaugural, east on Pennsylvania Avenue, past the stately buildings, their styles reflecting the entire panorama of American history. At the Capitol he proceeded across the park to the Library of Congress. He even went upstairs to the very room where he had done the third deed, following the pattern of the grand design.

It was thrilling to know that of all men, he alone had been chosen to be the lightning rod to warn this great nation of its peril. He alone! The instrument! Retracing his steps along the historic route, he moved westward to the Lincoln Memorial, standing in awe again at the remarkable likeness of the Great Emancipator, sculpted in perpetual reflection. He, too, had once saved America.

"You could be greater than Jefferson or Lincoln," his mother had assured him during one night of bliss.

He put his worldly affairs in order, leaving instructions for the disposition of his papers in his safe deposit box. On the chosen day, he would make arrangements for the key to be delivered to his lawyers, as well as the letter to the *Post*.

"This house and everything in it is to be kept intact in perpetuity," he had instructed, recommending how his chosen executors were to handle its financing, using the vast inheritance that would ensue, the entire proceeds of the family fortune.

At first, he knew, it would be a museum of infamy, but time would heal that. One day it would serve as a symbol to the concept of greatness itself, a historical memory to the one man who dared use the symbols of assassination as the lightning rod of communal memory. He also designated that space on his library shelves be reserved to the hundreds of books that were sure to be written about his divinely inspired acts. One day he would be revered as the apogee of human courage. America would heed his warning and acclaim him.

Yet he remained on the lookout for further trials. They were necessary to goad his courage, test his mettle. Euphoria was a dangerous condition.

When the call came from Fiona FitzGerald, he knew what it meant, another obstacle to be conquered.

"I must see you," she said.

"When?"

"Now."

It was, he was certain, the last gauntlet.

XXVI

THE MATTER with Bruce was beyond apology. When she faltered, her anger would come to her rescue. It was obscene to be used, manipulated, by someone to whom she had given her trust. Indeed, trust was the most enduring value she possessed. What was love against trust? That piece of herself would never be given away to anyone.

But that knowledge could not get her through the lonely nights. Nor could her obsession with the Kennedy assassination. The words in the endless testimony and books swam without meaning or comprehension in her mind. Finally, she could barely focus on the subject.

Yet whenever she was tempted to surrender, the unalterable fact remained. There was someone out there with a gun and some unsuspecting victim as well. Meanwhile, the tide of protests was rising. Jefferson was getting more edgy. The eggplant was leaning on both of them now. They had looked into every dust-covered corner, past and present. There were simply no other places to explore.

"Let's leave it alone, Fiona," Jefferson pleaded.

He was right, of course. A look in the mirror confirmed it.

The circles under her eyes had darkened and the network of red veins in their whites seemed a permanent fixture. Her color, too, was pallid and unhealthy.

"I appreciate your concern," she told him, trying to muster an air of sarcasm. It melted on contact. "I liked you better when you called me mama."

"Okay, mama. Let's get the hell off this case."

"What happened to that sense of ethnic revenge?"

He sighed. It was impossible for her to bait him and she finally gave up.

"Maybe you're right."

"Let's leave it alone. Let him become an inspector without any more hassles. I think we should make our peace. No skin off our asses. Call it a victory and forget it."

She might have taken his advice. She was that close. But Dr. Benton's call changed all that, changed everything. It came, as most cataclysmic events, in the middle of the night.

"I found something," he cried. "I'm coming over. You get Jefferson."

She made a pot of coffee and waited. She called Jefferson, who groaned a response. She heard a female voice of protest.

Dr. Benton's cottony hair was frazzled. His dress was careless and he needed a shave. Jefferson arrived soon after. She poured out three cups of coffee and for a long time they all sat in silence, sipping the hot liquid, waiting for Benton to begin.

"History," he muttered. "We seemed to have neglected history." He stood up and, in an odd gesture, clasped his hands in front of him as if to hold in his excitement.

"In less than three months it will be the hundredth anniversary of James Garfield's assassination." He watched them, savoring the suspense. "President Garfield." He unclasped his hands and waved a finger in the air. "It was in the newspaper, a tiny little piece. I nearly missed it. July second, eighteen eighty-one, President James Garfield was assassinated at the Baltimore and Ohio Railroad Station by a man by the name of Charles Guiteau, a disgruntled job seeker. July second." He looked at them. "Mean anything?"

"My God," she cried. "You said the Baltimore and Ohio Railroad Station."

"I did say that. And do you know where that station used to be?"

She tried to lift her coffee cup, but her hands shook too much.

"The National Gallery of Art," he said in a quivering voice.

"Sombitch." The revelation finally reached Jefferson. He slapped his thighs.

"And the other?" Fiona blurted. She wanted to reach out and embrace the doctor.

"I have this set of encyclopedias," Dr. Benton said, enjoying their reaction. "It only gives dates and a few details. President McKinley was killed in Buffalo."

"Buffalo?" She was disappointed. "Where's the connection?"

"At the Temple of Music . . ." He paused, relishing it. "On September sixth, nineteen hundred, at the Pan American Exposition."

"The Pan American Union Building." It came in a duet; Jefferson and she.

"With a revolver wrapped in a handkerchief," Dr. Benton continued.

"A witness had said a ball of fire shot out of his hand," Fiona shouted. "And the time?"

"I haven't had a chance to check, but if you would like to wager, I'll say that the time was exact, the wounds similar." His hand swept toward the piles of books in the apartment. "You've been on the right track, Fiona. But going in the wrong direction."

"I can't believe it."

"Shall I pinch you?" Dr. Benton said, his fingers gathering the skin on her arm.

"The old ammo. He used the old weapons?"

"As night follows day."

"The man's crazy," Jefferson said.

"As crazy as a fox," Dr. Benton said. "He's got this whole thing down to a near science, an elaborate delusional fantasy. He's also been quite brilliant in the execution."

"Either that. Or he's been phenomenally lucky," Fiona's mind was racing now. "I never heard of a case like this. Never. Some of his actions were so . . ." She groped for words. ". . . esoteric." She suddenly thought of Remington, who had inadvertently set off the chain reaction. Inadvertently! An idea struggled somewhere in her mind.

"It sure slopped over on a lot of people," Jefferson said.

"That poor painter," Fiona said. "All those loused-up lives. Innocents. The lot of them. What kind of a mind conceives this?"

"Who knows?" Dr. Benton said. "Someone seething with frustration, someone sad and sick and brilliant. A loner, probably, like the real assassins."

"Well, at least we know the MO," Jefferson said. "The chief will piss in his jeans."

"I rather think he might want to go public now," Dr. Benton said. "He could even get a commendation for having the foresight to keep the cases in active investigation. He could say he had to deliberately keep the matter under wraps."

"That still won't get the killer," Jefferson said.

"The good old bottom line."

"I'm not so sure," Dr. Benton said.

Fiona and Jefferson looked at him, pacing the floor now, his head down. He stopped abruptly and turned toward them.

"There were four."

"Four what?"

"Assassinations."

"Lincoln." Jefferson croaked. "Lincoln."

"Exactly"

She was already rummaging among the papers and books. She had screened out the material on everything but the Kennedy incident. Now she remembered that there was something in the Warren Commission report, a section on presidential assassinations that she had ignored. She thumbed through the pages and found it.

"Oh, my God. What day is it?"

"April tenth," Dr. Benton said.

234

"Four more days. It's going to happen in four more days. The theater," Fiona said.

"Ford's."

"Right fuckin' on," Jefferson shouted, slapping his thigh again.

"It was going too fast. Fiona felt the tangled energy as their minds raced.

"Let's face it. He's a sucker for authenticity. This is the real thing. What day is it?"

She looked at the calendar.

"Tuesday."

"I believe they're running something. It's the height of the tourist season," Dr. Benton said.

"We better let the muvva know, Fiona," Jefferson said.

She nodded.

"We just don't want to throw it at him. We need more facts. It's got to come out as more than just an educated guess."

She paused to read from the Warren Commission report.

"He'll be using a brass Derringer," she said. "One shot, percussion weapon. We better get him before he gets it off."

"It may be the only way we'll find him," Jefferson said. "Then I want the privilege of blowin' him away."

Fiona spent the morning at the Martin Luther King Library with Dr. Benton, gathering up books on previous assassinations. It crossed her mind briefly that, in the interests of time, she might have called upon Bruce's office to use the facilities of the Library of Congress. That was the past, and her rejection of the idea became, in her mind, the first line in a new chapter of her life.

While they were at the library, Jefferson was at headquarters going over the case files of both the gallery and Pan American Union cases, extracting relevant information to play off against the actual facts of each assassination. Later they met back at Fiona's apartment and began poring over the books, making notes. The material was formidable. It wasn't until late in the evening, their eyes strained and burning, that they decided to go on what they had. Amid a clutter of hamburger wrappings and denuded chicken bones, they began their comparisons. Dr. Benton worked on the earlier assassinations, while Fiona reviewed her Kennedy material; essentially, it had been validated before. This done, she had proceeded to gather the facts of the Lincoln assassination. Jefferson, too, studied a number of books on that subject.

"James Garfield was elected in eighteen-eighty," Dr. Benton summarized. "He was shot by Charles Julius Guiteau, a white male, thirty-eight years old, five foot five, one hundred twenty pounds. The weapon was a forty-four caliber English Bulldog with a white bone handle, which he bought for ten dollars..." He coughed. "This included a box of cartridges and, inexplicably, a woman's penknife." Fiona felt he was going into too many details. Sensing their impatience, he shook his head. "The damned thing is so fascinating, you don't know what material to screen out. I'll stay with the day of the killing." He continued: "Guiteau spent the night at the Riggs House, a hotel near the White House. He awoke at five, went to Lafayette Park, read a newspaper. At seven, he went back to the hotel, had a hearty breakfast, returned to his room, wrote a few letters, prepared a package of his autobiographical writings, put a revolver in his right hip pocket . . . note the details . . . right hip pocket. Wearing a clean white shirt, a black vest, coat, trousers and hat, he left the Riggs House a little before nine. He didn't even pay his bill. He was good at that. He was an expert at skipping bills. He took a horse car to the depot, located at Independence and Fourth Street, now the site of the National Gallery of Art. He even arranged for a taxi to get him away in case a lynch mob might gather after the shooting. Then he had his shoes shined. Also, he had only twenty cents left in his pocket; he owed the taxi driver two dollars. Apparently he planned to stiff him as well. He left his package with the newsstand vendor, went to the men's room to be sure the revolver worked, then waited for Garfield." Dr. Benton looked up. "Sounds so pedestrian, don't you think?

"The President arrived at nine-twenty. He and Secretary of State Blaine walked through the ladies' waiting room. Guiteau waited for them behind a bench. He drew the revolver when they were almost across the room, walked up behind Garfield, then calmly shot the President in the back. He fired a second time, but this one only grazed the collapsing President's arm."

"Check and double check," Jefferson said. "The man was shot in the gallery. Two shots, the fatal one in the back. Time. About nine-twenty. The gun. English Bulldog was one of the alternatives Hadley had cited. Was Garfield bearded?"

"Bearded and big." Dr. Benton said.

"Like Damato."

"Like Damato," Fiona repeated.

"It took Garfield ninety days to die. They tried everything. Today he would have lived. The bullet had entered through the tenth and eleventh ribs, nipped the vertebrae and an artery, then settled behind the pancreas. An aneurysm formed on the artery, halting the bleeding. Our killer's bullet was close, but more deadly and close enough for us to get the message."

"And the motive?" Fiona asked.

"In a nutshell?" Dr. Benton said, pausing. "God made me do it. The man was a religious nut, had been a shyster lawyer and itinerant preacher. He was a follower of a man named John Humphrey Noyes, a cult leader of the last century who had a commune in upper New York State called the Oneida Community. They even had their own version of the Bible, *The Berian.* It was all quite mad, but not much different from today's cults. Anyway, Guiteau was a frustrated nonentity who had begged the President for a job as consul to Paris. Had even met with him. That was the way jobs were given out in those days. The President was accessible. Anyway, Guiteau's trial was a media circus. They didn't hang him until nearly a year later."

"Obviously a nut case," Jefferson said.

Dr. Benton put down his notes and shook his head.

"Maybe. It seems somehow irrelevant. He was determined, obsessed, fanatical. To him, the reasons for the crime were quite logical. He was saving the country, removing what he thought was a controversial President, whose election had split the Republican Party. He died unremorseful, proud of his act, as if the President was more of a symbol than a human being. Also, he

237

wanted, above all, to be remembered as a hero. That's why he had bought a pearl-handled revolver instead of an ordinary one. He thought it might look better in a museum."

"So who remembers the dude's name?" Jefferson asked.

"The gun is in a museum and the killing is said to be responsible for the enactment of a law which created the Civil Service Commission."

"Thanks for small favors," Fiona said.

But the point of the exercise was to establish the similarities.

"Any doubts that the crime was a replication?" Fiona asked.

"Not in my mind," Jefferson said. "Down to the bullets. No doubt at all."

"Shall I proceed to McKinley?"

He searched their faces and when they had settled down, began:

"Leon Czolgosz." He spelled the last name. "Pronounced Cholgosh. He was twenty-eight, five foot seven, weighed one hundred and forty pounds. Conceived in Poland. Born in America. Little education, a shy, nervous man. He got turned on to anarchy a few years before. Anarchy was the big scare of that period. Another kind of cult. Anyway, William McKinley was an immensely popular President. Also a Republican. For some reason, the Republicans attract more presidential assassins than the Democrats. Kennedy was the only Democrat of the four, McKinley was elected to his second term in nineteen hundred. Teddy Roosevelt was his Vice President . . . there I go again . . . tangents. The material is simply not linear. You could spend a lifetime on this stuff."

"Many have," Fiona said, remembering her own recent obsession.

"McKinley was in Buffalo to attend the Pan American Exposition, a lavish spectacle. A few days before, on September second, Czolgosz bought a thirty-two caliber Ivor Johnson revolver decorated with an owl's head on the grip. On the day of the assassination, it was announced that the President would shake hands for ten minutes in the Temple of Music on the exposition grounds. The public reception opened at four P.M. McKinley had just returned from Niagara Falls. Ironically, so did Czolgosz. The President was guarded by soldiers, police detectives and the Secret Service. Apparently, the Garfield and Lincoln assassinations had taught the government something about presidential protection, although subsequent events prove the adage that if a killer wants to kill, he will somehow find a way. Despite fifty guards, there was little Leon, gun drawn, confronting the President. It was a blazing hot day. He was wearing a neat gray suit, another undistinguished anonymous man lost in the crowd. He shuffled forward. A Secret Serviceman nudged him to move quicker. When he reached the President at about eight past four, he extended his left hand, the President his right. Czolgosz pushed the President's hand away and fired. As he fired, the handkerchief went up in flames. Two bullets. The first ricocheted off the President's breastbone, the other penetrated his huge midsection, hitting the stomach, the pancreas and a kidney and coming to rest in a back muscle. The man died a week later. He, too, would have lived, if it had happened today. McKinley, staggered and collapsing, found the strength to prevent the guards from hurting his assassin. There's Christian charity for you."

"Check again," Jefferson said, looking at his notes. "Time and date. Two bullets. One of the gun possibilities mentioned in Hadley's report. And the wounds?"

"Close enough," Dr. Benton said. "Only more lethal."

"Terrorist attack!" Fiona laughed. "What the hell. It was as good a ploy as any. Think of the fallout on that one. Who knows how many heads have rolled in Argentina? The man who did it must be hysterical at our stupidity."

"We deserve the ridicule," Dr. Benton said. "People who forget history are doomed to relive it."

"Seems I've heard that before," Fiona said.

"We're cops. Not historians," Jefferson said.

"And this man's delusional system is, let's face it, quite unique," Dr. Benton said.

"How long did McKinley live?" Fiona asked.

"One week."

"And the motive?"

"Czolgosz believed that the President, or any man, should not have more . . . this is his exact words . . . more service than any other man. In other words, we're all equal."

"Under God."

"He was not into God," Dr. Benton corrected. "He was frying other fish. Trying to sell the anarchist concept. They eloctrocuted him fifty-four days after the deed. A quick trial. A quick verdict. They had learned something from Guiteau. But they beefed up the concept of better protection of the President and we got Teddy Roosevelt. It also broke the back of the anarchist movement. They also got into more narrower psychiatric definitions. Czolgosz had had a nervous breakdown a few years before. They said it had made him a schizophrenic . . . he had said it was his duty to kill the President. Duty!" He shook his head. "Madness."

"No remorse or contrition?" Fiona asked.

"None," Dr. Benton said. "How could they have had that? They had resolved that question by relegating it to some force outside of themselves. I suppose that was also the delusion of Booth."

"Yes. He thought God was commanding him . . . God again."

"And Oswald?" Jefferson asked.

"Nobody will ever know. If Oswald is the killer."

"You believe he wasn't?"

"I'm not sure. Not one hundred percent certain."

"The Garfield and McKinley killings were not without their own conspiracy theories."

"Nor was Lincoln's. It thrashed around for more than one hundred years."

It was after midnight. Fiona made more coffee. Not one of them made a move to adjourn. Like her, they were too fascinated, too exhilarated. The man, the killer, had forced them into history. But why? That question, she knew, was at the heart of the matter. And the heart was surging, pumping. After pouring their coffee, Fiona lifted her cup and sipped, glancing at her notes. It was her turn now. A drop of coffee fell on the paper, dissolving a word.

"The Lincoln killing was, unlike the others, a conspiracy. A group, led by Booth, was also out to kill Vice President Andrew

Johnson and Secretary of State Seward," she began. "But the others in the group were incompetents. Only John Wilkes Booth accomplished his purpose. Apparently Wilkes . . ." She paused. "They called him that, was a megalomaniacal figure, a brilliant actor with an obsessive wish to achieve everlasting fame by an act so outrageous that it would be forever engraved on the mind of man . . ." She laughed at her staginess

"Tell us when to applaud, woman," Jefferson said.

"I got carried away."

"We're all carried away," Dr. Benton said seriously.

"Anyway, Booth. I'd rather call him that. I don't know him that well. He learned that the President was going to Ford's Theater on the morning of April fourteenth, the day of the deed. He proceeded to the theater, checked out the presidential box. Boxes seven and eight. There was a partition in between that the management would remove. By some twist of fate, the lock was broken on the door that led to the box. With a gimlet, he made a hole in the wall to observe Lincoln's exact position when the time would come. The play was *Our American Cousin*, a potboiler of the period. Booth knew every line, including the one that got the biggest laugh, and he planned to pull the trigger at the exact moment when the roar would fill the house.

"Moments before the laugh line was to be delivered, Booth walked up the stairs to the box. Then came another quirk of fate. The man who was supposed to guard Lincoln and sit outside the box in the corridor . . ." She looked up from her notes. "He was a cop. Washington police. Unfortunately for Lincoln, he was a drunk and when the play started, he left his post to go downstairs to a next door tavern for a drink. Ironically, who do you think was drinking at the bar at the same time?"

"I don't believe it," Jefferson said, shaking his head. He had been listening intently, like a schoolboy.

"Could Booth have known that the man was the President's guard?" Dr. Benton asked.

"He could have, but there is no evidence to support it, at least not in the couple of accounts I've read. Think of this. If the guard was truly doing his job, he would have heard Booth come up the wooden stairs. He might, or should have, drawn his gun. Booth, although armed with two Colt revolvers, a large knife and his one-shot brass Derringer, would have had to stab the man, rather than attract attention by using a gun, an unlikely possibility if the man were alert." She paused. A shiver began at the base of her spine. "Booth seemed to have willed the circumstances."

"Coincidence, Fiona," Dr. Benton said. "No need to go cosmic."

"I'm sorry." She wondered why she had apologized, but let it pass quickly. "Booth fired the shot at exactly 10:15, point blank behind Lincoln's left ear. The ball lodged over his right eye. But the massive injury was enough to be fatal. He lived for ten hours."

"And Booth?" Jefferson asked.

"They cornered him in a barn in Prince George's County. He was allegedly shot by a man named Boston Corbett. But that was never proven. Fini. Like the Kennedy killing, the country went wild with conspiracy talk and investigation. All of the co-conspirators were hanged, although there was some question about the guilt of a Mrs. Surratt, in whose house the plan was allegedly hatched."

"April fourteenth, ten-fifteen," Jefferson said. He looked at his calendar watch. "Three fuckin' days from now."

"My God," Dr. Benton said hoarsely.

"The question, gentlemen: Will the eggplant buy it?" Fiona said. "We can't do it alone. Not now," she mumbled into the silence.

XXVII

H E LOOKED uncomfortable in her apartment, his big chunky thighs crossed, a cigarette mashed between his thick black fingers. When he inhaled, his eyes bugged out and when he let out the smoke through his nostrils, the smoke clouds obscured his dark face. As she talked, he became restless, a mass of little movements: a tremor of the lip, a nervous twitch in the eye, a foot in a perpetual staccato movement.

Jefferson, too nervous to sit still, leaned against the wall. Dr. Benton sat stiffly in a straight-backed chair. They had tried to sleep for a few hours. Fiona, her mind on fire, her heart pumping wildly from excitement or too much caffeine, had merely lain supine in her bed, tracking possibilities. What kind of a man was doing this? Why? The questions crowded into her brain, like a terminal point in some imaginary railroad. Whoever he was, he had transcended the category. According to the textbooks there were two types of assassins. One who wanted to get caught and one who wanted to get away. The last was more impossible to catch, the first more lethal. The killer seemed to be a combination of both. She tried to picture him in her mind, but the composite would not hold.

Was he some nonentity like Guiteau, or Czolgosz or Oswald, or some golden boy, like Booth, greedy for more than providence could possibly deliver? An image flashed in her mind and disappeared, like a flickering light extinguished by a faint wind. Somewhere deep in her subconscious, she was searching for something. Something.

Despite the lack of sleep, she was not fatigued. And by the time the eggplant had arrived, her mental state was clear. Confronting the three of them, the eggplant was instantly wary. She didn't give him any time for reflection, plunging right into the explanation.

During her presentation, he smoked a pack of cigarettes, a detail that she observed without missing a beat, hoping that the onslaught of pollution wouldn't kill him off until he had heard the end of her spiel.

"That is the damndest story I ever heard," he said when she had finished. He actually flashed a smile, which she interpreted as an uncommon sign of approval.

"That's what we thought," she said smugly.

"There is a bedrock of logic," Dr. Benton said, obviously relieved at the chief's reaction.

"It's like a fucking movie," the eggplant said.

"Maybe they'll make one about it. Like *The Sting,*" Jefferson said, also relieved.

"Okay," the eggplant said. "Let's say it fits."

"It fits," Fiona said firmly. She remembered her obsession with the Kennedy killing. Dr. Benton's discovery of the Garfield anniversary had led her to realize that she had been chasing a red herring. "It fits."

"Hey," the eggplant lifted his hands. "I'm not saying it doesn't. What it leads to . . . ," their nods encouraged him to continue, ". . . is that this weirdo is going to waste some poor innocent bastard in a theater at ten-fifteen the day after tomorrow."

"You got it," Jefferson blurted. The eggplant shot him a withering glance.

"Ford's Theater?"

"Maybe," Fiona said. "I've been thinking about that. There

are four legitimate theaters operating downtown. Actually, seven, if you count the Kennedy Center's four auditoriums. You've got Warner's, the National and Ford's. There's also smaller places."

"Are you saying . . ."

"I'm just speculating."

"I'm not as stupid as you think, FitzGerald. What you're saying is that we've got to man all the theaters. Every fucking one. You know how much manpower I'll need?"

"I know you're going to have to go to the top."

"Shit."

"If we're right, you'll be the biggest thing in town."

"Now I'm a potential hero." His eyes darted over the three of them. "You think I don't know what you think of me. The eggplant. The glory boy. The hot dog. You think it's easy for me to do this job?" He lit still another cigarette. "I'm not saying there isn't some ego in me. Hell, what's a man worth without an ego?" He puffed out some smoke and looked at Fiona. "Or a woman for that matter?" She knew she had him hooked.

"I'm not saying it's without risks," she said.

"Suppose we're all wet? Suppose we're just victims of a hyperactive imagination?"

Fiona noted the sudden use of the collective pronoun. He must have noticed it as well.

"If it works, there's more than enough credit to go around. I mean it, woman," the eggplant said. It was, she was sure, a major effort at sincerity. "Hell, you guys did the job. But remember who gave you the authorization."

She let it pass, knowing he was still working it out in his mind.

"But if we blow it, I'll be the department asshole of the decade."

She smiled, wanting to tell him that he had already acquired that title. Jefferson turned away to mask his own amusement.

"They better not try to take it away from us," the eggplant said, standing up. "It's our baby.

"And no press," Fiona said. "Not until we get him. Any leak now could scare him away." She wondered suddenly why the killer had gone out of chronological sequence. Perhaps he had meant to throw them off the track from the beginning. The Kennedy replication had been a test, she decided. Maybe he does want to get caught? She kept the speculation to herself.

"What kind of a man do you think he is?" Dr. Benton asked.

"He's obviously smart," Fiona said. "And he's studied the subject matter. A history buff. He also knows guns. Maybe he's even a collector."

"A brass Derringer would be hard to come by," Dr. Benton pointed out. "Maybe he'll use another kind."

"Not him," Fiona said.

"How the hell did you get on this track, FitzGerald?" the eggplant asked.

"God knows."

The flame in her mind sputtered to life again. Remington?

The events of inaugural eve returned, an oblique memory, filtered through the prism of her new knowledge. It had set off cataclysmic events in her life as well. A sliver of fear lodged in her gut, and the memories of her Catholic childhood rushed into her consciousness. God, the ubiquitous being! Was He also watching, listening, feeling, touching, seeing? God had no secrets. God knew. She shivered, unable to contain the enormity of her fear.

She could not wait for them to leave. When they did, finally, she reached for the phone. His voice was calm, unctuous.

"I have to see you today," she told him. He showed no surprise, the charm unflagging. There was a kind of serenity about his response. For some reason, nevertheless, her idea of him whirled around in the vortex of coincidence, drawing a strange heat. Guns. History. Perhaps his knowledge held the key to a locked door in her mind. She was certain there were things he knew, special things. His museumlike displays were a living testimonial to his interests and . . . She deliberately slowed down her thoughts. It's running away with you, she told herself, struggling for calm . . . His political frustrations. His Senate defeat. Oswald's bullet had aborted Remington's political life as well. What sets off a delusional system? she asked herself, as she applied makeup to her pallid face. New paths seemed to have developed in her thoughts. Thwarted ambition? The idea made her stomach queasy. She knew about that. Hadn't Bruce taught her something about that? Thinking of Bruce angered her. Politics was only a symptom. Ambition was the real disease. Perhaps Remington might offer some insight into that as well.

"Come at four," he said. "Cocktails."

She was at Remington's front door promptly. His Spanish maid opened it, offering a wide gold-speckled smile. She nodded recognition.

"Un momento. A moment. Mr. Remington will be right with you."

She had never been in the house without large groups of people, and her inspection of Remington's displays had been cursory, except for what was in his Rustic Room, the cases of guns. Her eyes searched now, screening out the profusion of scrimshaw, marine decorations, antiques, concentrating instead on what was absorbing her.

One thing was certain. Most of the autographs, photos, books and memorabilia displayed his passionate interest in the Presidency. Before, she had noticed only his obsessive interest in Kennedy. She could understand that now.

She thumbed through a catalogue, noting the preponderance of material about Kennedy, Lincoln, Garfield and McKinley. She stemmed the tide of speculation. Assassinated Presidents, if one were collecting, were certainly a special lure. Yet other Presidents, as the catalogue illustrated, were favored as well. Jackson, the two Roosevelts, Truman and Ford.

She was so absorbed in the catalogue that she did not hear him enter the room. His voice startled her.

"I'm sorry," he said, kissing her on the cheek. He motioned her to a chair near the fireplace, over which hung the heroic version of his younger self. He was radiant, self-confident, in command of himself, not at all like the frightened man she had seen on inaugural night.

"I make an excellent martini," he said, and went to the liquor table where the makings had been laid out. With a steady hand he presented her with a drink on a silver tray. He sat directly across from her.

"No problems over . . . her?" Her eyes gazed at the ceiling; her meaning was clear.

"A miracle," he said, smiling. "I owe you my gratitude on that one. And Bruce as well."

She averted his eyes and took a deep sip of her drink. If he didn't already know that they had broken up, she wasn't going to tell him. Besides, she thought testily, it was irrelevant to her visit.

"Now what can I do for you?" he said, flashing an ingratiating smile. She felt suddenly guilty, as if she were imposing on his privacy.

"Inadvertently," she began, watching his face. His eyes met hers squarely. "You set me off on a journey."

"How so?"

"We talked about the Mannlicher-Carcano and the three cartridges. Remember?"

"I do indeed." He smiled, showing his even white teeth.

"Then you said 'assassin.' You used the term."

"Yes?"

He waited calmly as she searched for words.

"It set off this long fuse." He nodded. "And I followed it."

"And where did it lead you?"

She looked at her hands. Her fingers seemed locked, like claws, holding back.

"Here."

Her swift response confused her. Yet he remained poised, waiting for her to continue.

"I mean you seem to know so much about the subject." She was fumbling her words, groping. "You know. About presidential assassinations."

"Ah. I see." He moved to the edge of his chair, his interest seemed piqued. "It's a bit morbid, don't you think?"

"No. I . . . I think it's fascinating. They cause quite a hullaballoo for a time. Then people forget."

"Until the act is repeated."

"Yes. I suppose you're right." She hesitated, watching him. "How many out there would remember names like Guiteau or Czolgosz?" Again she paused.

"Or even Tippet," she added. His face was bland, showing little reaction.

"Poor Officer Tippet," Remington said.

"Booth seems to have achieved the name recognition he craved."

"Well, he did want immortality." He sipped his drink, his hand steady. "Do you suppose it was because his name is so easy to remember? Booth. Only one syllable. The others seem harder."

Was she testing his knowledge? She searched for something esoteric.

"Garfield was shot with an English Bulldog."

"A forty-four," he said without missing a beat.

"You know that?"

"Oh, yes. He was shot at the old B and O Station."

"Is it still there?"

He looked at her archly now. Then he puffed out his cheeks and let out a trill of laughter.

"You're not serious."

"I am serious," she protested.

"They built the National Gallery of Art on the site."

"You know that, too."

"What is it? Privileged information?" His hand swept the walls. "It's my thing. They should teach it in the schools."

"Don't they?"

"A cursory pass at it. They are a manifestation of something deep in our national psyche, a clue."

For the first time, he seemed to drift off, his alertness fading. His eyes turned inward and he grew silent. For a moment she was confused. She felt inadequate. Intuition again. Not to be trusted.

"We have reason to believe," she began, her heart thumping in her throat, "that there's a killer loose who is replicating the assassinations of our Presidents. He's choosing the same time, same date, same gun. Only the places are symbolic."

"How imaginative," he replied, alert again.

"But he's killing innocent people." Compared to Remington, she felt awkward, naïve. What had she expected?

"What is tomorrow?" she asked. It seemed a last ditch ploy. Her clumsiness galled her. Why was she really here?

"Tomorrow?" He thought for a moment. "April fourteenth."

"Exactly."

"Why, that was the day that Booth shot Lincoln."

It was maddening. Was he playing with her? Teasing?

"What kind of a man would do that?" she asked.

"Kill Lincoln?"

"No. Replicate his killing. It has to have some purpose, don't you think?"

"Without question," he said innocently, widening his blue eyes, which caught the glints of the afternoon sun. "Why bother otherwise?"

"Why, do you suppose?"

"Maybe he's trying to tell us something."

"Us?"

"The world."

Aside from an intellectual interest, he seemed to betray no inner concern.

"Do you think he will go through with it?" she asked suddenly, hoping for some untoward reaction.

"Has he been on schedule up to now?"

His reaction was a disappointment.

"To the letter."

"Do you think someone who had gone to all that trouble would stop now?" he asked, as if reading her mind.

"No. I don't."

"Then at the appropriate time, he'll be there."

"You still didn't answer my question."

"You mean about the kind of man?" So he had been listening intently. She didn't know what to make of that.

"Yes."

"What kind of men killed the four Presidents?"

"Loners. Men frustrated in their aspirations. Even Booth, who had everything . . ." She hesitated, watching him, his face still bland, the lines and planes offering a sculpted impenetrable visage. "There are psychiatric explanations, of course."

"Oh." His interest seemed to quicken.

"Paranoid schizophrenia seems to be the most frequently heard diagnosis. All of them had maladjusted sex lives. Oswald was having impotency problems. Booth was overcompensating. He had six pictures of various girls in his wallet. Guiteau had bad relationships with women. And Czolgosz didn't appear to have any. There are some theories that portray all four as repressed homosexuals . . ."

She thought she saw a brief tic in his jaw, something uncontrollable, a tiny palpitation. Perhaps it is the light, she thought. But when it came again, she was alert to it. Something was stirring inside of him. He could not quite get it under control. To mask it, he began what seemed to her, a little stage business. Standing up, he moved to the liquor table and mixed up another batch of martinis, lifting one in her direction after he had filled it. She nodded no and he shrugged and began sipping. Somehow he had gotten the palpitation under control.

"The theory goes that the gun itself, the phallic symbol and the target, the President, represents the ultimate proof of the gender."

"Too bad psychiatry is not an exact science," he said, returning to his chair and crossing his legs. One foot dangled in the air. It had not done so earlier. He seemed to be waiting for her now. She groped for something rapier-sharp, something to puncture the bland facade. She felt her brain overheating again, regretting that she had not accepted the second martini.

"Would you have liked to be President?" she asked. In the long silence she could hear the relentless tick-tock of the antique grandfather clock in the hallway. Again, the palpitation began in his jaw.

"Yes. I would have liked that." He sighed. "But it wasn't in the cards. We tried."

"We?"

Again the palpitation.

"A collective pronoun," he said, smiling. "Often used as a euphemism, seems more modest." He was going to great pains to explain it. The eggplant had simply used it possessively, encapsulating them. Remington felt the further need to justify it. As if he had revealed something hidden, something he did not want revealed. Finally he said:

"Doesn't every mother want her son to be President?"

His foot was now beating a rhythm in the air. The palpitation continued, growing stronger as the declining light left deeper shadows on the planes of his face. Suddenly, he looked at his watch and got up.

"Another cocktail party," he said, offering the charming shy smile. "I'm caught in the Washington whirl."

She stood up awkwardly, still watching his face. Their flesh touched. His hand was strong and she gripped it hard, grasped it, as if the touch of it could transfer the information she sought. He was trying to disengage. She felt that, but continued to hold it.

"I hope you get your man," he said.

He walked her toward the door, gently nudging her elbow.

"If I can be of further help," he said, kissing her cheek. The kiss singed her flesh.

He closed the door behind her. What had she learned? she wondered; she was confused by the encounter. Something still nagged at her, uncontrollable, persistent. No! Not possible! *You women and your fucking intuition.* The eggplant's words echoed in her mind as she turned the ignition. The angry squeak of the tires as she pulled out reinforced the rebuke.

XXVIII

FROM ACROSS his desk the eggplant offered a tight thin smile. The meeting was scheduled in the department auditorium in ten minutes, but he had called them in, she suspected, for further reassurance. Jefferson stood beside her, his big black ham hands crossed awkwardly in front of him, feet astride, at parade rest. Like her, she was certain, his sense of anticipation was acute. Earlier he had opened his jacket and patted the Magnum, holstered beneath his right armpit.

"I want the first clear shot," he said.

If he shows, she thought. She had wrestled with this doubt for the past twenty-four hours. The pattern was irrevocable. It was the heart of her theory. Hadn't Remington agreed?

"If we're wrong, I've had it," the eggplant said. "And if I've had it, you're going to have it."

"They're in it upstairs, too," she said, feeling the bile rise in her throat.

"The bigshots always have a way of getting out of it," he sighed. "Anyway, we got our head. The ball is in our court." He put his elbow on the desk and cocked a finger at both of them. "I want this dude alive. You hear that, Jefferson?"

"You mean wait until he gets off his round?"

"It's only one shot," the eggplant said, lowering his voice.

"It's going to be a head wound, probably fatal," Fiona explained.

"I'm not saying that we deliberately let it happen."

"Then what are you saying?"

"I'm saying . . ." He was trying to keep his patience. "That . . . we get him alive. That's all I'm saying. The chances are he'll get his round off before he's spotted. That's what I'm saying." He waved his finger. "Of course, the only real evidence will be if he gets off his round."

"And blows some poor joker's head off," Jefferson snarled.

"You just keep that Magnum's fly buttoned." The eggplant's finger wiggled ominously. So he knew about that, Fiona thought. Maybe he wasn't quite the eggplant she imagined. Suddenly he softened. "Look, you got to trade off something. We want him alive to prove the other three killings. It makes sense. It's still just theory unless we sweat out a confession or work out a bona fide connection. We don't know if we'll find the weapons. The only sure thing is to keep the fucker alive."

"That means that some poor joker is going to die," Fiona said.

"Don't presuppose," the eggplant said with surprising gentleness. "I know," he whispered. A whiff of guilt mingled with her own. The scenario had to be played out. Perhaps that, too, was ordained. Someone had to die. There simply might be no alternative.

"We're going to have twenty people in plainclothes in all seven downtown theaters, with more than a hundred uniformed men in reserve. At least, the principal bases will be covered."

"What do they know?" Fiona asked.

"Only that we're after a screwball with a gun. A crazy."

"And how are they going to know that the crazy only has a single round? You want to take that responsibility?"

"Don't think I slept so good last night."

"Booth had two Colts on him. And a knife," Fiona said.

254

"I know."

"Nobody in their right mind wants to commit suicide. Even a cop."

"Maybe we should spell out the theory?"

"Absolutely not. It's not part of the deal. The upstairs boys don't want to look like horses asses if it blows up in our faces. It's one step at a time."

They were already late. The eggplant stood up and started out the door. In the squad room, he paused.

"Being a smartass has its drawbacks," he said, confronting her directly. She could see his agony. "It's just a job, FitzGerald. Just a fucking job."

The meeting broke up at six and the various teams fanned out to the theaters.

"Reminds me of Nam," Jefferson told her as they scurried for their cars. "Nothing worked then neither."

"Don't be such a pessimist."

A command post was set up in a room off the lower level of Ford's Theater, under a nest of pipes. Communications specialists had worked all day and the eggplant's voice rattled over the airwaves, staticy but clear enough. When they arrived at the post, the eggplant was already there. She was surprised to find Dr. Benton.

"You don't expect me to miss it, do you?"

He sat quietly in a folding chair, his arms crossed over his chest.

The theater managements had been alerted. Tickets to strategic seats were procured and plainclothesmen were stationed in various parts of the theaters. Because of their special position in the case, Fiona and Jefferson were given no specific assignment. They had agreed to roam, play it by ear, accessible to all theaters.

Fiona spotted Teddy standing in the shadows of the Presidential Box at Ford's, decorated on the outside with bunting and a portrait of George Washington, exactly as it had been at the time of Lincoln's death. The box, as a sign of respect, was never used, a memorial now. The theater itself had been rehabilitated a number of years ago and was operated as a museum and working theater under the sponsorship of the Department of the Interior.

Leaving Jefferson in the orchestra, she bounded up the stairs. Booth's route. The thought was disturbing. She saw Teddy, who was obviously assigned there.

"What's going down, Fi?"

"We're looking for a crazy."

"That I understand. It's the MO that's confusing."

"Let's hope it's all clear in a few hours."

She looked at her watch. It was nearly six. In another hour, the first patrons would be arriving. Standing in the box, near the rocking chair, authentically copied from the one Lincoln had actually sat in when he was shot, she sensed the historical connection and the span of dissolved time. He had sat in this place, living his last moments of consciousness. It chilled her blood.

When doubts flashed across her mind, she tried to reason them away. Would the killer strike at Ford's? It was the most authentic site. The performance was *The Fantasticks*, a light musical. Surely there would be moments of laughter. It was one of the points missed by the eggplant, and she activated her walkie-talkie to explain, as cryptically as she could, why each burst of laughter should be especially noted.

"Ten-four," the eggplant's voice crackled after his acknowledgment. Soon they would all get the message.

"Looks like you made a believer out of him, Fi," Teddy said. She detected a tinge of envy, the macho reaction.

"How are the kids?" she asked.

"I don't see them as much as I should." He seemed morose and bitter.

"Hang in there, Teddy," she said, bounding down the stairs. Again, she looked at her watch. Not yet. There was something that still had to be done.

"Do you think this will be the place?" Jefferson asked.

The Kennedy Center was doing a Noel Coward play, *Tonight at Eight-Thirty;* the National was doing *They're Playing Our Song* by Neil Simon; the Warner was doing a revival of

The Best Little Whorehouse in Texas. All comedies.

"This would be the most authentic." She looked at the straight-backed chairs ranged in a semicircle. Behind them, the stagehands were making last minute adjustments on the set. "Let's check out the other theaters."

Jumping into the car, they moved quickly through the traffic to the Warner Theater on Thirteenth Street, a converted movie house with a complicated array of box seats and balconies. They spent about fifteen minutes there, then proceeded across the street to the National.

"Who knows?" she whispered, surveying the faces of early arrivals. Was she looking for someone, a specific face? It nagged at her, inhibiting her concentration.

"Like playing Russian roulette," Jefferson said. "I still say Ford's." They left the National and jogged back to their car. Again, she looked at her watch. It was nearly seven. Crowds were beginning to form under the marquees.

She felt uncertain, confused, as if she were peering into the edges of a vast, impenetrable forest. The faces had a bland sameness, without any identifying features. Then, suddenly, a gesture emerged, a brief movement familiar in another context. She saw blondish, mustardy hair, a heroic profile, that vanished into the crowd.

Getting out of the car, she moved a few steps from the curb, briefly confronting an unfamiliar face. At that moment the image from all her intuitive meandering swept into the center of her focus. Remington! It came to her with all the explosive power of an epiphany. Remington! Could it be? She had bottled it up, banged shut the door to her intuition, in response to the eggplant's macho caveat. How dare they denature her instincts, she cried to herself, furious that she had joined in the conspiracy against her.

"A minute," she mimed to Jefferson, who watched her from inside the car. She entered an outdoor phone booth and dialed Remington's number. Breathing deep to calm herself, she listened to the rings, counting them out. After the fifth ring, she heard a woman's voice. It had a Spanish accent, Mrs. Ramirez.

"Mr. Remington, please." Her voice was tight, constricted.

"He's not at home," the woman said politely.

"Do you know where he is?" She felt her heartbeat accelerate. Her palms suddenly turned hot. There was a moment of hesitation.

"Sorry, no. Can I take a message?"

"Do you know where he went?"

"No."

"He doesn't tell you where he goes?"

She could hear the woman's breathing, the note of hesitation.

"I give him a message."

"I must know where he went."

"Out. He doesn't say. I take a message."

"To the theater. Did he say he went to the theater?"

"He don't say." There was a long pause. "I take a message."

Fiona hung up and dashed out to the car. At best, it had been a calculated risk. If her intuition was correct, she could have the blood of the victim on her hands. The thought gave her a cold chill.

"Who was that?" Jefferson asked, moving the car up Pennsylvania Avenue, past the rear of the White House, swinging left on Seventeenth Street.

"Personal," she snapped. He was silent for a moment.

"You don't go with that Congressman dude no more?"

"Mind your fucking business." She was instantly sorry. "You don't deserve that, Frank," she said.

"Say what?"

"You heard me."

"You called me Frank again. You're gettin' too familiar, Fiona." She hadn't realized he noticed such things.

They pulled up in front of the Eisenhower entrance to the Kennedy Center, pulled down the sun visor with the police shield, then walked through the tall glass doors. The red-carpeted foyer was filled with both tourists and theatergoers and they threaded quickly through the jostling crowds to the Grand Foyer, dominated by the huge tragic bust of Kennedy. The irony was not lost on her. Assassinations were a kind of theater of the absurd, and there was a bizarre appropriateness to Ford's and the Kennedy Center being memorials to martyred Presidents. She wondered why she hadn't seen it before. Mentally she rejected Warner's and the National as potential murder sites. The killer had too much of a sense of historic irony for that.

All of the Kennedy Center's four theaters, the Opera House, the Concert Hall, the Terrace Theater, as well as the Eisenhower, were in use that night. The Grand Plaza, with its massive chandeliers and huge expanse of red carpet, was crowded with patrons. Interspersed with the crowd were plainclothes cops, who nodded as they passed. They checked out each theater.

"The manpower's here," Jefferson said. "I hope it's enough. Hey, how do you guarantee we'll be at the right place at the right time?"

"I can't even guarantee that it's going to happen." Again, she resisted mentioning Remington.

They milled about in the Grand Foyer, watching the crowds converge. She searched each face. Nothing must slip by her. She remembered reading that Booth had left for the theater carrying a disguise, a beard, makeup. But he had used it after the killing, putting it on first at Dr. Mudd's house. It was maddening, trying to correlate details that were buried in historical fact and speculation nearly a hundred and twenty years ago.

And she could be dead wrong about Remington. It was simply that he had crossed her field of vision and was stuck in her frame of reference. Was it possible that her world had become so narrow? Then why did she persist in searching the crowd for him?

They had stationed themselves near the ticket taker stations at the Eisenhower, and when the line dwindled they stepped into the theater. Moving from vantage point to vantage point, she studied every face in every row. He wasn't in the balconies or the boxes. There were few bearded faces and those were quickly scanned and rejected.

When she was reasonably certain that he wasn't in the Eisenhower, she moved to the Concert Hall, repeating the process there. Then the Opera House and finally the Terrace Theater.

"I wish I knew what you were doing," Jefferson said, following her obediently. "You seem to be looking for someone in particular."

"I'm not sure."

Still, he followed her. They had checked the interior of the Warner and the National.

"You know something I don't?" he asked.

She looked at her watch. It was nearly nine. They drove quickly to the Ford's Theater where, once again, she checked the faces of the audience. Maybe he'll come in later, she decided. They went down to the command post where the eggplant was working the radio, barking orders, getting reports. He was wrapped in a haze of blue cigarette smoke. Dr. Benton still sat impassively, sipping coffee from a plastic cup.

"Everybody is in place," the eggplant said, looking at his watch. He got up and came over to Fiona.

"So far, nothing," he said, with a note of sarcasm.

"The time was 10:15 or thereabouts."

"He better not let us down," the eggplant warned.

"He won't."

The plainclothesmen on the scene reported the intermissions and she went upstairs with Jefferson to mix with the crowds. They seemed like all theater crowds she had ever seen, absorbed, anticipatory, some bored, others animated. She continued to search their faces.

"It's got to happen," she whispered to Jefferson.

"You never know what's in the head of a crazy."

"We know what's in this man's head."

She posted herself behind a red curtain to the left of the stage under an illuminated exit sign. Another plainclothesman stood there, surveying the crowd. Jefferson went to the opposite side of the stage to an identical exit. Through a slit in the curtain, she watched the crowd. The actors were involved in a song and dance number. Looking up, she could see the empty Presidential Box, the picture of Washington, the red, white and blue bunting. Just below it, she saw the curtain stir behind which Jefferson waited. Without actually seeing it, she knew he had drawn his Magnum.

Time seemed to crawl. At nine-forty-five, she went back to the command post. The eggplant's eyes lifted as she came in, then shifted to his watch.

"I've ordered them all to draw their guns, but keep them hidden," he whispered. "But I hope to hell they don't shoot." He shrugged. "Who knows with these trigger happy bastards?" She moved over to Dr. Benton.

"I'm scared," she whispered.

"So am I," he said, patting her back.

At five after ten, she walked up the stairs again and followed a corridor to her former position behind the curtain of the side exit. She nodded to her colleague beside her. In his hand, his gun was at the ready. Parting the curtain, she looked into the audience. A number of people stood along the back rail. Most of them were policemen. Again, she looked at her watch.

The music seemed to grow louder, keeping tempo with the maddening passage of time. Someone in the audience coughed.

Now, she screamed within herself. Now! The curtain across the auditorium stirred and suddenly she saw Jefferson's face and, below it, the muzzle of the Magnum. The actors sang, their shoes tapping on the stage. She waited a few minutes more and whispered into the radio.

"Anything?"

"Nothing."

Running back into the corridor, she came down to the command post again. The eggplant's eyes flickered gloomily.

"All fucking clear," he said.

"Give it time."

"That I've got," he said, his lips curling in a snarl.

"And the Kennedy Center?"

"Nothing."

By then it was 10:45. A voice sputtered over the radio.

"The show's breaking."

A roll of applause exploded above them and soon they heard shuffling feet and the clatter of voices and footsteps coming down the stairs.

"Nothing anywhere," the eggplant said, rubbing his eyes. Jefferson came up behind her.

"Anything?" He didn't wait for a response. "Sheet."

"Maybe we scared him off," Fiona said. Her insides seemed to have shifted position. She felt her pulse beating in her neck.

The eggplant said nothing, lighting a cigarette, inhaling. The smoke seemed to stay in his lungs forever. Finally, it emerged through clenched teeth.

"I bought it. I put my balls in your hands."

"I was sure," Fiona managed to say. "Everybody bought it."

"Yeah. But I'm the one that sold it."

A lieutenant came up.

"Wrap the fucker," the eggplant said. The lieutenant spoke into the radio, ordering the operation to cease. Technicians began to dismantle the equipment.

"I still say . . ." Fiona began, but the eggplant's look caught her short.

"I never did care what you thought. Fucking cunts in the police. Never could work. Never will work." He began to pace the room. "So I'm the department asshole."

Offering protestations now, she realized, would be futile. Turning away, she walked upstairs. There was a pay telephone against the wall and she dialed Remington's number again. Maybe she had rattled him. Yet her suspicion was obsessive, mindless. Her imagination had run away with her.

His voice was on the phone after two rings, firm, oozing resonant charm.

"Hello."

She did not respond, hanging up, suddenly feeling physically spent, emotionally done in. She went to the ladies' room and, squatting in front of a toilet, began to throw up.

XXIX

W HEN SHE awoke, she was wrapped in a sheet like a
mummy. Vague bits of memory, like a splintered mirror, rose in her mind, tormenting her. It was still night, pitch
black. Being locked in the wound sheet triggered a sense of
panic, awakening her from what must have been a nightmare.
Her pores had opened like floodgates and the sheet was satu-
rated with perspiration.

In disjointed fits her memory returned, the splintered bits
reforming to record the reflection of her humiliation. Jefferson
had driven her home, unable to penetrate her silence. His voice
had persisted. There was an effort at reassurance but, in the end,
she got out of the car and, without looking back, found herself
in her book-strewn apartment.

The rooms closed in on her. Expectations had driven her and
now that they had slipped away, nothing was left but a terrible
emptiness. For a long time she had sat slumped on her couch,
pasteboard covers of books denting her flesh, deliberately suffering her discomfort as a punishment for her self-righteous, self-
indulgent obsession. What she needed now was arms, muscled
haired arms, to envelop her, a hard male-smelling body to caress

her, reconstitute her shattered ego, a male pistoning to ram away reality, and give her back her sense of womanhood. She needed that flame of passion to warm her now. She cursed the trumped-up ideal that had disconnected her from Bruce. Loneliness, the parched infinity of emptiness, was more offensive, more debilitating than her high-minded ideas of independence. Everybody must act in their own interest. People manipulated others, according to their passions and compulsions.

"Shit," she cried into the unforgiving darkness. It was a sin against nature, her nature, not to demand the comforting touch of a male. She needed her body to be probed and searched and pleasured, her cheeks licked clean of tears, the burdens lifted, the afflictions soothed. It was no fucking fun coming home to nothing. Not after tonight.

Reaching for the telephone, she dialed his number. It rang interminably. Finally a hoarse voice cleared itself, croaking a reluctant greeting.

"Bruce."

Behind his voice, she sensed agitated breathing, a hurried whisper. A woman's bleat of annoyance. Then silence. He must have covered the mouthpiece with his hand.

"Fiona." She pictured the phone on its long wire carried to the privacy of the bathroom. His whisper gave it away. "Is there anything wrong?"

"Yes."

Another pause.

"Can it wait until morning?" he asked. The words came in a harried whisper.

Demand him, she goaded. But the image assaulted her. In the bed, their bed, the other female squinted into the darkness, waiting while his other life deflected his interest. If it could wait, why sound this alarm in the night? "Yes," she said, hanging up.

She dialed her parents' number, but quickly hung up before the ring. They would be startled out of their sleep. Cruel work. Besides, they had long ago ceased to offer the needed solace, two aging people with their own pallid, dead dreams.

The depression rolled over her like lava, penetrating her

flesh, burrowing into her bones. She had been so certain. Her doubts had been a deliberate hedge, a facade, unreliably constructed, a false protection. Her reason had been toyed with, like a woman's virtue in another age. It was that man. That man. His smug charm had oozed out of him like hog's sweat.

Humiliation doesn't come easy to Irish blood, someone had said once to her in childhood. They were always explaining away their stubborn pride and, in the end, it defeated them. Where in the name of hell did her brash certainty come from? This was no logical, ordered mind concocting fantasies of death, resurrecting history like some cosmic puppeteer. These events were being perpetrated by an aberrant mind, twisted, deluded by God knew what dark, tortuous motives, out of the slime of thwarted ambitions.

It was him. I know it is him!

But saying it did nothing to soothe her. Finally, she got up and paced the apartment, yielding to another dark prompting of her Irish blood, alcohol. But even that eluded her. There was less than a quarter bottle of Scotch left, and she nipped at it until it was gone.

Groping through the darkness, she lay supine on her bed, eyes open, determined to stare down the demons. But her mind would not cool, as she rehashed the material that had crowded into her brain. Assailed suddenly by an overwhelming urge to call Remington, she reached for the phone, partially dialed, then hung up. Her courage had failed her, and she quickly turned the phone button to secretarial.

She was offended, not only by the humiliation of defeat, but by the fact that she had implicated others in her fantasy. Somehow, she felt, they had fallen victim to her intensity, her obsession.

Yet, despite everything, the idea persisted. Someone out there was still doomed, whatever the break in sequence. Maybe she should make a clean breast of her suspicions, she thought, then quickly rejected the idea. Her credibility was gone. The eggplant would treat her, from now on, as a pariah.

The ring of the doorbell stabbed itself into the gloom and she quickly unrolled herself and put on her robe. Through the peephole she saw Jefferson's gleaming black face, and opened the door. He seemed wan in the cloudy post-dawn light.

"Better get dressed. They want us downtown."

His skin looked like slate and the network of veins in his eyes had multiplied since last night.

"What is it?"

"Trouble."

She dared not react, as if the slightest bark out of him would make her break in two. Dressing quickly, she attempted to hide the dark circles under her eyes and erase the haunted look that peered back at her in the mirror.

Beside her in the car, Jefferson was sullen, unapproachable.

"We should have left it alone."

It was all he cared to say. For a big man, the sense of defeat seemed incongruous, but the boy's fear filtered through the macho mask.

Chief Howard sat behind his big ornate desk, lips tight, dark eyes glaring behind horn-rimmed glasses. He was not a tall man, but behind his desk he seemed large, awesome. Cold silence greeted them as the chief pointed to two chairs in front of his desk. Dr. Benton was already seated. On another chair against the wall, slumped like a broken doll, the eggplant sat. Rage seemed to boil out of him, polluting the air.

"The door," the chief barked. The eggplant, reacting like a robot, got up and closed it. The chief tapped his fingers on the desk nervously, then picked up a pencil and broke it in half, flinging the remains into an ashtray.

"Do you know what this week is?" he shouted, his eyes shifting to the four frightened faces. Fiona searched her mind, confused by the man's rage. She needn't have been. The chief answered his own question.

"Easter week. The biggest tourist week of the year. There are more than a million visitors in town. To the business people, that is a bonanza. Am I correct?"

Fiona heard mumbling beside her. Turning toward the eggplant, she could understand his fear of the chief. "Am I?" he roared. Again, the question was rhetorical. He was working himself into a lather. Jefferson and Dr. Benton remained silent, perhaps understanding the peculiarities of ethnic rage.

"An hour ago." He looked at his watch. "An hour ago, I got a call from the *Washington Post*. Not just a flunky reporter. Himself, Bradlee. He asks me this question: Is it true that there is a psychopathic killer on the loose in this town bent on gunning down innocent people? He didn't wait for an answer. And did you not try to apprehend him last night in the theater, seven theaters to be exact?" His lips trembled and his nostrils quivered as he confronted Fiona.

"Now how would I answer that question, little lady?"

I'm not your little lady, she wanted to scream out at him. Instead, she bit her lip.

"I . . ." He punched himself in the chest ". . . approved last night's operation, which netted a big fat zero. So how do I answer that question, bearing in mind that it is Easter week and there are one million tourists in the city and this is the *Washington Post*, perfectly capable of scaring the shit out of any human being within spitting distance?"

Jefferson lowered his eyes. The eggplant did not move.

"Tell him the truth," Fiona said, her voice cracking.

"The truth." The chief nodded. "That two hundred cops were massed in town seeking a psychopathic killer who may be tied to four random killings? That three of the killings took place in or near public buildings? That one of the victims was a cop? That we've acted on some half-baked hypothesis having to do with the killer's acting out previous assassinations of our Presidents? That's front page stuff. Juicy. And how do you think we geniuses at MPD will look, especially since this fourteen-karat prick tried to cover up the fact that the first two killings were related, and he had deliberately tried to pin it on some spic country terrorists?" He shook his head sadly. The eggplant looked contrite. It was obvious that he had confessed, or it had been wrung out of him, when he sold the chief last night's caper.

"Do you think MPD, this great nest of incompetent nigger cops, would come out good in the press if I told Bradlee the truth?"

"We've gone through that, chief," the eggplant said. Fiona's heart went out to him. The poor sad bastard had tried, had really tried. She vowed tentatively never to call him the eggplant again.

"So what do you think I told him?" the chief said, dismissing the ex-eggplant with a contemptuous squint. A film of sweat had popped out on his upper lip. "I told him . . ." He looked at his watch again. "Over an hour ago, I told him that I would call him in two hours with the facts, the absolute facts. Now I know the paper's self-interest is involved as well and he wouldn't do anything to hurt their damned advertising, but if I said that to him, he would have my ass. It could be that he, too, will see the light and not wish to shake up the tourists, or hurt the night-out business."

Fiona was having trouble determining his thrust. Then the chief's eyes bored in on her alone.

"I want to tell him that we reacted last night to an anonymous tip. I do not want to tell him that it was a mission cooked up by our own people, responding to intelligence developed internally. In other words, until we have a killer, I want to tell a little white lie and keep a publicity avalanche from coming down on my head. Our head." He took a deep breath and leaned back in his chair. *"Kapish?"* His eyes rested on each one in turn. "I will not tell him about this presidential assassination stuff." He banged the desk with the flat of his hand.

"Can I count on this little circle to keep their lips zippered?" He drew in his breath. "Not a Watergate here. No cover-up necessary. We don't want to impede our investigation and we don't want the business community to get upset, or Congress, or the mayor. See, it becomes an ecological problem. Besides," he looked at Fiona, "your theory is out to lunch now that your loony missed his date with destiny. *Nestpa?"*

"Well, I . . ."

"I'm glad you agree, Officer FitzGerald."

He turned to the eggplant.

"I want this investigation to proceed with dispatch. I want this killer."

Fiona, Jefferson and Dr. Benton were dismissed together

while the eggplant stayed behind. As soon as they were far from his office, Fiona turned to them.

"My theory is correct. Something went wrong. I'm not sure what."

"Leave it alone," Dr. Benton said. "Why belabor the obvious? They did their dance of self-defense."

"And now they're going to sit on it."

"Not necessarily," Fiona said.

They looked at her and shook their heads together.

"I don't want to hear it," Jefferson said.

"Leave it alone, Fiona," Dr. Benton said. "You're a cop in a bureaucracy. The game is to make the guy ahead of you look good. Look. We all gave it our best. All of us. Even them in there."

"But I think I know . . ."

He lifted his hand, palm outward, like a traffic cop. It was the signal to stop.

"Just try. Cold turkey. Later, maybe, you can confront it. Not now."

She tried to follow his advice. She took the next three days off. She cleaned her apartment, brought most of the books back to the libraries. Then she spent long hours in the police gym, working herself into a lather. She took long walks along the river, hired a bicycle and pumped for miles on the tow path. She visited Jefferson's monument and caught the last lingering gasps of the cherry blossoms. She toured the Smithsonian, went to the Mint, joined the endless line of tourists on the FBI tour.

She tried. She really tried, but she could not escape. Leave it alone, Fiona. Leave it alone, Fiona. It became a litany, and finally it grew meaningless with repetition. Her secretarial service picked up Bruce's call, but she declined to call him back. That was over irrevocably. A need demanded to be filled at the time of its greatest urgency. For her, that had been her lowest point. Never again, she promised, will I allow myself that kind of vulnerability.

Unfortunately, she discovered, loneliness was corrosive and without a human support system, her will cracked and by the third day she was back at her research. She reviewed her findings. The accuracy of the three previous episodes foreshadowed what must come next. She went back to the library and pored over whatever she could find on the criminally insane. Almost always the pattern was irrevocable in mass killers. They perpetrated murders with exactly the same MO in spaced intervals, responding to some inner need. A sexual psychopath attacked women only, mutilated them, performed sex on their corpses, but always it was the same. A killer in Atlanta attacked and killed only black children.

As for Remington—if, indeed, he was the killer—the investigation required a massive commitment of time and effort to determine where, exactly, he was at the time of each previous killing. Surveillance had to be established around the clock. If she approached them now, they would think she was crazy. She could, of course, do it herself, but that required total immersion. One person was not enough. And if she was wrong, he could scream police harassment which wouldn't sit too well upstairs. Besides, it was still only a hunch, the hated intuition, and it annoyed her to be afflicted with it.

On Friday, she got into bed early and turned on the radio, half-listening as her mind tried to cool itself down. Even her excitement at what she considered her new theories on the Kennedy killing was losing its power. It was all theories, unprovable, although, she conceded, there would still be mileage in it for years to come. Especially for a politician. The Lincoln killing raised questions for more than a hundred years. Hadn't Carter pardoned Samuel Mudd who had innocently set Booth's leg? One could spend a lifetime on the research.

She listened to a clergyman give a mini-sermon on the meaning of Good Friday. Then came the news. The President was going to see the Coward play. It was nearly nine and she began to drowse, succumbing finally. Her mind relaxed.

Suddenly, as if her brain had been jolted with a bolt of electricity, she sat up in bed, her mind racing. Reaching for the telephone, she dialed Jefferson's number.

"You're home?" she gasped, as she heard his voice. "I have it. I have it."

"What?"

"Proof positive. Good Friday. It was Good Friday."

"What the hell . . ."

"Just trust me, Frank. Trust me. Lincoln was killed on Good Friday."

"Say what?"

"Not now, Frank."

"Sheet."

"The President. I just heard it on the radio. He's gone to the theater tonight. The Kennedy Center."

She turned on the light and looked at the time. It was nine-fifteen.

"Pick me up in fifteen minutes."

She bounded out of bed and jumped into her clothes. Before putting on her holster, she checked the cylinder. As she put on her jacket, she stopped and reaching again for the phone, dialed Remington's number.

The Spanish lady answered.

"Where is he?"

There was no effort at politeness, no preliminaries.

"He has gone to the theater."

She hung up quickly.

XXX

H E HAD floated through the last three days like a cork on a river's tide, certain that the relentless flow would be inexorable and that, at the appropriate moment, there he would be, bobbing in open sea. Not a doubt assailed his calm. Even the policewoman's visit had left him unshaken. Indeed, he had actually enjoyed the cryptic duel. When the sun rose and set on April fourteenth, he merely refocused his expectations, and when the phone intruded on the Good Friday calm, he knew even before he picked up the instrument that the moment had arrived.

It was his friend at the Kennedy Center. There was, he knew, nothing really sinister or suspicious in his request. By now, the theater management had been alerted and the elaborate preparation required for a presidential movement was in operation. The man was, after all, only going to the theater. He had explained to his friend that he was intent on putting together a theater party on the day of the President's attendance. A party. Wasn't that the principal business of Thaddeus Remington III, the capital's most illustrious host, the multi-millionaire political contributor, friend to the powerful?

272

Friday was the ideal day. Most of Washington's social schedule, the state dinners, the embassy parties, the six to eights, all the demanding little entertainments of the capital's official life, were scheduled Tuesdays through Thursdays. The weekends were for the plebians. On those days, the elite rested.

There were eight chairs in the box in two rows, four abreast, and he planned to fill seven of them with suitable personalities, whose presence would continue to agitate in the wake of his cataclysmic act for years to come. Perhaps a millenium. When the Soviet ambassador, now dean of the diplomatic corps, accepted the evening's outing, he knew that his little party would be a resounding success.

Had he made it sound as if he were part of the President's party? They would, after all, be occupying the box directly next to him. The penultimate symbol of power was always a seductive inducement. Wasn't he the flame they all danced around and wasn't the Soviet ambassador symbolic of the other superpower? He relished the conspiratorial theories that such nearness would suggest. Ambassadors always reacted with an eye on their home governments. Look, the Soviet ambassador would be telling his Politburo leaders, I am in the box next to the President. See what my connections are to the new American leader. Proximity, as they well knew in the Soviet Union, was a tangible measure of power.

It was the same reason that induced the Saudi Arabian ambassador and his lovely wife to attend, another ingredient for his witch's brew. Weren't they the holder of the keys to the American energy prison? Certainly, the presence of the principal representative of such an aberrant power would spice the brew with a perpetual aftertaste. Naturally, the Saudi accepted, despite the fact that his country did not have diplomatic relations with the Soviets. The event, after all, was of too special a nature to be missed. Besides, the Arab mind relished symbols.

To complete the seven, a number charged with its own mystique, he invited Bruce Rosen and, in a touch of irony that induced a giggle at the moment of its conception, Louise Padgett. She would recall a connection with that other assassination and Bruce, poor Bruce, would provide a line with another bizarre event in the Remington home. It would not take much digging to find a connection between Bruce and his former mistress, that suspicious detective lady.

Everything would connect, assuring the world of a momentous explosion that would propel his name to instant immortality, beyond all the others that went before him and sending out the ultimate message. Denying him, Remington, the Presidency was, of course, part of the grand design, set in motion at the beginning of his life, at the moment of conception in his mother's womb.

It was all there to be savored, a gigantic feast, foreshadowed by the God-driven Guiteau, the anarchist Czolgosz, the twisted, impotent Oswald and the egocentric, willful Wilkes, to whom honor must be given for the final replication. It was in Wilkes that the force began its relentless march, illustrating its manipulative genius and perfection.

The foreshadowing was pristine. A child could have seen it. But it had to be seen whole, in one flash. In the box with Lincoln, a wife who went mad, the woman later murdered by her husband, he, too, ending his days in an institution. Four ciphers brought together in one ill-starred night, destined for either murderous death or madness. Did this not transcend fate?

And Wilkes, cornered in a barn ten days later, felled by an impossible shot alleged to have come from a man, Boston Corbett, who later castrated himself, and after his appointment as doorkeeper of the Kansas state legislature, closed all the doors and with two revolvers began to fire away at the members. Neither Corbett's gun nor Wilkes's were ever examined to determine who fired the fatal shot. Years later, the gun that Jack Ruby used to shoot Oswald was also never examined, the assumption being that millions had seen him do the deed and, therefore, it was not necessary to offer absolute proof. Little details meant to perpetrate mysteries. His would last the longest of all.

Even those who played minor roles in the Lincoln drama showed the hand of the cosmic genius. The two men who barred the daughter of one of the alleged conspirators, Mrs. Surratt, from the White House to plead a pardon for her mother, a senator and a customs collector, were both killed by their own hands within eight months of the execution.

And so it went. Connections! On the day Lincoln was shot, a crowd of fifty thousand armed with knives, guns and sticks were on the verge of smashing the office of Southern sympathizers when one man climbed on a platform and calmed the crowd. He was General James Garfield. An endless train of odd happenings, hints, clues to the transcendent power.

There were the missing pages of Booth's diary, implicated through a coded book found nearly a century later in a secondhand bookstore, that accused Secretary of War Stanton of having masterminded the Lincoln assassination; these connected as well to Nixon's Watergate tapes. Nixon, who missed by a hair being elected in 1960, was accused of excising eighteen and a half minutes of damning tapes. How many pages were missing from Booth's diary? Eighteen!

The Kennedy matter, too, was an endless trail of odd signs that defied explanation. An autopsy without a forensic surgeon, an alleged second gun, the mystery of Jack Ruby. Oswald's denial. An avalanche of theories that would never be fully proven, leaving the lingering doubts forever.

They would be nothing compared with what he would leave them. Nothing. Because he was aware of the power within him. Every tissue, every cell, every nerve end had been dedicated to this one supreme moment.

Hadn't he tested and retested the credibility of his role, the linkage to a divine power that mocked any speculation that the mind of ordinary mortals could devise?

"You must stay tonight," he told Mrs. Ramirez, whose pattern was to visit her daughter every Friday night at her home in Arlington. He wanted to be sure his house was in order when they came to inspect it. Someday it would be a museum. He spent the day arranging the weapons he had used during the three previous episodes in his gun cases and carefully labeled the clothes he had worn.

That finished, he picked up the letter he had prepared for the *Post*. He would mail it himself. Wilkes had given his letter to a fellow actor who later destroyed it, although he had read it first and reconstructed it for the investigators. He went to the post office where he paid the clerk extra for the overnight service.

"Will it get there tomorrow for sure?"

"We guarantee it."

He smiled at the black woman who stamped the letter and passed along his change, oblivious to the role she would soon play. Everything, every detail, every imagined nuance would be analyzed and reanalyzed. In this age of technical miracles, there would not be a detail that would escape the repetitive scrutiny of an army of investigators, legions of historians. His grave, in that spot next to his mother's in the little cemetery on Nob Hill, would be a shrine to the man who warned the world of the fragile vulnerability of the Presidency and the need to elect the best, the very best, to fulfill the solemn task. As he might have been.

He held the brass Derringer in the palm of his hand, reviewed the way he had loaded it, the insertion of the percussion cap, the tamping of the powder, the wadding and finally the ball. Laying it carefully aside, he assembled the other artifacts that he would carry with him, essential symbols of comparison; the false beard, the makeup pencil, the gimlet, the Sheffield knife. Wilkes had carried two Colts as well, but he had needed them for his planned escape. He would have no need of them.

He had instructed his male guests to wear black tie, which meant gowns for the ladies, implying an after-theater social event. The idea amused him. It was so in keeping with his life style and certain to add elegant spice to the historical details.

After shaving carefully, he showered, lingering in the steaming water, cleansing every orifice. If he did not survive the evening, he wanted to present them with a well-cleansed and groomed corpse. In his bedroom, he watched his movements in mirrors, his flesh reflected in an aura of pink health. It was his mother's flesh remembered as he had seen her in her full womanly glory. Those parts of him in the mirrors that did not reveal his sex, offered a reminder of days past, the curve of a buttock, the patch of a shoulder, the curly beginnings of his auburn pubic hair. Hers! His blood surged and he felt the old excitement as he watched that part of him twitch to life.

"One more time, mama." He felt her tousled delicate hair brush him there, her soft lips caress the ivory hardness. It came quickly, the joyous elixir of their consummated passion. I am here, my son, my man, her voice said.

After dressing, he added the final touch, an evening cape with red silk lining.

Before he left, he walked through the rooms of his house. Lovingly, he touched his scrimshaw, his marine artifacts, his exhibits of presidential memorabilia. If a picture seemed angled, he straightened it, an object out of place, he put it where it was supposed to be. Everything must be in its proper place. So it would be, for all time, beyond the memory of living man.

"What time you come home, Señor Remington?" Mrs. Ramirez asked as he pushed open the front door.

"Late." He paused. He had rarely informed her where he was going, a private fetish. Servants need know of no life beyond the household. Tonight, he decided to violate the caveat, perhaps giving her a greater role in the event, a parting gift.

"You are a good woman, Mrs. Ramirez," he said, smiling. He reached out to touch her arm, confusing her. Then he said:

"I am going to the theater."

He closed the door behind him and stepped into the crisp April evening. Breathing deeply, he savored the odors of the awakening earth, noting that the tulips along the driveway were showing their first delicate blooms.

He arrived early, stationing himself at the ticket taker's stand of the Eisenhower Theater, which gave him a high vantage over the broad expanse of the Grand Foyer, overlooked by the sad heroic sculpted head of the martyred President. Symbols were everywhere. One need only to use one's eyes.

The Saudis arrived first, she elegant in the latest Paris fashions, he appropriately mysterious with his goatee, dark face, and a long Semitic nose over which his brown curious eyes observed a lugubrious world. Remington kissed the ambassador's wife on both cheeks and shook the ambassador's hand.

"I hope you enjoy it," he said.

"I love Coward," his chic wife smiled.

277

Small talk, he thought, that soon would be immortalized. The Soviet ambassador's big lumbering figure strode into view, his chubby, dumpy wife beside him. He wore his usual jolly smile and shook hands all around. Diplomats were adept at dissembling, and he could detect behind the eyes of the two ambassadors the guarded suspicion that lay masked and cunning behind their good humor. Nothing among diplomats in Washington was purely social. He was sure they were wondering why Remington had gathered them together, an unlikely and very odd group.

"We will have much fun," the Soviet ambassador boomed. "Although I don't know this Noel Coward." His wife smiled sheepishly. Her English was not good and she remained silent as the ambassadors chatted amiably.

"That I absolutely guarantee," Remington said as his eyes searched the growing crowd. He had asked Bruce to pick up Louise. As expected, Bruce had not protested. His docility had been bought and paid for. He saw him now, ambling forward in the crowd, Louise beside him. As he came closer, Remington could see his discomfort. As a politician, he liked the idea of the company and the proximity to the President, but the escort chosen for him was decidedly not to his taste.

He kissed Louise, who looked surprisingly fresh and well groomed, a marked contrast to their last meeting.

"It was wonderful, Tad," she whispered. "Your inviting me. I'm so embarrassed. Your invitation tonight is like a . . ." she faltered and he was afraid she was about to burst into tears of gratitude. But she held on gamely. ". . . a resurrection."

He patted her arm.

"I'm just happy it turned out all right," he said.

"You don't know what it means to me . . ." He interrupted her to nod toward Bruce, who was vigorously shaking hands with the two ambassadors. Obviously, the ambiance and the prospects of sitting in the box next to the President had placated him and he was now beaming.

"Well, I did my duty," he said. "Although I don't for the life of me know why you invited her."

"I thought it would be a nice gesture."

"After what she did."

Remington led them up the red-carpeted stairs, to the wide vestibule which led to the horseshoe of box seats. Earlier, he had recognized the unmistakable signs of the Secret Service, their tiny microphones planted in their ears, the color-coded lapel buttons, their unsmiling faces and hawklike darting eyes. As they passed through the vestibule, they attracted hardly a glance from the guardians of the President. As if to further defy them, he put a hand in his pocket and caressed the Derringer.

In the box, he seated the two ambassadors and their wives in the front seats, while Bruce and himself, with Louise between them, brought up the rear. Beside him was the President's box, still empty, although a Secret Service man stood at the entrance. He could see others behind him as well. Below in the orchestra, other men were already at their posts, watching the audience as it slowly milled about, filling the auditorium.

"He's late," Bruce whispered as the theater lights dimmed.

"A precaution," Remington whispered back. The dimmed houselights filled the theater with hushed anticipation. The curtain rose. At that moment, a stirring began in the box next to them and he could see the President, his wife, and others in their party take their seats. The President took his seat to the right of the others, nearer to Remington. He began calculating the position that would give him the clearest shot to the back of the man's head.

The President turned and saw the distinguished group sitting next to him. He seemed surprised and mimed a greeting, flashing his broad ingratiating smile. Turning slightly, he saw Remington over his shoulder and waved a special greeting.

Again, Remington put his hand in his pocket and caressed the Derringer. He looked at his wristwatch. There was time. More than two hours. He could relax, watch the show, enjoy the wit and sophisticated Coward dialogue.

A wave of laughter passed through the theater. He could hear the President's warm throaty guffaws and see his sidelong glances as he beckoned those beside him to join in the fun.

"He's having a ball," Louise whispered. "Just like Jack." Like her, the people in his party were amusing themselves more with the President's reaction than with the play itself. Below, people who sensed the presence of the President had begun to look up, signaling their neighbors with a jab in the arm and pointing.

He could, of course, do it now. His hand reached again for the Derringer. No, he decided. It would be wrong to break the rhythm of the replicated act. Good Friday. Ten-fifteen. The moment would come in good time.

When the lights went up again, a wave of applause rippled through the theater, acknowledging the President's presence. He and his wife stood up and waved. Many in the audience below simply stood in the aisles and gaped while others made for the rear of the theater and the Grand Foyer.

The President turned toward them, leaning over into their box, and shook hands with the ambassadors.

"I didn't know you Russians had such a sense of humor," he said to the Soviet.

"That is our strongest suit," the ambassador replied.

"I'm happy to see you enjoying yourself, Mr. President," the Saudi ambassador said.

"We former colonists still eat up the stuff from the mother country," the President said. He turned to Remington and put out his hand.

"Good seeing you again, Tad," he said, offering his most sincere boyish smile. Remington gripped the President's hand. He had been toying with the Derringer in his pocket. All he had to do was to take it out, point and pull the trigger. It would all be over in a split second.

"They love to see you out, Mr. President," Remington said. The President laughed, leaned over to him, and whispered:

"It's like getting out of stir."

"That doesn't seem to stop people from wanting to get in," Remington said. Bruce, trying hard to listen, chuckled. "Like him," Remington pointed.

Bruce blushed and Louise giggled nervously. Then the President turned back to his group and chatted until the lights dimmed again. Remington looked at his watch. It was 9:45. The audience settled down.

Remington leaned over and whispered loud enough so that all in the front row of the box could hear.

"I saw this recently at the White House." He pointed. "So did he."

The curtain went up. The actors began to deliver their lines. Again, he put his hand inside his pocket, felt the cool metal, and gripped the handle, his finger touching the trigger. He would not cock it until he removed it from his pocket. Again he looked at his watch. Time was moving inexorably now. There was nothing to hold him back, only the replication of the exact moment. It would be forever engraved in the minds of men. The connection would be unmistakable. With his left hand, he felt for the knife tucked in his belt. He doubted that it would ever be used as Wilkes had used it on Major Rathbone.

His concentration was interrupted by activity in the President's box, a hurried whisper, a movement of chairs. Someone had bent over the President. There was shuffling of feet, bodies moving. His hand tightened over the Derringer. A flash of panic assaulted him as he saw the President and his wife stand, their seats taken by two men. He started to withdraw the Derringer. In a moment he knew why. The President did not leave his box, he had merely shifted chairs and was now sitting within touching distance of him. He resisted the impulse to reach out and touch the man's arm, clamping his right hand more tightly around the Derringer.

Ignoring the spectacle on the stage, he listened with all the intensity he could muster. Was it the man's heartbeat he could hear, the relentless tick of the life force, flooding him with energy and being? The sound seemed to draw him into the man's body, his own substance slithering through the man's pores, pulsating now with the same rhythms. Surely, he cried within himself, this is the ultimate validation, the final truth. He was the President.

A trill of laughter passed through the theater, recalling the lines of the play. Piggie, Mr. and Mrs. Wadhurst, absurd names, no less absurd than Mrs. Mountchessington or Asa Trenchard from *Our American Cousin.* He looked at his watch. A shiver of pleasure passed through him; the denouement, so irresistibly conclusive that he could not resist an exclamation.

"What?" Louise asked.

He did not answer. "How's your daughter?" The words crackled from the stage.

His hand brought out the Derringer, his thumb put the pressure on the cocking device.

He stood up. In another moment . . . immortality.

XXXI

JEFFERSON'S HUGE body sat propped forward, his body angled toward the windshield, his big hands manipulating the wheel. The car moved in gasps, bursts of sudden speed and abrupt stops as it snaked through traffic heading south.

Bracing herself with the handstrap, her feet pushing against the slope of the car, Fiona tried to ignore the near misses and dangerous turns. He was taking chances for which the car was not built. But her anxiety propelled her courage. It was necessary. It was up to destiny to decide.

Had the split second of revelation come too late? It gnawed at her, despite the consuming agitation. She looked at her watch. It was three minutes to ten when the car literally jumped through the traffic at Fourth Street, ignoring a light, swerving to avoid the traffic's crosscurrents. Behind them, they heard the grating squeak of tire on asphalt.

Their reactions had been instinctive and his car was in front of her apartment as she dashed forward, hastily dressed, still wiping the cream off her face with the sleeve of her jacket. He was tireless and his beer breath filled the car with its sour stench.

Both knew that their actions were beyond consequence, raw intelligent energy reacting by rote.

"Time?" Jefferson shouted, as they sped past the Tidal Basin. "Ten-oh-one," she fired back.

"Fuck."

Through the thicket of self-disgust, her mind groped for a plan. There was little time for explanations. "Just trust me," she would shout at them. The chief's voice roared back its answer: "Trust you?" Confronting the Secret Service was awesome in itself. They always seemed so dead certain, so arrogant in their sureness.

"I won't think about it," she said, her voice a croak.

"What?"

She looked at her watch again. The car swung past the Lincoln Memorial, offering a fleeting glimpse of an unwanted irony. The watch's face had blurred.

"There's an entrance along Rock Creek Parkway."

He slowed as he saw the wooden guardrail, but the hesitation was temporary.

"Ease it. Don't crash it," she cautioned, her mind recognizing the reality. The Secret Service would crowd in on them, misunderstanding. He obeyed and the car reacted, jostling them, as it decelerated. The brief shake-up sharpened her, like a strong hand quieting a hysteric. Her mind cooled, splitting her intellect from her emotions. A wrong move could trigger a wrong reaction. Was it possible in their state to be credible? Deliberately, she wiped her face and smoothed her hair. We mustn't look like madmen.

The car reached the outer island in front of the Kennedy Center, directly across from the Eisenhower Theater entrance. Jefferson was reaching for his Magnum.

"Don't draw," she barked, her hands reaching for her own piece, feeling the cool leather of the holster.

They ran across the island, through the tall glass doors, slowing abruptly as they saw an iron-jawed Secret Serviceman react quickly, blocking their way. She looked at her watch. Ten-ten.

Jefferson's oncoming menacing black face triggered a quick response by the white Secret Service agent. His fingers flicked toward his belt. She flashed her badge and ID

"MPD," she cried. The badge and ID trembled in her hand. "In five minutes, someone is going to shoot the President."

His eyes darted from face to face, evaluating them. He was wasting precious time. His fingers groped for his holster.

"No time for that," she shouted. Her knee lashed out, crashing into his groin. Doubling up, he sank quickly, and they dashed forward, slipping through a side door that she knew led to the corridor outside the auditorium, used primarily for an exit.

In the corridor they hesitated.

"You bad, mama." His eyes searched hers. It was her show, her judgment. Again she looked at her watch. The second hand was relentless. What she wanted was for time to freeze. Her stomach lurched. She berated her lack of insight. Damn! How had she missed it? It had been there all the time. Jefferson looked at her helplessly, waiting, his Magnum drawn. The exit door was closed, perhaps locked. A Secret Serviceman surely was posted inside. Alert eyes were watching. They should have run up the balcony stairs to the box seat vestibule.

Her mind calmed again. Remington would be up there, in point blank range, the Derringer cocked, his finger on the trigger. For him, confusion would be an asset.

"The President's box?" she whispered.

Jefferson nodded.

"Just react," she pleaded. "I know he's there."

"I'm with you, mama."

She heard a wave of laughter. "Don't think," she begged herself, pushing open the door to the orchestra. In the sliver of light, she caught a peripheral glimpse of a Secret Serviceman's startled face. Jefferson, like a big silent cat, bounded past her, moving up the aisle, the Magnum balanced in both hands. Another wave of laughter exploded; her eye, in a swift miracle of magnified vision, saw him move, a slow motion danse macabre. She saw the President's head, unmistakable even in the shadow, and the outline of the rising Remington. Others moved as well.

"*Him.*" She pointed. "Shoot the mother."

The split second expanded in a bubble of stopped time. She saw the big black hands clutching the gun, his arms outstretched, making a human barrel, his thick legs braced, as he sighted. The explosion ripped through the auditorium, freezing time at last.

The rolling laughter stopped abruptly. The interval passed in a mini-second, shattered by a staccato burp of the Secret Servicemen's suddenly revealed Uzzi machine guns, which quickly created a cast-off rag doll out of the black man.

"No!" she screamed. It was a clarion for life to begin again. She heard others scream. The audience erupted in panicked movement and she had to fight the oncoming crowds to get to Jefferson's torn and battered body. The Magnum's trigger guard was clasped in his rigid fingers.

Strong hands gripped her shoulders, lifting her, and she fought to shake them loose, bending over him again, cradling him in her arms. Rage clamped her chest, and her tears came without sobs. Through the mist, she saw his smiling open-eyed death mask, hard ebony, without anger. Again she fought them off as they tried to lift her.

"Leave her be," a voice said, with the disembodied ring of authority. "They saved the President." The hands left her, and she continued to cradle him until she could not bear his empty eyes. She closed them gently and stood up.

"I want to see him," she murmured, looking up. A crowd had gathered in the vicinity of the President's box. They let her pass and she walked through a cordon of hard-eyed Secret Servicemen, through the auditorium, then up the steps to the boxes. They made way for her.

She saw him lying on the floor of the box, face down, the cocked Derringer still poised in his hand. Kneeling, she touched his hair, fine spun, still neat. The familiar aroma wafted to her nostrils. Lifting his head, she saw his face, still smoothly handsome and patrician, even in death. The bullet had caught him dead center in the right eye, leaving a large spongy blank spot. She let his head fall, and, still kneeling, reached into the pocket of her jacket for her credentials.

Secret Servicemen crowded around her in a semicircle. She flashed her badge.

"I am an officer of the Homicide Department of the MPD. This is my case. I don't want anything touched. Anything." The men looked at one another, confused. In the distance, she heard sirens.

"Do you understand?" She glared at them, then turned back to the corpse, her mind beginning to absorb the essential details through clear eyes.